# THE KIDNAPPING OF ROAN SINCLAIR

ASHLYN DREWEK

FOX HOLLOW BOOKS

Cover design by Teresa Conner at Wolf Sparrow Creations

*For my readers.*
*Without you, none of this would matter.*

# FOREWORD

A warning to the reader — this book contains references to alcohol/drug use, sexual assault, graphic violence, self-harm, ethnic and homosexual slurs, and a lot of profanity. Reader discretion is advised.

# 1

# ROAN

"I'M NOT HAVING THIS DISCUSSION WITH YOU AGAIN." MY father slammed his briefcase shut and locked it, along with any hope of this exchange ending peacefully.

"No, of course not. Why would you want to have a reasonable, adult conversation about anything?" I knew provoking him wouldn't help my case in the long run, but I didn't care about that right now. I was tired of him running every time I tried to talk to him, because having a real heart-to-heart with your twenty-two year old son was apparently the most horrifying thing on the planet. It's why I never even bothered trying to tell him I was gay. His head probably would have exploded.

"Roan, I have to be on a plane in—" he punched his left arm into the air, glaring at the Chopard on his wrist "—one hour."

"You said you were leaving at six."

"They moved the flight up. Is that ok with you?"

"No," I huffed in exasperation. "I came here to talk to you! I just sat in traffic for over an hour and a half to get here in time."

"Schedule something with Joyce and we'll talk about it when I get back. And take that shit out of your face before your mother sees it."

Snorting, I rolled my eyes, catching a glimpse of the stud in my right nostril that had him so pissed. It was either that, or the small, silver hoops in my ears. All things considered, a couple piercings were the least rebellious form of body modifications available these days.

"She's not coming home from Phoenix until Sunday, remember?" I shot back, half tempted to go home and switch the stud for a more noticeable hoop that very minute.

He didn't acknowledge the fact he wasn't aware of his wife's whereabouts. The calculator that served as his brain was probably too busy tallying up my mother's latest expenses. Flight, luxury retreat, shopping, meals. She'd easily blow tens of thousands by week's end.

"Do you always have to argue with me?" he snapped after a moment of tense silence.

That hardly qualified as arguing, but pointing it out definitely would have. So, I folded my arms over my chest and watched him gather up the rest of his belongings from the desk. "What if I just do it? What if I up and leave one of these days?"

He scoffed, not even bothering to look up. "Be my guest."

Ouch.

I swallowed thickly, entirely unprepared for how much that stung. Shaking my head, I tried to recover some semblance of confidence. "It's really more of a courtesy at this point. I'm graduating in three weeks. I don't *need* your permission to defer grad school."

"No, you just need my money." Dad shot me a cold look, moving for his office door.

Anger surged to the surface, obliterating what composure I had. My carefully rehearsed speech crumbled to bits under the weight of his indifference. "I don't need *shit* from you."

He lingered in the door, throwing an unimpressed look over his shoulder. "Whatever you say." With that parting barb, he walked out, barking at Joyce on his way.

"Such an asshole," I hissed under my breath, tromping out of the office. Joyce and I nearly collided as she rounded the corner. She shrieked and dropped a stack of files, papers scattering over the marble floors.

"Oh, I'm sorry, honey," she said, touching my cheek gently with a wrinkled hand before reaching down for the first folder. "I didn't see you there."

"No, it's my fault. I wasn't paying attention." I dropped to one knee and scooped up as many papers as possible, trying to keep them in some sort of order.

"How did it go with your dad?" She sounded so hopeful, I felt like an asshole for snuffing it out.

"Same as always," I replied with a grim smile, handing her the stack. "If it's not about Georgetown, he doesn't want to hear it."

"What does your mom say?"

"'Know your truth.'" Rolling my eyes, I grabbed the rest of the folders and stood. "Whatever the hell that is supposed to mean. I'm guessing she picked it up from her latest 'guru.'"

"Well that's a load of horse crap." Her coral lips twisted into a frown. "Did you tell him about the senior showcase next week?"

I leveled a look at her. Music, and anything to do with music, was at the very top of the list of things Dad refused to discuss. It didn't matter that I was actually good at composing *or* performing, or that I'd already gotten jobs collaborating with musicians in Chicago, or that I was currently learning the production side as well. To Phillip Walter Sinclair, the controlling interest holder and chairman of the board for Northern Illinois Bank & Trust, the only thing that mattered was money and amassing it in droves.

"Well, I'll be there," Joyce said with a smile.

Before I could reply, a series of gunshots rang out. My blood ran cold before my brain even registered what the sound was.

People started screaming while men shouted commands — *Get on the floor. Shut the fuck up. Don't fucking move.*

It was an assault of noise and commotion that turned my stomach inside out.

It was a robbery.

Grabbing Joyce by the arm, I hauled her into Dad's office and pushed her toward the desk. I hit the lights and locked the door, hoping they'd bypass the room if they thought it was empty.

"Oh my God!" Joyce whispered, grabbing my hand and yanking me down behind the desk. "I can't believe this is happening. We've never been robbed!"

"We'll be fine. Just keep quiet." I squeezed her bony hand in mine, hoping she believed me.

More gunshots echoed in the lobby, along with shrieks and yelps. I could hear Cindy's voice clearly, acknowledging the order to do something. As the head teller, she had access to all of the cash that wasn't currently locked up in the vault. Of course they'd grab her.

Heavy boots stormed back and forth, shouting commands that were hard to understand with the distance.

"Did you hit the button?" I whispered, glancing up at the panic alarm beneath Dad's desk.

Joyce nodded emphatically.

I nodded too, patting her hand. Then we just had to wait for the police. How long had it been? A minute already? A police response at this time of day would be fast. The robbers knew they had to move quick. We just had to stay quiet and out of sight.

I'd no more than reassured myself when the door handle jiggled. Holding my breath, I strained to hear anything else above Joyce's whimpering and the wild pounding in my chest.

Something heavy smashed against the door. It flew into the wall, impaling the handle into the drywall.

Joyce shrieked, her hands flapping to her face.

The next thing I knew, a gloved hand grabbed the collar of my shirt and pulled me up vertically. I saw a flash of a gun in my face and little else. The man shoved me out of the office and grabbed ahold of Joyce, forcing her out behind me.

"Take it easy!" I said, catching her before she tripped over her own feet on the gleaming floors.

"Shut the fuck up and get over there," the man snapped in accented English, using his gun to point in the direction he wanted us to go.

Keeping an arm around Joyce, I led her away and helped her to the ground next to Cindy. Some people were laying facedown on the floor with their arms over their heads. Others were kneeling, some crying, some praying. I was more concerned with watching the robbers as they moved around.

There were four of them, dressed identically in black hoodies and jeans, with black neck gaiters pulled up. They were all armed with some sort of gun — one kept an eye on us, another cleared out the registers, and the third guy ran around collecting everyone's cell phones, car keys, and wallets.

The one who found us disappeared again. Glass shattered in Dad's office. A moment later he reemerged, obviously pissed off. He kicked a potted plant over, spilling soil all over the place, and yelled something in a language I didn't understand.

The one standing guard over the people looked at his watch, but didn't reply.

"Wallet! Cell phone!" another one snapped, shoving a backpack in my face.

I dumped the items into the bag, mentally cataloguing all the credit cards I'd need to cancel as soon as I got to a working phone.

Zeroing in on Joyce again, the pissed-off guy strode forward, nearly bowling his partner out of the way. "Where's the master key?"

Joyce shrank back, every muscle in her old body quaking. "I, I don't know!"

The man pressed the gun into her temple, lowering his masked-face closer to hers. "Where is it?!"

Bursting into tears, Joyce yelped. "I don't know!"

"You don't know?" the robber taunted, pushing harder with the gun. "You don't know?!"

"They don't leave it here," I interjected, like an idiot. But I was desperate for him to stop torturing Joyce. She was on the verge of a heart attack as it was and after her bypass last winter, I didn't want to see her drop dead from the stress.

The man's attention whipped to me, along with the gun. "The fuck you say to me?"

"It's not here," I ground out, trying not to have my own heart attack with the barrel of a gun a millimeter away from my nose. "The master key for the vault? It's not here. And if you don't leave now, the cops are going to get here and we all know how that'll end." Forcing my gaze away from the gun and up into the man's black eyes, I held his hard stare.

The guy standing guard whistled sharply. The other two went to his side, no questions asked.

The one in front of me squinted, right before he grabbed the front of my henley and yanked me to my feet. Jamming his gun into the back of my head, he shoved me toward the other three, snapping something in the foreign language.

I put my hands up and went along, even though I felt like I might puke at any minute.

"No, don't!" Joyce shouted.

"Roan!" Cindy yelled at the same time.

Any thought of reassuring them was gone immediately when the robber who whistled stepped forward, stopping me in my tracks.

For starters, he was huge. I was six foot and he still had several inches on me. From the breadth of his chest, I was sure he could bench me if he really wanted to. His eyes, a shocking ice-blue color, met mine, freezing the air in my lungs. Thankfully, they darted past my head to the guy behind me, allowing me to suck in a quick breath. He also spoke in a foreign language. At least, I think he spoke. The guttural syllables were more of a growl, sending a shiver down my spine.

The gun nudged the back of my head, but I couldn't exactly go anywhere with the second guy right in front of me. When the gun pushed again, I stumbled forward a step, right into the whistler.

Cocking his head, his pale gaze dropped to mine as I bounced off of his torso. Before I could decide what my next move should be, if I should apologize or just keep my mouth shut, he fisted the front of my shirt and reeled me in even closer. Hissing something to the guy behind me, the whistler's handgun came up into view, turning toward me.

I grabbed at the hand holding me with both of mine, trying to pry his ridiculously strong fingers open, but it was pointless. "No, I'm sorry! I didn't mean—"

The gun came down swiftly, crashing against the side of my head. I crumpled under the blow. The floor rose up to meet me, welcoming my head with a hard 'thunk.'

The last thing I saw was a pair of black boots striding away.

## 2

## SASHA

"What the fuck is your problem?" Yuri yelled in Russian, slamming the sliding door of the van as Gregor punched the gas and sped out of the parking lot.

"Hostages were not part of the plan," I yelled back, yanking the itchy black mask off my face.

"He knew about the key! He could have gotten us what we wanted!"

Fixing him with an unimpressed glare, I bit my tongue to keep from replying. I gave orders, not explanations. And in our chain of command, *my* orders didn't come from a goddamn idiot like Yuri.

"Igor." I turned my attention to the man at the back. "Open the doors."

"For what?" Yuri demanded.

Igor was smart enough to nod and crawl to the door, unlatching one side and then the other.

Without wasting another second, I unholstered my gun and fired a round into the center of his face. Blood splattered on one of the doors, along with squiggly chunks of his brain. The impact from the bullet knocked him backward and gravity took care of the rest.

The car behind us laid on their horn when his body tumbled out. Tires screeched as other vehicles swerved to try and avoid it. Somewhere in the back, two vehicles collided.

"What did you do that for?" Yuri shouted.

I stared at him for a moment, trying to decide if he really was that stupid or if he was just mad I killed one of his lackeys. "His information was flawed."

"Are you fucking kidding me?!"

"He failed." I leaned my elbow on my thigh, aiming the gun in Yuri's direction. "That means *you* failed. Do you want to tell your uncle what happened, or should I?"

Yuri ripped his mask off and whipped it toward the back of the van. "Fucking animal."

"That's what I thought." I returned the gun to the holster in the small of my back, disappointed he didn't give me a reason to use it on him.

Eduard snorted and shook his head. "Viktor is going to be so pissed."

I ran a hand through the longer part of my hair, pushing it back into place. Pissed was an understatement. Viktor brought me in so this bullshit *didn't* happen, so he got what he wanted out of that fucking vault and kept his idiot nephew in line. And now look.

I told him I didn't do bank robberies. They were messy and chaotic and prone to going to hell, like this one did. The fact Yuri was the mastermind behind it didn't help. Why he thought he could make the leap from running girls and drugs to bank robbery was beyond me, but this was the first and last time I'd ever pull a job with him.

Now my ass was on the line thanks to Igor's shitty

information. If I didn't find a way to make up for the mistake, we'd all face the firing squad.

Eduard, meanwhile, rifled through his backpack, sorting the stolen goods into different piles; car keys, cell phones, wallets. He flipped through the wallets, taking whatever cash he found and tossing it into a pile separate from the credit cards and IDs. "Shit, Sasha." He slapped my bicep and shoved a wallet under my nose. "Look!"

"What?" I made a face and snatched the wallet out of his hand, reading the name on the driver's license.

Roan Sinclair.

It was the kid Yuri tried to kidnap — the one who knew about the key.

"Sinclair..." My lips pursed as names cycled through my head. Men I'd killed, men I'd tortured, men I'd stalked. Men like Phillip Sinclair, the one who, for all intents and purposes, owned Northern Illinois Bank & Trust.

Eduard's eyes lit up and he nodded, a smile stretching across his face.

Sliding the license out, I stared at the tiny picture for a moment. Roan Sinclair — blond and blue-eyed, with a smile that undoubtedly got him whatever he wanted. A little ray of sunshine if I ever saw one. The kid's address was the same as his father's but after all of the surveillance I did on the mansion, I knew he didn't live there.

Digging through the rest of his wallet yielded little insight. A few credit cards, receipts for a coffee shop in a town I'd never heard of, a Chicago transit card. There wasn't anything remarkable until I found a student ID for Braeburn University.

Perfect.

"Get me everything you can on Roan Sinclair and Braeburn University," I said, handing the wallet back to

Eduard. "We might be able to salvage this fuck up after all."

# 3

# ROAN

THE HAIR ON THE BACK OF MY NECK STOOD UP.

A knot formed in the pit of my stomach.

I was being followed. I was sure of it.

Throwing a glance over my shoulder, I stopped on the sidewalk, looking for any sign to confirm my suspicion. The dark street was still and quiet. A breeze rustled the leaves overhead, the scent of lilacs and cigarette smoke wafting by.

There was no one behind me, but I couldn't shake the feeling I was being watched.

After the robbery, I went back to school, like normal. I went to class, like normal. I even went to the stupid therapy appointment my mother insisted on. Needless to say, it didn't really help. I constantly had moments like this, where I would have bet money someone was watching me. There were times I swore I saw those pale blue eyes in the middle of a crowd. PTSD, the shrink said, and threw a prescription for benzos at me.

Mom told me I had to 'reclaim my power,' with zero input on how to actually do that. She meant well, but sticking a crystal on my forehead and meditating wasn't going to reclaim shit.

And my father? I hadn't talked to him since he stormed out of his office that day. He didn't bother checking in after his precious bank was robbed. According to Joyce, he was *very* busy with the investigators and she assured he'd be in touch soon. Ever the optimist.

Quickening my steps, I dug my keys out of my pocket.

I hated this feeling. I'd been on edge ever since I woke up to paramedics poking and prodding me. They had to actually stitch the gash in my head where that asshole hit me with his gun. I mean, I suppose I should have been grateful he didn't shoot me. But Jesus. I think I'd had a continual headache thanks to him. Between my senior showcase and actually graduating, pounding headaches and paranoia was more stress I did *not* need.

Thankfully the showcase was a breeze. The music majors spent a week in Chicago rehearsing before ultimately performing for a group of agents, producers, and other industry professionals. I had a collection of business cards on my desk and a meeting already lined up with one of the theater managers downtown. I was on Cloud Nine, except Georgetown and my father loomed on the horizon like a storm blowing in.

One year, that's all I wanted. One year to see if I could make music a viable career. If it didn't work, I'd resign myself to the cold, calculating world of finance and take my place at NIB&T like a good little Sinclair. But he couldn't even give me that.

Shoving the key in my front door, I turned the lock and reached for the handle.

Something rushed out from around the corner. No, some*one*. They slammed right into me with a war cry.

I stumbled back a couple steps, grappling with the dark-haired person squeezing my midsection.

"Frankie!" I huffed, trying to force my lungs to work once my heart started beating again. "What the fuck?"

"Did I get you?" she asked with a grin, brown eyes shining brightly.

"Yeah. You almost gave me a heart attack." I shoved her away and opened the door. "What are you doing here?"

"I was bored. I missed you." She darted inside and did a pirouette before flopping backward on the couch. "Can I crash here this weekend?"

"If you want..." I dropped my backpack onto the floor and kicked my shoes off before joining her in the living room, collapsing on the other side of the sectional. "What's up?"

"Freddy's home," she groaned. "He finished his classes early and has been a royal pain in my ass all day. I had to get away."

"That's no way to talk about your brother." I lobbed a pillow at her. She whipped it right back at me.

"Says the only child. You don't know how good you have it."

"Oh yeah, it's great. You get spoiled beyond belief, you're constantly the center of attention, and oh, my personal favorite, you get to carry *all* of your parents' expectations and be an epic disappointment when you ultimately fail to measure up and crush all of their hopes and dreams. Yay!"

Frankie snorted. "What about *your* hopes and dreams?"

I sighed. "Maybe that's how the Starling household works, but my hopes and dreams are completely irrelevant unless it involves sitting upon the NIB&T throne and making my father even more money."

"So what are you going to do about Georgetown?" She rolled over onto her stomach to look at me, swinging her feet in the air behind her.

Shaking my head, I searched the ceiling, like I could find the answer to my predicament amongst the many layers of paint. "Hell if I know..."

"You should come with me to New York," she said, grinning from ear to ear. "We can be starving artists together. I'll be the beautiful ingenue and you can be the brilliant musician."

I had to admit, it was tempting — the idea of giving my dad the finger and doing what *I* wanted for a change instead of following His Majesty's royal decree that I get my Master's in Finance (not Economics, not an MBA, only Finance — he was quite clear about that) and join him in expanding the NIB&T empire.

"Yeah, but you'll meet some guy and I'll get the boot and then where will I be? Homeless and penniless in New York or living as your third wheel?" I shook my head. "Hard pass."

"Or *you* could meet some guy and *I'd* be the third wheel," she countered.

I rolled my eyes. "First of all, I don't have time to meet anyone. And second of all, I don't *want* to meet anyone."

"Still hung up on Wyatt?" she asked with a grimace.

"No," I sighed. It was fun while it lasted, but I wasn't going to drag his ass out of the closet. I'd never been the type to beg for anyone's attention, no matter how desperately I might have wanted it.

"Pierce?"

"No. Jesus." That one was maybe a little true... He was tall, dark, and moody, a puzzle I was always working on. I should have known better than to get involved with an art major, but I liked his unpredictability. It kept me on my toes, until the drama got to be too much. As a musician, I had my own creative struggles, thank you very much. I didn't need to suffer for the sake of his art, too. "I'm not hung up on anyone."

"You can say it," she sighed, batting her lashes at me. "You made a mistake with the whole 'gay' thing and now that it's out of your system, you're ready to come back to the love of your life."

"You got me." I shot a finger-gun at her with a wink. "I've been biding my time until you broke up with that last asshole to swoop back in and reclaim my woman."

"I know." She beamed at me. "I'm simply irresistible."

"You're something alright."

She gasped and launched another pillow at me. I caught it with a laugh and tucked it under my head. The invisible knot in the middle of my stomach finally began to unwind. For the first time in weeks, things felt normal again.

# 4

# SASHA

VIOLIN MUSIC FILTERED THROUGH THE NIGHT, SOFT AND sad. The breeze shifted, rolling through the open car windows and blowing my cigarette smoke out into the atmosphere.

Closing my eyes, I tipped my head back against the headrest and allowed myself a moment to relax. Whenever Roan was playing, I didn't need to watch him like a hawk. I could keep tabs on him, and his mood, through the music alone.

If he was playing the piano, he was downstairs, working, writing new music. It was a constant starting and stopping, minute modifications, and lots of pacing around, humming to himself.

If he was playing the guitar, he was still downstairs working, but usually it was lyrics, so there was more writing and less moving.

And if he was playing the violin, like tonight, he was stressed — or sad — and he was only playing for himself. Given the low tones of the song, I was betting on sad tonight. Further confirming my suspicion was the fact he was on the balcony off of his bedroom, as opposed to inside, playing for no one but the stars.

It was a stark contrast to how he'd been earlier in the day.

He and his female companion spent most of the day out and about. Breakfast, followed by shopping (her, not him, though he carried all of the bags and didn't appear to complain), and a trip back to the townhouse he lived in. The female had been staying with him for the past week, though I had yet to develop a solid understanding of their relationship.

According to the dossier we'd been compiling, her name was Francesca Starling. A childhood friend, it appeared they had an on-again/off-again romantic relationship, at least if the pictures were to be believed. While she'd been staying here, she slept in his room, but there wasn't any indication of anything transpiring between the two. Guess they were off-again.

After they dropped off her shopping bags, Francesca stayed home while Roan went to the park and played football with a group of guys.

At least this part of the job wasn't boring. It was almost as good as watching TV and a hell of a lot better than staring at his house or the building where his classrooms were. At the park, I felt secure enough to leave him for a while to grab something to eat and come back for the rest of the game.

Cheeks flushed and glistening with sweat, Roan sprinted easily from one area of the field to the next. His team had apparently been chosen for "skins," since he ditched the gray t-shirt from earlier and was only wearing a backward baseball hat and black shorts.

From his position and the plays he made, it looked like he was one of the attacking midfielders. Given his height and lean build, it made sense, though he could have easily been a forward. Unless he didn't want the attention. Midfielders tended to be the brains of the game, but forwards got all the glory.

It didn't seem to matter who won. The guys all high-fived and fist-bumped, laughing and talking over one another. One of his teammates, their giant of a goalkeeper, grabbed Roan from behind and lifted him off his feet. Roan was smiling when he yelled something over his shoulder. It must have taken the goalkeeper by surprise, because he dropped his hold and took off running. Roan loped after him with a water bottle, easily closing the distance.

As soon as he was close enough, Roan threw most of the water on the guy and bolted in the opposite direction, keeping out of his opponent's hands with a laugh and a smile that lit up his whole face. He radiated warmth no matter what he was doing. And like the sun, he seemed to pull everyone around him into his orbit. It was strange — the complete opposite of the world I lived in. You couldn't afford to be warm and kind. Those traits would get you killed in a heartbeat like the fool you were.

If anything, the football game gave me more insight into the kid's physicality. Whatever method we used to subdue him, it would have to be near-instantaneous. If he managed to slip away, there's no way I'd be able to run him down. I was tall — taller than him by at least seven centimeters — but my muscles were *not* build for speed or agility. I was solid and bulky, meant for crushing, not chasing.

Roan finished his game and went home for a much-needed shower, which I was privy to thanks to a conveniently placed camera in the neighbor's tree. When the door was open, it covered part of the bathroom and most of the bedroom.

He peeled the sweaty shirt off and tossed it into a laundry basket before turning the shower on. After screwing around with his phone for a bit, his head bobbing to whatever song he'd clearly selected, he slipped out of his shorts. No surprise, his ass was as perfect as the rest of him — round, defined, and just asking to be grabbed.

Jesus, Sasha. You've been awake for too long — you're on the verge of hallucinating or some shit.

As soon as Roan turned toward the camera, I dropped my gaze, shaking a cigarette out of the pack. Lighting it quickly, I took a drag and exhaled slowly. By the time I looked up again, he'd disappeared from view and the bathroom door was mostly shut.

When he reappeared, he was clothed in a t-shirt and a pair of gray sweats. Raking a hand through his wet hair and messing it around, he headed for the stairs. Francesca made food and they settled in on the couch to watch TV. It looked like she'd chosen a sweet romantic movie. *Again.* I didn't know if he was sick of watching impossible love stories with simpering women and weak-willed men, but I sure as shit was. At least when Roan controlled the remote I knew we'd be watching something entertaining.

Hours later, she was still on the couch and he was on the balcony with the violin. I, in the meantime, had gone through a pack of cigarettes and started on another, sipping tepid tea out of a thermos.

"Are you sleeping?" a voice asked through the open window, ruining my moment of peace.

I opened my eyes to see Eduard's smirking face. "What do you think?"

He laughed and leaned against the car door. "How's the golden boy?"

"Sad," I replied automatically, taking another drag off the cigarette.

Eduard lifted his dark brows at me. "Sad?"

"Listen." I held up a finger. The morose melody, accompanied by the rustling trees, demonstrated my point.

"What does this fucking kid have to be sad about?" He shook his head, eyes rolling.

I shrugged. Sadness — or any feeling, really — didn't register with me. The only acceptable feeling in my world was anger. Even if I did manage to feel something else, what purpose did it serve? I had no use for anything besides anger and indifference. So, I couldn't begin to fathom what a rich American had to worry about. His father had everything. The house, the job, the car, the wife, the all-star child. By extension, Roan had those things too — minus the wife and child. Yet, every time he hung up the phone, he picked up the violin and played, sometimes for hours.

Eduard stood straight, slapping the car door. "Go home. I'm parked down the street."

Nodding, I flicked my cigarette out the window and started the car.

Up on the balcony, I gave Roan's shadowy figure one last glance before driving off.

# 5

# ROAN

"NO, YOU CAN'T MAKE ME!" FRANKIE CRIED, TIGHTENING her arms around my neck.

"You have to let go," I said with a laugh, trying to peel her off before she strangled me. The pleading look I directed at her brother went unanswered. Instead of helping, he just rolled his eyes.

"No!"

"Frankie, move your ass!" Freddy yelled from the doorway, checking his watch for the twelfth time. "Mom has a reservation for seven and you're going to make us late!"

"Fuck off!" Frankie snapped. "I'm saying goodbye!"

"You've been saying goodbye for fifteen minutes already!"

"My lease is up next week," I said, pulling back as much as possible to try and look at her. "Then I'll be back home for the rest of the summer and you'll be absolutely sick of me."

"And then you're going to Georgetown and I'll never see you again!" she wailed as dramatically as possible, smashing her cheek to mine.

"You're going to New York, so what do you care?" Freddy snapped.

"God, can you give us two seconds already?" Frankie shot back over her shoulder.

"Whatever. I'll be in the car." Freddy grabbed all of her bags and hauled them outside.

She was only supposed to stay the weekend. It turned into three weeks, in which time she managed to buy a replacement wardrobe and a slew of crap for the kitchen and bathroom. Not that my stuff was "bad," it just wasn't her "style." So she said. And since she couldn't lug everything home on the train by herself, Freddy had to suck it up and make the drive from Chicago to pick her up — her *and* her crap.

"What is your mom dragging you to tonight?" I asked, hoping to distract her while also sidling toward the door.

"Dinner at some restaurant with some chef that's trending. The waiting list is ridiculous, but you know how it goes. Mummy Dearest called in a favor and poof! We're dining at the chef's table tonight." She pouted and grabbed my hand. "I wish you were coming. Can't you go back to being my boyfriend? Seriously!"

"One little problem with that..." I blinked at her pointedly.

"You're still a good lay, even if you're gay. Hey, that rhymed!" She laughed at her own joke while I shook my head.

"Thanks. I think…"

Freddy honked the horn.

"I'm coming!" Frankie yelled out the door.

"I actually have to go, too," I lied, taking another step closer to the threshold. "And you don't want to get stuck in traffic. That means you're in the car even longer with your brother."

She made a horrified face. "Oh my God. You're right! Ok. Call me tomorrow. And let me know when you're back at your parents." Pecking me on the lips, she twirled on the ball of her foot and darted out the door. They started arguing the minute she climbed in the car, hands flapping and mouth moving a hundred miles a minute.

In the twenty years I'd known the Starling twins, nothing had changed except their fights were louder and their insults meaner. Freddy and I got along just fine, but Frankie was the one who kept me sane while growing up in the gilded cage of the Sinclair household. Together, the two were like oil and water.

The couple years Frankie and I were boyfriend/girlfriend were actually great. She was everything anyone would want in a girlfriend, even a teenage boy who didn't know who he was or *what* he wanted. When I finally figured it out our senior year of high school, she was incredibly supportive — not that I expected anything less.

Still, as much as I loved having her around, I didn't mind the peace and quiet left in the wake of Hurricane Frankie. I kicked back on the couch and settled in for a war movie, ironically, thrilled to have the TV back after weeks of being subjected to rom-coms and cooking shows.

The movie was almost over when my cell phone rang.

It was my dad, of all people.

Hitting pause, I sat up and stared at the phone. It was always a toss up if I should answer and be pissed off immediately, or let it go to voicemail and be pissed off after the fact. Apparently I was a masochist, because I opted for immediately.

"I'm calling to confirm the moving truck will be there in two days," Dad said without a proper greeting. "Do you have your apartment in D.C. lined up, yet?"

My pulse kicked up a notch. "No." Silence. "We're

supposed to talk about it, remember?" I said slowly, trying to cut all emotion out of my voice and be as cold and calculating as he was.

"If you wait much longer, you're going to end up in an undesirable neighborhood."

"If I defer for a year, then it doesn't matter."

There was a sharp click. I thought he hung up, but when I saw the line was still open, I figured it was his perfect white teeth snapping together. "Why do you insist on pursuing this ridiculous notion? Music isn't going to get you anywhere in life. It's bad enough you already majored in it! You're lucky Georgetown took you with just a minor in business!"

"It's a twenty-one *billion* dollar industry," I said, trying not to lose my cool — and failing miserably with each sentence out of my mouth. "I'd say people are getting pretty far with their 'ridiculous' music dreams. And, for your information, I've already had paying jobs. People *like* what I do, not that you'd know anything about it."

He snorted. "Please tell me you're not mad I wasn't there for your little singalong. You know I had—"

"No, Dad, I'm not mad because at this point I expect nothing less from you. The flowers Joyce got in your name were really nice. You should think about giving her a bonus. Oh, you know what? Maybe a week's paid vacation so she can relax a little after having a *gun* pointed in her face last month! I'm fine, too, by the way. Too bad you weren't there for it. It was really something."

"I don't have time for this."

"You never do." I rolled my eyes and hung up. I don't know why I even bothered answering anymore. Growing up, I didn't understand the weeks of silence from him. I blamed myself for not seeing the faults he obviously did and tried to be better, until I was fucking *perfect*. Perfect student. Perfect athlete. Perfect musician. Something he could be proud of. None of it mattered. He still found something to criticize.

Turning off the TV, I stuffed my earbuds in and set my phone to "Do Not Disturb" before cranking up the angriest rock music I could find on my playlist. Yanking my shoes on, I stormed out the front door.

One nice thing about living near the university were the perfectly manicured walking paths everywhere. I headed toward the lagoon, one of the more relaxing spots on campus, in the vain hope I could leave my anger behind me if I walked far enough or blew out my eardrums with enough thundering music.

Stopping for a red light, I slipped my phone out of my pocket and skipped through a couple songs, looking for something that matched my mood.

A mass of black swooped in front of my face, blinding me. Whatever it was yanked back on my throat, negating the ability to yell or even breathe.

I fell backward, crashing into something — no, someone. They wrapped their arms around me, squeezing the air out of my lungs, while someone else grabbed my legs. I tried to jerk myself free, but my thrashing got me nowhere. The two of them were too strong.

The sensation of floating hit me as I was carried sideways for a moment. I landed hard on my hip and shoulder on something cold and metal. Whoever had my arms let go and switched to crushing my torso with their weight. Likewise, their partner sat on my legs.

A sliding door slammed shut next to me.

Shit, I was in a car. No, a van. And we were moving quickly.

A sharp sting pierced my shoulder, followed by a sudden burn down the length of my arm.

As soon as the weight on my legs lifted, I kicked out as hard as I could. I caught the fleshy part of someone's body, based on the grunt and the fact the fucking mammoth on my chest threw his elbow into my stomach.

What little air was in my lungs immediately rushed out. Try as I might to stay awake, my eyelids weighed a thousand pounds. It was getting harder to keep them open until finally they slammed shut altogether.

# 6

# SASHA

"Goddamn motherfucker," Eduard hissed, hunched over and holding his balls.

I suppressed a laugh and ripped the bag off of Roan's head so he didn't suffocate. "No fun at the Birdcage for you tonight."

"Fuck off."

Smirking, I tapped a cigarette out of the packet and handed it to him as a peace offering before retrieving one for myself. I lit up first and tossed him my lighter.

"Now what?" Eduard asked, tossing it back.

Throwing a glance at Roan's unconscious body, I exhaled a cloud of smoke. "Take him to the warehouse. Ivan is going to deliver the package tomorrow. And then we wait."

"Sounds fun."

"Better than trying a second robbery."

Eduard shook his head and flicked ash off the end of his cigarette. "I don't know why Viktor let Yuri take the lead on that. Even if it *was* Yuri's idea, he's a fucking idiot.

What the fuck is in that safety deposit box that is so important anyway?"

"Viktor said it's a bunch of emeralds," I replied with a shrug.

Eduard leveled a skeptical look at me. "Seems like a lot of trouble for some emeralds."

I agreed but I didn't say it out loud. I wasn't in a position to question what Viktor wanted, at least publicly. Privately, I thought he'd lost his goddamn mind. Emeralds were technically worth more than diamonds, but as with any stolen item, if you didn't have a buyer, then it didn't matter what the value was. I didn't know what he was playing at, and I didn't want to know. All I wanted was to get the fucking things and move on with my life while I still could.

"Hey, are you two hungry?" Gregor yelled from the front seat. "I can stop somewhere real quick."

I exchanged a look with Eduard before I rolled my eyes skyward. God give me the strength to not fucking snap.

Eduard did it for me. "With a fucking body in the back?" He reached between the seats and smacked Gregor's head. "You fucking moron!"

"He's not even awake!" Gregor bit back in his defense. "It's not like they'd even know."

"Just drive," I said with a sigh, holding my forehead with one hand.

"Yes, boss."

---

Gregor drove straight into the warehouse, which made carting Roan to the cell that much easier. Thankfully he was still out when I grabbed his arm and slung him over my shoulder like a fireman, winding my arm through his legs and holding onto his thigh. He smelled like some sort of cologne, citrusy and aquatic all at once. It reminded me of summer in the Mediterranean. For a moment, I wondered where he'd be come summertime — if he'd even still be alive.

Ducking through the door of his cell, I slid him off of my shoulder, pretty much dropping him onto the floor. I aimed for the blanket that was in there, but there was only so much I could do to cushion the impact.

The sight of him laying there, looking like a broken doll, gave me a moment's pause. It was strange seeing Roan so still. Every other time I'd had him in my sights, he was moving. Constantly moving. Even when he was on the couch, there was some part of him that twitched or tapped. He was like a hummingbird, like the music he played was constantly at work inside his brain and his body couldn't help itself. Except now, the only movement came from the rise and fall of his chest.

After waiting for more than a minute, I yelled for Ivan.

He scurried around the corner, eyes wide. "Yeah, boss?"

I gestured to Roan impatiently. Why did I have to spell everything out? What was the point of a plan if I had to hold everyone's fucking hand along the way?

"What? Oh! Oh. Yeah, got it, boss." Ivan darted into the cell and pulled his phone out, snapping a couple pictures of our hostage. "You want me to go now?"

"No, I want you to go tomorrow, like I told you."

"Oh, ok. What do you want me to do now?"

My gaze fell to Roan, considering him for a moment. Ivan was young and dumb, but Roan would be fine. The drugs I gave him would keep him unconscious for a while and as long as he was asleep, he wasn't in any danger.

"Watch him," I replied. "I'm going to sleep for a few

hours." I stepped out of the cell and headed for the office, slipping my phone out and dialing Viktor's number. "It's done," I said when he picked up.

"Problems?"

"No."

"Then move to the next step."

I didn't acknowledge the command. I simply hung up and eased myself onto the couch, covering my eyes with my forearm. Hopefully I could get a few decent hours of sleep now that something had finally gone right.

# 7

# ROAN

The world around me was fuzzy and dark. And quiet. The only thing I could hear was my own breathing, which meant I was alone. I didn't know if that should be comforting or not. After having Frankie with me for the past few weeks, it was strange being by myself again.

Pushing myself into a sitting position, I held my pounding head in one hand. My throat was raw and scratchy and my tongue felt like sandpaper. I forced myself to swallow, hoping to encourage more saliva to make things tolerable.

I felt... off. Not quite dizzy, but the world was moving at a sluggish pace. And my fucking body hurt. My shoulder, hips, ribs. Was I run over while I was sleeping?

A shiver rippled down my spine and I realized I was on a concrete floor, on top of a thin, ratty blanket. A single lightbulb, high overhead, cast a circle of pale yellow around the small space. Glancing up, I shielded my eyes with my hand, studying the enclosure.

It was all chainlink. Like a dog kennel. Except someone added chainlink across the top, too. If I wanted to, I had enough room to move, which I suppose was a good thing. Other than the threadbare piece of fabric, the only other thing with me in the kennel was a bucket. I didn't even want to investigate what was in it. The entire place smelled like a weird combination of motor oil and urine and I'm sure the bucket wasn't helping matters.

The space I was in was on the end of what looked like a row of similar kennels. How many, I couldn't tell. I couldn't see what was beyond them. It was too dark. Of one thing I was certain, though — I was *not* the first person these people kidnapped.

I was fucking kidnapped!

It was blurry, but I remembered it now.

If I was in a frat, I'd think this was a hazing ritual. But I wasn't. And *this* wasn't. This was very real.

The why eluded me entirely. I was generally a nice person. I didn't go out of my way to intentionally piss people off, unless you were my father. No frats, like I said. There was no way my friends could pull off an elaborate prank like this, complete with the fucking drugs and creepy warehouse.

I was a no one. Yeah, my dad was rich, but *I* wasn't. Between busting my ass in school and giving music lessons to kids in town, I was busy trying to get a career started before my imprisonment at Georgetown began. How could you make an enemy doing any of that? And even if I somehow managed to, who the hell would want to kidnap me over it?

What felt like several hours later, I still hadn't come up with any bright revelations.

A large metal door screeched somewhere in the dark and heavy footsteps echoed in the distance.

Scurrying to my feet as quickly as I could, I pressed myself against the chainlink at the far side, opposite the door, waiting. My heart pounded with each thud from the boots until it quickened on its own, outpacing the person the closer they got.

Emerging from the shadows, a giant of a man appeared before me. Head held high, he strode forward with a look of determination on his terrifyingly handsome face. His black hair matched the fitted t-shirt he wore, showcasing his muscles in a casually intimidating way. Unless he wore a tent, I'm sure any shirt was going to show off how big he was. Jeans and black boots completed the look, along with dozens of tattoos scattered across both of his hands and arms.

Without hesitating, he unlocked the door and walked in, ducking as he did so. He left the door open behind him, probably because he felt comfortable knowing he had at least fifty pounds of muscle on me. I'm pretty sure he could crush my skull between his hands if he tried hard enough. Was he the fucker who crushed my ribs, too? My guess was "Yes."

I didn't want to be the first one to speak, even though a thousand questions screamed inside my head. I swallowed each one of them back, waiting to see what he was going to do.

He was equally silent, watching me with a blank expression on his face. Every so often his jaw shifted to the side, the dark stubble drawing attention to how sharp his features were. If he wasn't a fucking kidnapper, I would have said he was hot. Lie. He *was* hot, even if he was a kidnapper. But he lost major points for being a criminal.

When his hand drifted behind him, I jerked back enough to make the chainlink rattle. I cursed myself for flinching, especially when the corner of his mouth quirked into the smallest smile imaginable before vanishing.

Still without speaking, he withdrew his hand again,

slowly, holding a water bottle aloft. He glanced between me and the blanket before lobbing it to where I'd been sitting.

"Thank you," I murmured. Did I just thank my jailer? Seriously? This was what happened, apparently, when your mom made you go to etiquette school in the twenty-first century during her Stepford Wife phase. You thank people, even when they clearly didn't deserve it.

His black brows slanted in question, but he didn't reply. Rude. Even if it was a ridiculous situation, he could at least say "You're welcome." With his mission accomplished, he turned to go.

"Wait!" I took a step after him. "Why are you doing this?"

He kept walking; so did I.

Naturally he got to the opening first. He stepped through and closed the door the moment I reached it, though his movements weren't hurried in the slightest. Clicking the lock into place, he arched an eyebrow, but stayed where he was, like a silent declaration of victory.

"Tell me why," I repeated, threading my fingers through the chainlink and holding his gaze in the hope he'd tell me *something*. "Why am I here? Who are you? What do you want?"

His face was as expressionless as before, but his pale eyes swept over me slowly, from head to toe and back again. He looked familiar, but I had no idea from where. Maybe he just had one of those faces. No, his face was too striking to be common. There's no way I would have forgotten running into him. The snarling tiger's head tattoo on the side of his neck made him all the more distinguishable.

His Adam's apple bobbed, indicating a swallow of his own. I thought the movement would precede an answer, so when he turned and left, all without ever making a single noise, frustration exploded inside of me.

"No, wait! Don't go! Come on!" His steps never slowed. Head up and shoulders as straight as a fucking linebacker's, he strode away like he couldn't hear me at all. I smacked my palm against the chainlink. "Goddamn it!"

Watching his broad back disappear into the darkness from which he came, I slumped against the kennel door, helpless to do anything as my answers strolled away.

## 8

## SASHA

It was hard not to answer Roan when he asked why he was here. I could have given him a one- or two-word reply. It wouldn't have hurt anything and maybe it would have put his mind at ease, but I wasn't here to put his mind at ease. I was here to use him. That's it. He was a tool, an object, a thing. *The* thing to get me what I wanted — a giant payday from Viktor and a one-way ticket out of this city.

Ivan delivered the package to Roan's father earlier in the day. The instructions were simple — if he wanted to see his son again, call the number we provided.

We waited all day, and nothing.

"Are you *sure* he got it?" I asked Ivan, arms crossed over my chest to keep from slapping the stupid out of him.

Ivan shifted his weight from side to side, alternating between staring at me and staring at the phone on the table. "I'm sure! The housekeeper picked it up from the porch. And I saw him there eating breakfast. She had to have given it to him."

Hours later, when I was about to send Ivan back with

another letter, the phone rang. Phillip Sinclair had had the envelope for over eight hours. I didn't know what the fuck he'd been doing the entire time. Gregor was monitoring the house, so we knew he hadn't called the police. In the end, I didn't really care now that he was finally calling.

"What do you want?" Phillip demanded.

Using a voice changer, Eduard answered in English. "The master key for the bank vault."

"Never." He didn't even hesitate. Did he miss the part in the note where we said we had his son? He couldn't have. It was before the fucking phone number.

"We have no interest in your money," Eduard continued patiently, "only the key."

"Do you know who I am?" His outrage reverberated through the phone.

"Yes, Mr. Sinclair. We are well acquainted with you and your family, as you should know by now."

He glossed over the response. "Then *you* should know who you're fucking with."

Eduard made a face and pointed at the phone, as if I wasn't paying attention to every word coming through the speaker. And I thought Russian fathers were assholes.

"It's a simple trade, Mr. Sinclair," Eduard huffed, letting his exasperation show. "Do we have a deal or not?"

"Just so we're clear, you want me to trade the *key* for my *son*?"

"Yes."

Click.

We both stared at the phone, hovering over it in disbelief. It sat on the table between us, staring back, mocking us with its silence.

"Did he just fucking hang up?" I grabbed the phone and looked at the screen. Sure enough, Roan's father disconnected.

"Maybe it was an accident?" Eduard shrugged. "He'll call back."

He didn't.

We waited for hours. There was no return phone call.

"Well *now* what?" Eduard asked, raking a hand through his dark hair, finger-combing it to the side.

I laced my fingers behind my head, holding onto the nape of my neck and trying to think of something. Needless to say, that was not the reaction either of us had been expecting. I was truly at a loss, but I'd be damned if I admitted it out loud. "Let me call Viktor and see what he wants now."

Eduard nodded and left the room while I dialed.

"Is it done?" Viktor asked as soon as he answered.

"No. He's refusing." I couldn't believe I was actually saying those words. It was a fucking key. It would cost the man nothing to hand it over but for whatever reason, he treasured it more than his son's life.

"He's refusing to get his son back?" Viktor made an irritated noise. Something thumped in the background, like he slammed his fist against something hard.

"He won't give up the key," I repeated. "So now what? If we go back to the bank and force our way in, they're going to know the emeralds are gone." Which defeated the entire fucking purpose of trying to be stealthy about it.

Viktor swore under his breath. "Maybe you should cut something off his son and send it to him. Let him know you're serious."

The thought of permanently depriving Roan of any of his appendages made my stomach inexplicably sour. "I don't think that would convince him. He seemed pretty certain."

"We'll let him think on it for a few days. When his son doesn't return home, he may have a change of heart."

"Yes, sir."

A few more days?

A few more days watching Roan? Being in the same space as him? Dodging his questions and the beseeching look in his brilliant blue eyes?

Sure. No problem.

## 9

## ROAN

THE NEXT DAY A GUY ABOUT MY AGE SHOWED UP WITH A grease-soaked paper sack in hand.

Unlike the tattooed guy from last night, this one opened the door just enough to throw the bag in and yanked it shut again. And unlike the other guy, I stood a much better chance against this one, which he probably acknowledged as well. We were the same height and roughly the same weight. I knew by looking at him I'd be able to outrun him.

"Thank you," I said automatically.

He made a face, clicking the lock shut. "You're welcome?" Yes! An answer! His accent was strange, foreign. It seemed familiar, like German or something, and I was eager to keep him talking.

"I'm Roan." I didn't want to freak him out and chase him off, so I stayed where I was instead of retrieving the food. "What's your name?"

Licking his lips, he shoved his hands in his pockets. "Ivan."

Ok. So, Russian? Something Eastern European.

"Do you know why I'm here, Ivan?" He started to turn away, so I got to my feet quickly and held a hand out, like that would help. "No, wait! Please. I won't ask you about that. Just don't go. Please?"

Shockingly, he paused and turned toward me again. He eyed me warily, which was simultaneously amusing *and* confusing since I was the captive here. "I'm not supposed to talk to you."

"Says who?"

Heavy steps thundered across the warehouse, silencing whatever Ivan was about to say. I stood tall, waiting to come face-to-face with the tattooed guy again. In lieu of an actual name, I'd dubbed him Mr. Black, trying to bring some sense of order to this fucked up situation.

Except, it wasn't him. It was a different tattooed guy with slicked-back blond hair and a big, gold cross around his neck. The new guy cracked Ivan upside the head so hard it made *me* wince and snarled at him in another language.

In that moment, I was teleported back to the bank. Every feeling of fear and helplessness I had that day flooded through me again. Everyone always talked about "Fight or Flight," but they didn't mention the third option — "Freeze." That, sadly, is what my body chose to do then, like it chose to do right now. Not that I could flee anywhere or successfully fight anyone while locked in a goddamn dog cage.

At least now I knew why Mr. Black seemed so familiar. It was his eyes, the only part of him that'd been visible that day beyond his obvious size. A blue so pale and shocking against black lashes, they almost looked inhuman. Eyes like that were wasted on an asshole like him.

But why the fuck would a group of bank robbers come back a month later to kidnap me? Me?! I didn't even work at the fucking bank! If they were going to kidnap any Sinclair, why the hell didn't they go after my dad? He was the one with more money than he knew what to do with. Mom and I were just ornaments in his life — easily replaceable when lost or broken.

I didn't have the chance to ponder my circumstances for long.

Ivan said something quickly and hurried away, holding the side of his head.

The blond man stormed up to the kennel and slammed his fist against the chainlink. "Don't fucking talk to him or anyone else. Got it?"

"Or what?" I smirked at him. God, fear made me stupid. Why couldn't I keep my mouth shut like a normal person?

"I'll cut your fucking tongue out." As if I needed a demonstration, he pulled a knife out of his pocket and flicked it open. "And make you eat it."

"Be my guest." My father's dismissive words tumbled out of my mouth before I could help it.

The dickhead said something in his foreign tongue and pointed the knife at me. I'm sure it was a threat, or a promise, of what pain lay in my future. Spitting through the chainlink, he sniffed and stomped off.

Real smart, Roan. Real fucking smart. Antagonize the guy with a knife.

Shaking my head at my own stupidity, I took a cautious step forward and snagged the paper bag off the ground. Carrying it back to the blanket, I sat down and peered inside. It looked like a cheeseburger and some fries. It even included a handful of napkins and some ketchup packets. How considerate.

I unwrapped the burger and took two bites before my stomach twisted itself into knots. I wrapped it up again and tucked it away for later. The same went for the remainder of my water. Ever since Mr. Black dropped it off, I'd been rationing it. So after one measured sip, I secured the lid and set it down.

Aside from preserving what little I had, rationing also helped avoid the inevitable — the bucket. Peeing wouldn't be so bad. But I did *not* want to have to shit in a bucket. Blame my spoiled upbringing or a stupid sense of pride, but I refused to be broken down like an animal.

Drawing my knees up to my chest, I wrapped my arms around my legs and buried my head against my forearms. Despite being summer, it was cold in here. The fact my nerves were fried didn't help. It made everything that much worse, from the temperature to the dread twisting through my body.

At least now I knew why I was here. Silver linings and all that. It was the bank robbery and my big fucking mouth. But if they thought I was the solution to getting them whatever they were so desperate for, they were wrong. Dead wrong.

## 10

# SASHA

WATCHING THE KID PROWL AROUND HIS CELL WAS LIKE watching an animal in the zoo, pacing a well-worn trail back and forth. He didn't even need to look up as he moved, like he'd memorized every inch of it. Then again, it wasn't hard to do in such a small space. I did the same thing when I was in prison.

Sometimes he did push-ups or squats instead of pacing. Other times he sang while his hands mimicked the motion of playing his instruments or conducting. I'm sure he missed his violin, given how much he'd been playing in the days leading up to his abduction. He had a good voice — something he didn't demonstrate during his performance at school, but did at home. Unlike the other instruments, the singing didn't seem to correspond to a mood at all, so I didn't know how to interpret it while he was here.

It had been two days already and Viktor hadn't decided what to do with him yet. By now someone other than his father had to have realized he was missing, yet no police reports were filed. Gregor sent another demand but, for whatever reason, Phillip Sinclair didn't answer. This wasn't the *worst* kidnapping in history, but it was definitely one of the most confusing.

"Just kill him!" Yuri snarled. "If he can't get us what we need, then he's a liability. We need to cut our losses."

"*You're* a fucking liability," Eduard snapped. "Can we kill *you*?"

"Don't go near him until we hear from Viktor," I said, pointing at Yuri.

The asshole wasn't even supposed to *be* here, but here he was. I didn't trust him as far as I could throw him. Ever since he showed up, I'd gone through a carton of cigarettes and a box of tea, standing guard in the shadows, making sure no one went near Roan unless it was to hand off food or water. The only time I dared to sleep was when Eduard was around.

"So you think you're in charge now?" Yuri stared at me.

"After you fucked up the bank robbery, yeah. Don't like it? Call your uncle." I pulled my phone out of my pocket and tossed it on the table in front of him. "Explain to him why you deserve a second chance. Or is this your third? Fourth? Fifth? I can't keep track."

"Who is going to watch the kid?" Eduard interrupted. "We have other business this week. I cannot be in two places at once." The last part was meant for me. My vigilance hadn't gone unnoticed by him, but at least it went without commentary.

I folded my arms over my chest and settled into my stance. "I'll look after him myself."

"Oh, is that so? The big, bad Aleksandr Vassiliev is a baby sitter now?" Yuri stepped forward, lifting his chin. "So much for the Wolf of Verkhoyansk."

"Watch your fucking mouth, Yuri," I snapped with a glare.

"What happened? Finally lose your teeth?" He leaned forward and chomped the air right in front of me.

I lowered my face closer to his, my voice along with it. "If you don't get the fuck out of here, I'll do to you what I did to that family in Tomsk. I don't care who your uncle is."

Yuri looked like he wanted to say something, but he snorted instead and stalked off. He made sure to slam his shoulder into mine on the way. I rocked with the motion, but kept my footing. I should have taken him down right then and there for such disrespect, but somehow I refrained. Probably because I was distracted by the memory of my own threat.

Tomsk.

I could still smell the blood and the shit, even after all this time. The first true slaughter to be associated with my name. I was merely following orders, but to everyone else I was a fucking animal. My hands would never be clean and I was fine with that. I was even fine with the stupid nick-name — The Wolf of Verkhoyansk, the one who killed so savagely they couldn't believe a man would do the things I did to another human.

What I wasn't fine with were pieces of shit like Yuri getting in my way or using the moniker as an insult instead of respecting the brutality of what it meant.

"I'll make sure Ivan is around to give you a hand," Eduard said on his way out.

"No. He's still too soft. Take him with you."

Eduard nodded and disappeared.

As soon as everyone was gone, I grabbed some food and carried it to the kid's cell.

He was asleep when I approached, curled up into a tight ball on his side. Even though it was warm outside, it was considerably cooler in the warehouse. I'm sure the concrete didn't help. He was still wearing the clothes we grabbed him in, which was nothing more than a blue t-shirt and black jeans. I considered getting him a hoodie or something, but hopefully he wouldn't be here much longer.

Unlocking the door quietly, I eased inside and set the fresh bottle of water and a protein bar on the floor near him. He didn't seem to be eating much of anything, or drinking, either. I didn't know if it was because he thought we might poison him or suddenly withhold food. Either way, he was wrong. It was bad business to hurt your hostage any more than you had to.

I was on my way out when his voice stopped me in my tracks.

"Thank you." So quiet, I almost missed it. But he always said it. No matter who it was or what they brought, he said "thank you" every single time.

Bracing a hand against the door frame, I angled myself toward him. He was still laying on the blanket, only now he was clearly awake, watching me intently.

"Why do you do that?" The question rumbled out of me before I thought to stop it.

"Do what?" His blond brows dipped.

"Say 'thank you.'"

Blinking, he pushed himself up into a sitting position, his brow still furrowed. "I don't know."

I squinted at him, looking for insincerity in his face. I doubted he had an insincere bone in his body, but why the fuck was he being so cordial to the people who were holding him captive?

"Because you don't have to?" he offered at last, looking at me like he hoped it was the right answer.

"Well, stop." I crossed the threshold and slammed the door shut.

# 11

# ROAN

The next time I woke up it was to the sound of girls screaming. A dozen different voices, shrieking, crying, and shouting in another language, the sounds echoing off the metal walls around us.

I got to my feet quickly and watched the dickhead blond guy and another guy shove a group of girls toward the cages next to me. When one of the girls didn't move fast enough, the blond backhanded her, sending her sprawling across the floor with a yelp.

She tried to crawl away from him, holding her face while the angry red handprint swelled on her skin.

He snarled something in his language and grabbed a handful of her long, blonde hair, dragging her across the floor by it.

One of the girls ran forward to try and help her, but the second guy shoved a gun in her face and pushed her back toward her own cage. He holstered his gun again beneath his black Adidas coat and secured the lock before moving down the row, depositing a single girl in each cell.

If they resisted, he slapped them or jabbed their stomach so they doubled over before he pushed them inside.

Clinging to the chainlink, I watched in frozen horror, helpless to do a goddamn thing.

The Dickhead, meanwhile, was still taunting the hysterical blonde on the floor. She screamed back at him in the same language, kicking viciously and clawing at his hands to try and free her hair.

"Hey!" I yelled the word before I even realized what I was doing. "Asshole!"

His dark gaze snapped up, his lip curling. "Shut your fucking mouth, boy, or—"

"Or what? You'll cut out my tongue? Yeah. You said that already. Original. Why don't you leave her alone?"

Stepping over the sobbing girl, he strode to my cage in no time flat.

I stayed exactly where I was. If he wanted to use someone as a punching bag, I'd rather it be me than a girl who was half my size. It was stupid as hell, but it was the only thing I could do to help her.

He unlocked the cage and walked inside, producing the same knife as before and flicking it open. "Since you can't shut your fucking mouth, maybe I should put it to good use, hmm? I'll fuck it so hard you'll be gagging for a week."

"You think pretty highly of yourself." I glanced at the front of his pants pointedly.

"Come here and I'll fucking show you."

I held my ground, but with each step he took, I seriously regretted my decision to fuck with this guy. Did he know I was gay or was that a standard threat he used on all of his captives? I really didn't want to find out. The good thing, if you could call it that, was the fact he was leaving the girls alone. For now, anyway.

He grabbed my chin and slammed me against the back wall of chainlink, angling the knife at my cheek. "Get on your knees, boy."

"Fuck you," I seethed.

His knuckles cracked across my cheekbone, whipping my head to the side. I was still seeing stars when he grabbed the front of my shirt and swept my legs out from underneath me, slamming me onto the concrete floor. He dropped his knee into the center of my abdomen, pinning me like an insect. A crazed smile twisted his face as he grabbed my jaw. "Let's see if you're still pretty by the time I'm done with you."

He swiped forward with the blade, aiming for my face.

Instinctively, I threw my left hand up to block the knife while I turned my face away. The blade bit into my palm, slicing through the skin like it was fucking paper. I swore loudly, but the voice roaring through the dark space wasn't mine.

Mr. Black appeared in a flash. He stormed through the door and drove the barrel of his gun into the Dickhead's forehead. My kidnapper/savior snarled something in what I was almost one-hundred percent certain was Russian. I didn't have a clue what he said, but the way he said it gave me goosebumps.

My kidnapper/abuser, on the other hand, stood slowly, though he looked less than pleased to be doing it. The blond threw back a reply and spit. Again. Except this time it was directly *on* me. Fucker.

Mr. Black pulled the gun away and pointed to the guy's left hand with it. When the Dickhead didn't immediately do whatever it was he wanted, Mr. Black snarled the command again. The urge to crawl over to Mr. Black's side of the cage hit me hard. I wanted to put as much distance between me and the other asshole as possible, but for once I played it safe and stayed exactly where I was before one or both of them turned on me.

The blond guy said something and lifted his left hand, flipping off his partner.

I blinked and the gun went off.

Something hot and wet splattered onto my face. I scrambled away from the sensation until I was trapped in the corner of the kennel, the blast ringing in my ears, along with the girls' shrieks.

The Dickhead screamed, cradling his bloody left hand to his torso.

Tucking his gun in his waistband, Mr. Black seized the back of the guy's head and threw him out of the cage.

As soon as they were in the open, it turned into an all-out beat down. Mr. Black and the Adidas guy both pounced on the blond, pummeling him with fists and elbows until he collapsed at their feet. Even then, the beating continued until the Dickhead stopped trying to fight back. Blood oozed from various places on his face, but his chest was still moving. I didn't know whether to be disappointed or not.

Once they were done, Mr. Black leaned over and seized a handful of the asshole's shirt, hauling his limp body up so he could growl something directly in his face. He punched him one last time and let go, standing triumphantly over the unconscious man, his fists bloody and chest heaving.

Adidas said something and Mr. Black looked up, following his gaze to the cages. I flinched when Mr. Black's eyes met mine. Even from a distance I could see the rage in them.

Fuck, was I next? I'd started it. Adidas saw that. Was it my turn to get my ass handed to me by these two?

The thought barely formed before they both left without another word.

I turned my attention to my bloody hand, staring at the dark red pooling in my palm.

What the fuck just happened?!

# 12

## SASHA

I WAS SHAKING I WAS SO FUCKING ANGRY. GODDAMN YURI and his goddamn ego. Now the kid was hurt, which meant if his father ever pulled his head out of his ass and agreed to the deal, he was more likely to renege when he saw what condition his son was in. Not to mention the girls Yuri roughed up during transport would need extra time to heal. If he wasn't born into Viktor's family, there's no way any other boss would have kept his ass alive. I know I wouldn't.

My fist flew out and connected squarely with the mirror in front of me. The glass splintered and cracked, reflecting my pissed off expression in a dozen facets.

Fucking Yuri!

Grabbing the first aid kit, I stomped out of the bathroom again. I stopped to fill a bucket with water and walked back to the cells with my supplies, glad to see someone managed to drag Yuri's ass out of sight.

The kid hadn't moved. Pressed in the corner of the cell, he was still staring at the bloody splatter on the floor. Or his hand. It was hard to tell from the angle. I deposited the stuff on the floor and retrieved one more item before unlocking his cell.

When the door squeaked open, Roan turned his head, watching me with a guarded expression. It was the first time I didn't see hope flicker in his eyes. He actually looked afraid, like he had at the bank, caught between Yuri and I with nowhere to go.

I pushed the door open and motioned him to his feet.

A muscle twitched along his jaw, like he was trying to decide what to do. Not listening was *not* a fucking option. I'd never had vast reserves of patience and the little there was was running thin.

"Get up," I added in English.

He complied, but remained standing where he was.

"Come." I beckoned him forward with one hand. Still, no movement. He was so fucking stubborn. No wonder he got under Yuri's skin — he was under mine in three seconds. "Now!"

Relenting, Roan trudged forward, his gaze locked on me the entire way. Speckles of blood dotted his face; Yuri's backhand made his cheek red and swollen. He was going to have one hell of a bruise in the morning.

"What do you want?" he asked, stopping at the cell door.

I took his right hand, slapped a handcuff to it, and tugged him along behind me. Hooking the other cuff to the side wall of chainlink, I arched a brow at him, waiting for his next question.

Shockingly, he didn't seem to have one. He continued to watch me glumly, chewing on the inside of his lower lip.

With a satisfied nod, I grabbed the bucket of water and splashed waves of it onto the floor, sending Yuri's blood flowing into the drain. The last thing we needed were fucking rats in the building. I hated rats.

Once that was done, I picked up the first aid kit and made my way back to the kid.

He glanced between my face and the distinct red and white cross on the plastic box, clearly confused why I would bother tending to his hand. He must not have understood his worth.

Uncapping a bottle of water, I poured some over his palm and used a couple of cotton pads to wipe away the blood. He should have probably gotten stitches, but that wasn't going to happen, so I used the tiny strip bandages to pull his skin taut. After decades of putting myself back together, I was fairly certain he'd be alright.

"What's your name?" he asked as I worked.

I ignored him. It was actually strange to hear his voice so quiet, yet so close. Normally there was more distance between us.

"I know you can speak English," he added.

Fixing him with a glare, I stared pointedly for a minute before resuming my ministrations. I *could*. That didn't mean I was *going* to. And certainly not at his insistence.

"I didn't mean anything by it," he said, his voice trailing off as he looked away. "I just wanted to know who to thank this time."

Exhaling sharply, I paused and looked up. His gaze returned to mine, still wary, but that tiny shard of hope was back. "What did I say about that?"

"I don't listen," he replied offhandedly, his head tilted to the side, like he was studying me.

"Obviously," I snapped.

A small smile curved his mouth. "Is that a joke?"

Resuming my silence with a scowl, I wrapped his palm with gauze. His hand had been cold when I first started cleaning him up, but now it was warm. I really should get him a hoodie. Despite his sunny disposition, he didn't seem to generate nearly enough body heat for himself. God, he'd never survive a Siberian winter.

Shaking my head, I dispelled the thought immediately. But I kept shaking my head at the whole damn situation. It was brave to stand up to Yuri. Brave and fucking stupid. Especially for some girl he didn't even know and would never see again.

"Thanks anyway, Mr. Black," Roan muttered after a minute, shifting his weight away from me.

Furrowing my brows, I looked up, releasing his hand. Mr. Black? What the hell kind of a name was that?

His bright blue eyes met mine, blinking serenely. The purplish facets scattered in his irises didn't reflect an ounce of fear anymore. He *should* have been afraid, not trying to figure out my name so he could fucking *thank* me. I didn't thank the man who bought me when I was twelve and shipped me overseas. I didn't thank the men who beat me at the start and finish of each day and sometimes in between. And I certainly didn't thank the ungrateful fucks I worked for now. So why did he keep *thanking* me?

The blood on his face was a welcome distraction. Wetting another cotton pad, I dabbed his forehead, happy to have something else to concentrate on. "What did Yuri say to you?"

"Yuri?"

Fuck. I yelled at Ivan for being too soft on the kid and here I was, conversing just as easily. Ok, not quite as easily, but conversing nonetheless.

I ground my molars together and forcibly pushed Roan's face away from me, wiping blood off of the side of it.

"Why do you care?" he asked. The pulse in the side of his throat jumped. I trailed the damp cotton along it, mesmerized by the beating and how it aligned with his breathing. His smart mouth may have been playing it cool, but his heartbeat gave him away.

Realizing I hadn't answered, I spat out a reply quickly. "I don't." At least that part was true. I didn't care. It was a matter of curiosity — and covering my own ass. I wanted to have all of the facts when I told Viktor how his dumb-fuck nephew ended up with a hole through his hand.

Before Roan could open his mouth again, I shoved his face in the opposite direction to assess Yuri's handiwork up close. Despite the swelling and redness, the skin wasn't broken. Still, the mere sight of it made my blood boil all over again.

"Why did you shoot him?" Roan asked, his gaze sliding to meet mine.

I slapped another cotton pad on his cheek, right on top of the knuckle marks.

He hissed and pushed back into the chainlink with a grimace.

"Stop talking," I said, enunciating each word. Letting go of the pressure, I turned his face toward me once more. There was a bit of blood on his chin, right where it dipped in the center beneath blond stubble. Not enough to be a cleft, but enough to give it definition, a sign he'd crossed the threshold from boy to man, even if the rest of his features remained youthful.

The tip of his tongue slipped out, swiping across his bottom lip. Fuck me... The curiosity to taste him hit me out of nowhere. I was fixated on his mouth, momentarily lost in wondering what it would look like after being kissed mercilessly. Just like his creamy skin, I was sure his lips would turn a darker shade of pink, showing the marking for hours, if not days, later.

Revolting, Sasha.

Vile.

Disgusting.

I had to get away from him.

Clearing my throat, I threw the cotton pads into the bucket with the rest of the garbage.

"Thank you," he murmured. It may have been exhaustion, but he almost sounded dejected, like he sensed his time outside of the cell was coming to an end.

I refused to acknowledge his ridiculous gratitude. Instead, I left him standing there while I cleaned up and put everything back where it belonged.

Part of me wanted to leave him standing there all night as punishment for not listening to me. When I told him to stop thanking us, I meant it. I didn't need his fucking gratitude — I needed a goddamn key!

The other part of me didn't want him left out alone, exposed and vulnerable. Roan wasn't like the usual bodies we moved through here. He had value to Viktor, which meant he wasn't here for Yuri to fuck *or* fuck with.

Hopefully now the greasy bastard got it through his thick skull Roan was completely off limits. An eye for an eye, or a hand for a hand as it were. And a beating to make sure he never stepped out of line with me again.

One more fuck up and I'd be all too happy to show him the Wolf still had his fucking teeth.

# 13

# ROAN

Shifting my weight from one foot to the other, I rubbed my handcuffed hand, trying to work some feeling back into it. It wasn't super high up, but the bend in my wrist was enough to impair the circulation. My left hand was already fucked, I didn't need my right getting nerve damage or something. I could still move all my fingers on the left side, but there was no way I'd be able to play any instruments anytime soon. Not that I knew *when* I'd see my instruments again. Or *if*…

The good thing from this whole cluster was that I had one more name. Yuri. The blond asshole.

Ivan and Yuri.

Two down, two to go. Considering how rarely I saw Adidas, I didn't count on getting his name.

But Mr. Black? His name was the most important one. He was clearly in charge, despite Yuri's feelings on the matter. *He* was the one I needed to focus my attention on. Not that it was easy.

Between his refusal to talk and the permanent scowl etched on his face, I found myself getting caught up just watching him. The way he moved, the way he stood. He was huge and he knew it. He filled up every space with his hulking form, exuding alpha vibes simply by breathing. It's probably why he didn't have to say anything at the bank that day until the very end. A whistle was all he needed to summon people to his side, because even the criminals bowed down to him.

I *should* have focused on details that would help me escape, or something I could tell the police when I finally got out of here.

I *shouldn't* have noticed how the muscles in his neck tightened every time I talked to him, making the tiger's head tattoo practically snarl. I shouldn't be hopeful whenever I caught a whiff of cigarette smoke, wondering if he was nearby. I shouldn't have been able to feel his gaze on me, even from a distance. But I did. And, like a fucking masochist, I wanted more of it. I didn't miss the way his gaze lingered on my mouth, even while he manhandled me with the worst bedside manner known to man. In spite of myself, I was fascinated by him, trying to figure out why the hell he wanted *me.*

I was beginning to think he'd left for good when the sound of his heavy steps returned.

Unlocking the handcuff from the chainlink without a word, he dragged me back to the front of the kennel. Instead of stopping at the door and pushing me in, he actually walked in first and pulled me in after him, like he was leading a horse into a stall.

Once I was inside and he was effectively blocking the opening, he unlocked the cuff from my wrist.

He started to turn when I stupidly reached out and touched his left forearm. "I just wanted to say—"

Before I knew what was happening, he grabbed my hand and wrenched it behind my back. His other hand clamped around my throat from behind, ready to strangle me or crush my windpipe at a moment's notice.

"Don't you fucking dare," he growled in my ear, bringing about another wave of goosebumps. "I am not here to make your life easier. I am not your friend. Don't think for one second good manners will spare you."

My mind processed what he was saying — not to mention the sheer volume of words he'd actually spoken. My body, on the other hand, was more concerned with the fact his chest was pressed into my back. Being tossed around wasn't something I was used to, but I was too awed by him to be pissed, not to mention warm. His hands felt like fire on my skin and after days of living with a perpetual chill, it was a twisted form of relief.

"Spare me from what?" I asked, trying to look over my shoulder. His fingers tightened, putting the kibosh on that idea.

"Fate." His lips brushed the shell of my ear. A shiver ran through me at the ambiguity of his answer, or maybe it was his breath, a surprising burst of wintergreen.

Shoving me forward, he exited the cage quickly and locked the door before disappearing with thundering strides.

As soon as he was gone, the girls in the other cages started whispering, like a messed up game of telephone. A couple of them were crying again, while the others shushed them.

I turned my attention to the blonde Yuri was tormenting and knelt next to our shared wall, shoving all thoughts of Mr. Black out of my mind. Christ, the girl couldn't have been any older than twelve or thirteen. Her face was bruised and she gingerly touched her scalp, probably where that asshole ripped her hair out.

I laced the fingers of my right hand through the chain-link and cleared my throat quietly. "Hey. Are you ok?"

She scooted over to me, wiping her face with the edge of her jean jacket. Her answer came in a flurry of Russian. By the inflection alone, I assumed she was asking questions. Even if I knew the language, I sadly had no answers to give. As she spoke, she covered my fingers with hers, her blue eyes flooded with tears.

I shook my head with a wince. "I don't speak Russian."

Either she didn't understand, or she didn't care, because she said something else, gesturing helplessly to our shitty surroundings.

"I'm Roan," I said, touching my chest with my left hand. People were people, no matter what language they spoke. If the only thing I could give this poor girl was a little humanity, that's what I was going to do.

"Roan?" she repeated it back, brows furrowed.

Nodding encouragingly, I gave her a small smile. "Yeah, Roan."

She tucked a lank of hair behind her ear, blinking back her tears and frowning. I empathized with her frustration with me, with the situation we were stuck in the middle of. At least I had the so-called wisdom of adulthood to fall back on and try to make sense of it all. What did she have? Every fairytale and childhood hope had been smashed to pieces.

Mimicking me, she laid a hand on her chest and cleared her throat. "Katya."

"Katya," I repeated with a nod.

A small smile flashed over her face. She shifted and leaned against the chainlink, pulling her bare legs beneath her. Unlike me, she didn't have the luxury of a blanket. If I was cold in full-length jeans, she had to be freezing in a miniskirt.

"Here." I leaned over and grabbed the blanket.

Thin as it was, I was able to slide it under the metal base of our wall. She pulled it up on her end and wrapped it around herself. Resting her head against the chainlink, Katya wormed her hand through one of the diamond openings and held it out to me.

I leaned back against her, lending whatever warmth I could through the metal and took her small hand. She clung to me tightly for the rest of the night. Even after I lost feeling in my ass from sitting on the concrete for so long, I didn't dare move. I stayed right there, singing every relaxing song I could think of, clutching her hand between both of mine and praying we made it through another day.

## 14

## SASHA

"COPS!" IVAN SHOUTED AS HE RAN BY, HEADING FOR THE cells. "The fucking cops are here!"

Swearing under my breath, I took off after him, yelling for Eduard as I ran.

"Where the fuck did they come from?" Eduard asked, jogging beside me. "We didn't get any warning."

"It doesn't matter. Just get out of here." I turned to Ivan and barked at him next. "Call Yuri. Get the girls out of sight and stay the fuck off the streets until you hear from someone."

"Yes, sir!" Ivan shouted, yanking a brunette out of her cell and shoving her into line with the others.

"What about him?" Eduard asked, his chin jutting toward Roan.

"I'll deal with it," I said, not even thinking twice.

Eduard nodded and opened the second-to-last cell, ripping the tiny blonde girl out.

"Roan!" She screamed his name, stretching her hand toward the kid and clawing desperately at the air.

"Katya!" He was on his feet, shaking the chainlink, like

he was seconds away from tearing the entire structure down. If I hadn't welded the thing together myself, I would have been more concerned. "Let her go!"

I slapped a hand on the chainlink in front of his face. "Shut up!"

Roan glared at me, his teeth on edge. "Where is he taking her?"

The balls on this kid…

I didn't have time to admire his tenacity. Spinning the dial on the lock, I ripped open the door and gestured for him to come out.

He shook his head and took a defiant step backward.

"Out. Now," I growled.

"Nyet," he spat back, doubling-down on his withering glare. For a moment, I was frozen by the Russian word on his American tongue. Did he speak Russian? Or was it a lucky guess? Either way, we *really* didn't have the time to play games.

Charging in after him, I latched onto his bicep, dragging him out of the cell like a bratty child. Fighting me the entire way, he alternated between punching any part of me he could, including a well-placed aim to my kidney, and hanging onto the chainlink.

With one final yank, his fingers dislodged from the door and he stumbled out behind me.

As soon as we were out, I drove the barrel of my gun into his ribcage and steered him toward the back door. It was amazing how compliant he became with an H&K aimed at his lung. If I would have known he was going to be such a defiant little shit, I would have started off with the gun and saved myself the agony of pissing blood later.

"What's happening?" Roan asked, his long strides easily matching mine. "Why are we leaving?"

I swore under my breath while also asking God for

patience before I shot him. Ignoring his damn questions, I shouldered open the back door and took a quick glance around.

Seeing no one, I tightened my grip on him and sprinted across the parking lot to where I parked my Mercedes. The front of the warehouse had to be swarming with cops by now. Hopefully I still had time to get out the back way.

"What's going to happen to Katya?" he asked, planting his feet firmly in protest while I opened the driver's door.

"Get in the fucking car." I didn't wait for an answer before I shoved him into it headfirst. Before he got the idea I wanted him to drive, I grabbed a handful of his ass and pushed him over the center console, into the passenger seat.

A cop came around the corner of the building, shouting orders at us. Like that ever worked.

I took aim in the V between the frame of the car and the door, squeezing off a round. A second later, the cop's face crumpled inward and his body dropped like a sack of potatoes.

"Fucking Christ!" Roan shouted, ducking and covering his ears with his hands. "You just shot a cop!"

Ignoring the panicking to my right, I watched as the cop's body disappeared back around the corner from where it came. The next head that peeked out got a matching bullet like his partner.

From what I knew of police tactics, they wouldn't try to make another move until they replenished their numbers. That gave me a small window to get the hell out of here. American prisons may have been easier than Russian ones, but I had no desire to see the inside of either ever again.

"If you move, I'll shoot you," I barked as I climbed up into the driver's seat. Starting the engine, I steered the

SUV in the opposite direction of the cops and peeled out of the parking lot.

"Who *are* you? Who the fuck kills two cops like it's nothing? They have helicopters, you know! And cameras! How far do you think you're going to get now that you've—"

"Shut up!" God, his fucking mouth would.not.stop! I couldn't think with him yammering on. There were plenty more where they came from and I needed to sort through my options before I inadvertently drove us into a roadblock or right over spike strips.

Because he couldn't seem to help himself, Roan kept going. "Where are we going? If this is some suicide-by-cop shit, let me out right here. I'm not fucking dying for you!"

"I swear to God, if you don't shut your fucking mouth, I'll shut it for you." In case he forgot I *did* have a gun and I *wasn't* afraid to pull the trigger, I aimed it at his head.

He swallowed hard, pressing himself into the corner of his seat, his eyes locked on the barrel hovering right in front of his face. "What's going to happen to Katya? Is that guy going to kill her now?"

Rage coursed through my veins. Always a challenge. Always pushing that little bit more. He saw what I was capable of and he still thought it was a good idea to test me. I was beginning to think bravery and stupidity went hand in hand with him.

Instead of shooting him, I did what I did the first time we ever stood face-to-face — I slammed the heavy barrel of my gun into the side of his head as hard as I fucking could.

He slumped against the door, a rivulet of blood trickling down the side of his face.

Maybe now he'd stop asking so many fucking questions.

## 15

# ROAN

Someone took a sledgehammer to the side of my head. Or, at least, that's what it felt like. I was pretty sure I had a concussion. The pain, the wooziness, it all reminded me of any number of head injuries I got playing soccer or fucking around with Freddy through the years.

I reached for the side of my head, but my arms wouldn't move. Jerking up, I looked right and immediately whipped my head left. Both of my wrists were handcuffed to a wooden headboard. I yanked against the restraints, but they didn't give. All I accomplished was rattling the bed and tiring my arms out.

Letting out a string of curse words, each one came out muffled. I tried to open my mouth, but it was stuck shut. Tape, or glue, or something. That fucker.

He wasn't even here for me to silently seethe at. There wasn't anywhere in this tiny motel room for him to hide, except the bathroom. The door was open and the light was off, so I doubted he was in there. How could he tie me up and leave? What if I asphyxiated? What if my brain swelled and I died right there?

Unable to do a damn thing, I glared at the dusty popcorn ceiling and took stock of my new situation.

Not only were these mystery Russians into bank robbing, they were also clearly involved in human trafficking. Is that what they had planned for me? I didn't think I really fit their demographic, but what did I know? Maybe there was a market for tall, lean, blond-haired, blue-eyed guys.

Except, Mr. Black didn't send me with the girls. Did that mean he had a different fate planned? Or was it some fear that I'd spoil the goods, so to speak, before the girls got to their new buyers?

I snorted at the thought. Aside from the fact I wasn't a rapist *or* a pedophile, there was the tiny little detail of my sexual orientation. Yuri's threat could have all been for show, but I didn't want to take the chance. As far as I knew, *they* didn't know about my sexuality and I'd prefer to keep it that way.

Admittedly, it was sometimes difficult whenever my silent captor was around.

No, Roan!

Tall, dark, and murdery were *not* admirable traits. He wasn't even nice. Nice to look at, but *not* a nice person.

Jesus Christ. He was holding me captive, killed two cops right in front of me, and handcuffed me to a fucking bed. *None* of that was ok. He was a fucking psychopath. But try telling that to my dick, who had a shitty track record when it came to choosing men, and was now awake and in search of release.

As if my life couldn't get any worse, the deadbolt turned and the door swung open.

I squeezed my eyes shut, willing my hard-on to dissipate that very instant. Maybe if I ignored it, it would go away. *Not* looking at my smoldering kidnapper was a good start.

The mattress dipped to my left.

My eyes flew open, right as Mr. Black's hand hovered over my face.

Even if there was something over my mouth, I still tried to ask what the fuck he thought he was doing.

My mumbling must have amused him, since I saw a flash of his perfect white teeth for a nanosecond. Paired with his dark hair and icy eyes, he looked like a Siberian husky — one who was two seconds away from devouring me.

"I should have done this a long time ago," he murmured. His gaze dropped to my mouth and he ran his fingertips across my lips. There was a barrier between them, which led me to believe it was tape, not glue, that kept me silent.

The angry "Fuck you" I tried to throw at him didn't sound anything like what it needed to, but I think I got my point across with the death glare I gave him. Yeah, sure, he was hot as hell but I wasn't going to lay there while he molested me or whatever the fuck he thought he was going to do.

He chuckled quietly and looked up, brushing his hand over the side of my head. His fingers touched something on my forehead and a burning sensation jolted through the left side of my body.

I winced and jerked back, glaring again. What the fuck was that? My head was pounding, but what in God's name was the *burning* all about?

Ignoring me like usual, he rifled through a plastic grocery bag and pulled out the rudiments of another first aid kit. Wiping around my temple, pad after pad came away with crusty brown blood.

Then I remembered.

He hit me with the gun. Again — like he had in the bank. Motherfucker. That was twice now. If I survived this ordeal and had any permanent brain damage, I'd know exactly who to blame.

Blistering pain shot across my lips when I wasn't paying attention. Without warning, he ripped the tape off and held two pills out to me, pinched between his fingers.

I bit my lips with a whimper and opened them slowly, mindful of any adhesive residue. "Thank you," I snapped, because I knew it would piss him off.

Predictably, he responded by glaring and holding up the pills, like I couldn't see them without his impatient reminder.

I eyed them warily. "What is it?"

"Pain killers," he replied through gritted teeth.

"You're a sadist," I hissed at him. "You knock me out and then you bandage me up and give me medicine? What the fuck is your endgame?"

The corner of his mouth twitched into a smirk. "I don't want to listen to you whine. So we can do this nicely, or *not*."

Fair enough.

I leaned forward and opened my mouth.

He slipped his fingers inside, depositing the pills on my tongue. His piercing gaze was locked on mine the entire time. If he was worried I was going to bite him, it didn't show. At all. And by God was I tempted. If I wasn't currently chained to the bed like Jesus, I might have done it.

His fingertip grazed the edge of my tongue on the way back out. For a moment I thought I saw something in his eyes that wasn't outright anger, but before I could even begin to imagine what it was, it was gone again.

Uncapping a bottle of water, he held it out at an angle and motioned me forward. When I tipped my chin up, he poured some of the ice-cold liquid in, a bit at a time, until I had enough to swallow the pills.

They probably hadn't even made it through my esophagus when he pulled out a roll of duct tape and ripped off another piece.

"No! Wait!" I leaned back as far as I could, like I could avoid the inevitable. "You don't have to do that."

He arched a disbelieving eyebrow.

"I won't talk," I said quickly, licking my lips. Pretty sure they were missing the top layer of skin now. "If—"

"If?" Both eyebrows went up. "You don't make demands."

"If you'd please let me take a shower," I continued. "I've been in these clothes for… I don't know how long. I just want a shower. That's all."

Instead of growling out a "No" right away, he packed up the garbage from his impromptu patch job, his dark brows furrowed.

I watched him in silence, waiting. He didn't give any indication one way or the other what his decision would be.

When he leaned over me again, I was hopeful. Then he picked up the piece of tape and slapped it over my mouth.

Motherfucker!

Yanking on the handcuffs, I swore beneath the tape.

My pathetic protest ended as soon as he reached for my jeans and popped the button open.

Frozen, I listened as the metal teeth unzipped.

Oh, fuck. Oh, fuck. Fuckfuckfuck.

One of his large hands gripped my hip and pushed it

over, twisting my lower half as much as it would go with my arms still stretched out to the sides.

He yanked the waistband of my jeans away, his fingers grazing along the small of my back in the process. They stopped right at the top of my ass and… did nothing.

Fuck! What was he doing?

And then, just like that, the weight on the mattress lifted. The door opened and slammed shut and he was fucking gone.

Without him holding me in a twisted pose, my body rolled back into its original position. Closing my eyes, I exhaled slowly through my nose. So much for getting rid of my hard-on.

# 16

# SASHA

SASHA, YOU FUCKING IDIOT! YOU'RE SICK, SICK IN THE head.

I grabbed a pair of pants in Roan's size and threw them into the shopping basket. Staring at the heaped fabric, I shook my head and pulled them out again, trading the gray sweats for black instead.

This was a first — shopping for a victim. But who knew how long we'd have to be shacked up in that motel room. He had a point about the shower. And we'd both need some extra clothes if we wanted to be comfortable.

Comfortable? Christ Almighty. Who gave a fuck if he was comfortable?

Cursing myself, I stopped in front of the socks and underwear, grabbed the stuff I needed and wandered over to the shirts.

I had no idea what size shirt to get — I hadn't bothered to check. My clothes would be huge on him, but he wasn't small, either. Yeah, he was lean, but I had to accommodate for his height.

Before I overcomplicated everything, I grabbed a

medium t-shirt and threw it onto the pile. A few more things rounded out this bizarre little shopping trip and I headed toward the cash registers, scanning my own shit and paying in cash.

Bags in hand, I walked back to the motel. It would have been faster to drive, but I wanted the time to myself. I hoped fresh air would help me get a grip on whatever the fuck my problem was.

He was a fucking meal ticket, Sasha, nothing more.

He was your captive.

And he was a *he*.

One made him off limits — the other made him a death sentence.

I raked a hand through my hair and scratched the part where it faded down to bare skin. Just a few days. We had to lie low for a few days until the heat cleared, then I could take him to another safe house. Hopefully by then, Viktor would know what the fuck he wanted me to do with Roan now the original plan had gone to hell in a hand basket.

Keying myself back into the room, I kicked the door shut and secured the deadbolt and the chain. For good measure, I shoved a chair up under the handle at an angle. Once I knew the room was as secure as it was going to get, I turned my attention to my captive.

He watched me with a glare, mumbling his displeasure beneath the tape.

"Don't talk. Got it?" I pointed a warning finger at him.

He nodded.

I picked at the corner of the tape and ripped it off in one quick motion.

He groaned and closed his eyes, rolling his lips together. I tried to ignore the fact my dick perked up with the sounds and focused on unlocking the handcuff from his right wrist.

"Don't even think about trying to run," I growled.

Glancing at him as I circled around the bed, I expected a verbal answer, but he shook his head. Good. Progress. Unlocking the left handcuff from the headboard, I held onto it, like a little metal leash, and led the way to the bathroom.

"Get in." I slid a pointed glance at the tub/shower combo.

Expelling an irritated huff, he stepped into the tub as directed.

"Take it off." I jerked my chin toward his dirty shirt. I suppose I should have been happy he was doing what he was told for a change, but it was like dealing with a toddler. I shouldn't have to instruct him every goddamn step of the way.

There was still no verbal reply, but he didn't jump to and follow the order, either. He watched me warily, as still as a statute.

"Or I'll rip it off," I added.

His blue eyes dropped to the discolored tub. For a minute I thought he was going to keep refusing, but he finally moved. With the one hand still handcuffed, he reached behind his head and gathered a fistful of fabric, peeling it over his head and shaking his right arm free.

I purposely kept my attention on the shirt and not the outline of his abs. Exchanging my hold on the extra handcuff for his actual wrist, I slipped the t-shirt off the rest of the way and dropped it on the floor before securing the cuff to the fall handle in the shower.

"What?! No!" He yanked against the cuff. Thankfully the cheap plastic rod held. "How the fuck am I supposed to take a shower wearing handcuffs?"

"Figure it out." I stomped out of the room, leaving the door open, to which he also protested. Snagging a conveniently pre-packaged bag of toiletries I picked up at the store, I marched back into the bathroom and crushed it against his chest. "You have ten minutes. And the next time I hear anything out of your mouth, I'll carry out Yuri's threat."

"You're going to fuck my face until I gag?" He lifted a challenging brow before his gaze drifted to the bulge in the front of my pants. It wasn't a full-on erection, but it wouldn't stay that way for much longer if he didn't stop looking at me like that, like he was fucking daring me.

Slamming my forearm against his chest, I heaved my weight against him, pinning him to the shower wall. "What the fuck did you say to me, you fucking queer?" I meant cut his tongue out! Had I fucked up the English translation that badly? No. No, I *know* I didn't. That's what Yuri said he was going to do. Cut his tongue out and make him eat it. I heard him.

Roan's blue eyes flashed, surprise and stubbornness at the same time. "*That* was Yuri's threat right before you shot him. And if you're planning the same thing, then I'm pretty sure that makes you the—"

My first blow was a closed backhand across his mouth. One way or another, he'd learn to shut the goddamn thing. Threats of violence obviously didn't work. It was time to show him I wasn't fucking around.

The second and third blows landed in the center of his diaphragm, dropping him to his knees with a ragged gasp for air. I didn't let him have it. Seizing him by the throat, I bent my face close to his, watching red-tinged saliva rush over his bottom lip and drip down to his bare chest.

"You better pray to God your father comes through, because if he doesn't, I'll be all too happy to break your fucking neck."

His lashes fluttered, but he didn't look afraid. Instead, he laughed, his white teeth outlined by blood.

I squeezed harder, but he didn't stop laughing, even when he was gasping for air.

"Just kill me then," he rasped. His watery eyes found mine and stayed locked in place, not fearful, not angry — resigned. A memory I'd long since buried flashed to the forefront of my mind, another blue-eyed boy staring up at me, waiting to die.

I jerked my hand away and climbed out of the tub, storming out of the bathroom as quickly as I could.

## 17

# ROAN

I SPAT OUT A MOUTHFUL OF BLOOD AND WATCHED THE RED swirls slink down the side of the tub. Heaving a breath, I coughed it all back out, only to repeat the process until oxygen actually made it into my lungs.

At least now I had my answer.

They took me for ransom.

They must have figured out who I was after the robbery and thought I'd be an easy payday. Too bad nothing in life was easy. My father would never pay, no matter how little they asked. Like the US government, he did *not* negotiate — with anyone, for anything. Mom had zero financial control, so she was of no help. At least now I knew I was living on borrowed time. Cold comfort.

Another laugh spilled out of me, until the absurd reaction turned to tears. Smashing the heel of my hand against my eyes did little to stop the dampness. Dad was as likely to go to the police as he was to pay the ransom. No one was going to swoop in and rescue me. I was completely and utterly on my own.

I should have pulled myself together and showered,

like I wanted. But I couldn't. I just sat there with blood in my mouth, one arm dangling in the air, staring at the shower curtain and trying not to think about what sort of STDs were crawling all over the yellowed plastic.

The enormity of the situation was crushing and I was powerless to do a goddamn thing.

I didn't know how much time passed. It was definitely longer than my allotted ten minutes. My arm fell asleep by the time Mr. Black's massive frame filled the doorway again. He had to have known I didn't shower, considering he left the door open and I hadn't turned on the water. Still, his dark brows furrowed as he stepped into the bathroom.

Wordlessly, he closed the distance between us and stepped one foot into the tub. I caught more than a whiff of cigarette smoke. Did he smoke a whole pack? Jesus. Well, good. Maybe he'd have a fucking heart attack.

I should have been worried he was coming back to actually kill me, or at least beat me some more, but I didn't care. The numbness in my arm spread through the rest of me as well. It was better than feeling any sort of real emotion.

He unlocked the handcuff from the plastic rod without a word. I waited for the vicious tug upward, or another punch. Neither of them came. Instead, he took the cuff from my wrist and let my arm fall to my lap.

By the time I had the energy to lift my head, he was gone, closing the bathroom door behind him.

I stayed sitting for a minute, unsure if it was a trick or not. Although, on some level I knew it wasn't. The one thing I could say for my warden was thus far he hadn't been manipulative. On the contrary, he'd been direct and to the point, brutally so. He, himself, may have been a mystery but his likes and dislikes were pretty clear.

Forcing myself to my feet, I stripped out of the rest of my clothes and turned on the shower. It was the least I could do to feel normal right now. Since there wasn't a razor in the little kit, the shower was quick, even with the added time it took to brush my teeth and try to wrangle my wavy hair into submission. At least I had it cut right before the showcase, so it wasn't terrible, just long and messy on top, as usual.

The real problem came after the shower was over.

There was no way I putting dirty clothes back on when the whole point had been to get clean. Wrapping a towel around my waist, I scooped up the clothes and dumped them in the tub. Like a washerwoman at the river, I did my best to scrub the soap through the dirty fabric and rinse it all out.

I'd just finished wringing out my jeans when the bathroom door opened. I tossed them over the curtain rod and threw a questioning glance over my shoulder. I mean, I knew who it was. It was what he wanted that remained to be seen.

He froze in the doorway, which was very unlike him. Over the past few days, I'd seen him barge into a variety of spaces without hesitation. So what was his deal now?

I leaned down and snagged my t-shirt from the tub, wringing it out too. If he wanted silence, I'd give him fucking silence. Besides, knowing he was waiting on a payout that was never coming made me less inclined to humanize him. I didn't want to get too comfortable with the man who was ultimately going to murder me.

With my clothes taken care of, I turned to face the mountain in the doorway. He hadn't moved an inch, nor had he taken his eyes off of me. The blazing awareness I felt on my back was now focused on my front, traversing from my face to my chest and down my abs.

Self-consciously, my hand drifted to the knot in the towel, holding it securely in place. The last thing I needed was to be completely naked in front of this guy after getting smacked around for even mentioning his dick.

His narrowed gaze leapt back to my face. He held up another grocery bag before tossing it into the sink. "Get dressed."

"Da, comrade."

His dark brows slanted as he gave me another once-over, his mouth twisting into a deeper scowl. Shaking his head, he snapped himself out of whatever he was thinking and closed the door.

Padding over to the sink, I pawed through the bag, surprised to actually see clothes. New clothes. Suddenly the pants thing from earlier made sense, although he could have fucking *asked* what my size was instead of mauling me. Then again, he probably didn't *ask* for anything. Someone like him made demands or took what they wanted. He and my dad would get along swimmingly.

Dressing quickly, I opened the door and walked out into the room, waiting for the next battle to begin.

He was texting on his phone, apparently oblivious to my return.

"Thank you," I said, more out of habit than anything, and resumed my spot on the bed.

His head whipped up, eyes narrowed. A growl rumbled in the back of his throat and in two steps, he was in my face. The first thing that came was the strip of duct tape.

I didn't even bother protesting. I didn't have the energy. The second I saw the handcuff emerge from his back pocket, I gave him my wrist. He took it and held it, his thumb pressed along my pulse point, while he scrutinized my face. I studied his in return, memorizing each line, each little scar — things that would be an imperfection on anyone else only added to his lethal visage.

My compliance seemed to confuse him. He hesitated for another moment, eyeing me suspiciously, before securing the handcuff to the headboard. To further his confusion, I stretched my other arm out, waiting for the second cuff. It was coming anyway, so I might as well roll with it.

He muttered something under his breath in Russian, locking the second cuff quickly. Snatching the remote off the nightstand, he turned the TV on and flicked through the channels before landing on an action movie. Tossing the remote on the table by the window, he disappeared out the door without so much as a backward glance.

My head thunked back against the headboard.

## 18

# SASHA

This fucking kid. One minute he's mouthing off, refusing to do a damn thing I tell him, and the next he's going along with the program without complaint. Rubbing my forehead in a laughable attempt at alleviating my headache, I set off down the stairs and jogged across the street to the pizza place.

While I waited for our food, Viktor called.

"What do you want me to do?" I asked, walking outside and leaning against the side of the building. Staring at the rundown motel across the street, I lit a cigarette. Just looking at it made my skin crawl. I'd lived in worse, but it was close enough to resurrect memories of flea bites and freezing cold — all shit I purposely chose to forget.

"Are you sure you grabbed the right kid?" he asked.

I ripped the cigarette out of my mouth and blew out a sharp steam of smoke. "Are you fucking kidding me? I've never failed you."

"His father hasn't answered our demands."

"His father is a fucking prick," I muttered.

"Well, I'll give this prick until the end of the week. Then we will see," he said before disconnecting.

I smothered my groan by sucking more nicotine into my lungs before flicking the butt out into the parking lot with the rest of the trash. Shoving the phone back in my pocket, I went inside to pick up my order.

Food in hand, I returned to the room at a snail's pace. Just a few more days. No problem. Other than eating, I'd keep Roan's mouth taped shut and we'd be fine.

When the door opened, Roan looked like he was asleep. His head was tipped back against the headboard exposing the smooth whiteness of his throat. I was able to get three steps into the room before he stirred, blinking against the sudden light.

Once the door was secured, I tossed a bottle of water in his lap and set the pizza on the bed next to him before unlocking one of the handcuffs. Flipping open the lid, I grabbed a slice for myself and hooked the second chair from the table. I dragged it away from the window and across the room, where I could watch him, the door, and the window all at once.

Roan picked at the tape on his mouth and pulled it off slowly, questioningly, watching as I settled into my chair. Unholstering the gun from the small of my back, I couldn't help the sigh that escaped as the pressure lifted from my spine. Balancing the gun on my thigh, I took a bite of pizza, acutely aware Roan was still watching me.

"You are *not* welcome," I said, between chewing. There. Pain in the ass. Beat you to it this time.

The little shit smirked, picking up his own slice. He dropped his food suddenly and spun the box, squinting at something on the lid. "Sasha?"

Without even thinking, I looked up at the sound of my name.

He blinked at me, a smile spreading across his face as he put two and two together. "Your name is Sasha?"

Fuck me!

Why did that girl have to ask what my name was? And why the fuck did I answer with the real one? Because I was on the phone with Viktor, paying more attention to his hemming and hawing than the teenager batting her lashes at me behind the counter.

"Aleksandr," I corrected with a growl, tearing off another bite.

"But you go by Sasha." I grabbed my gun and was halfway out of my chair when he held up his free hand and dropped his gaze. "I'm just saying, it's better than 'Mr. Black.'"

Easing back into my chair, I kept glaring at him. He peeked up after a minute, meeting my gaze once more — boldly, stupidly, and unafraid as usual. His smirk was back as he retrieved the piece he dropped, but at least he kept his mouth shut this time.

We ate in silence, explosions and gunfire in the movie filling the quiet.

Roan only had one piece and a few sips of water before he slid down the mattress and rolled onto his side, the side that was still handcuffed.

"I'm not starving you. Eat," I said, inexplicably irritated by his timidity.

"I just want to sleep," he murmured, closing his eyes and nestling into the pillow. His nose twitched and he swiped at the silver hoop in his right nostril before settling again. It was the first time I realized he had changed it from the stud he usually wore.

*Why* did I know that?

I gave myself a mental slap. I didn't exactly believe he wasn't hungry, but I wasn't going to argue, either. At least he'd be quiet for a change without having to resort to duct tape.

Finishing the movie and my dinner, I stood, accompanied by a series of pops and crackles as I stretched my back.

Once he assumed his position, Roan didn't move. His breathing deepened and his fingers twitched, the first signs of falling into a deeper sleep.

I should have made him roll over so I could restrain his other hand. For some reason, I didn't. Maybe it was because he was curled up into himself, with his free hand tucked tightly against his chest. Or maybe it was sheer confusion at how well he was sleeping given his situation. Then again, I'd learned to fall asleep whenever and wherever I could. Apparently being held against your will gave you that capability.

Grabbing the edge of the blanket, I tugged it up over his shoulder. He still didn't move.

I turned off the light above him and returned to my chair with the remote. Lighting a cigarette, I flicked through the channels until I found another movie and settled in for a long ass night of standing guard.

## 19

# ROAN

For the first time in days, I woke up feeling refreshed. Ok, not like I was ready to conquer the world, but like I'd actually managed to give my body the rest it needed after so many nights of quick, uncomfortable cat naps. I was warm, for a change, and my body wasn't screaming at me in pain.

Rubbing the sleep from my eye, it suddenly dawned on me my hand was free. Nor did I have tape over my mouth. My head whipped to the left, deflating slightly to see the other handcuff was still there. Of course. Sasha was mean, but he wasn't stupid.

It was strange I finally knew his name, but exhilarating in a way. Like knowing it gave me some sort of power over him. He was no longer a nameless figure controlling my existence. Aleksandr. Sasha. The nickname didn't make sense, but maybe it did in Russian.

Speaking of… where was Sasha?

It didn't take long to pick up on the sound of water running. The door to the bathroom was half-open, steam drifting out lazily along the top of the ceiling.

In the two seconds it took me to realize he was showering, my brain and my body each came up with a plan. The brain said now was the chance to escape. Find a way to break the headboard and get the fuck out. My body, however, decided it was the perfect time to stir up a little morning wood and fucking immobilize me.

As soon as the bathroom door opened the rest of the way, my jaw dropped and my brain stopped working altogether.

Strolling out in nothing but a towel, Sasha was every bit the bad boy of my fantasies. His clothes hadn't disguised how muscular he was, but watching droplets of water roll through those ridges and valleys was something else altogether.

A dusting of dark hair spread across his massive chest and tapered off the further south it went, each of his tattoos still visible beneath. Like his arms, the tattoos were a mix of symbols and writing, not one solid piece or style and certainly no color. There were stars on each side of his chest, along with a pair of eyes on his pec. A dagger looked like it was piercing through the skin on his sternum, blood dripping down onto a snarling wolf's head in the center of his abdomen with some writing beneath it. It was hot. And terrifying. Mostly hot. No, terrifying. Crazy, Russian criminals were terrifying, Roan. But also really fucking hot.

It took him a couple seconds to realize I was awake. "What the fuck are you looking at?" he snapped.

A Russian god sent to torment me? Literally.

Knowing that was definitely not the right answer, I swallowed any thought of a reply and kept my mouth shut.

Apparently satisfied I wasn't going to speak, he turned his back to me and grabbed a handful of clothing from the top of the dresser. His back had even more muscles. And more tattoos, including a giant one of the Virgin Mary and baby Jesus. He didn't strike me as the religious type, but what the hell did I know? There was a double-headed eagle and a knight thrown in the mix, along with dozens of other, smaller tattoos I only caught glimpses of as he moved.

My traitorous dick completely tented the front of my sweat pants, begging for attention. I bit my lip and waited until Sasha ducked back into the bathroom before I reached down and tried like hell to adjust it so it wasn't so obvious. Fat chance. No matter how I tried to disguise it, it was fucking obvious.

Sasha rounded the corner of the bathroom, fully dressed in a dark gray t-shirt and jeans, and his eyes immediately fell to my hand.

I expected derisive questions, or outright yelling. I even expected another backhand to go with my growing collection of bruises. What I didn't expect was for him to swagger forward, step by step, his head dipped low like a predator on the hunt. And I certainly didn't expect him to kneel on the bed or reach over me to unlock the handcuff.

Even after I was no longer cuffed, I stayed right where I was. Did he *not* see? He had to have seen. He saw everything.

It wasn't until he tossed his head toward the bathroom that I eased out of bed, watching him like a hawk. He didn't make a move to restrain me, or even go with me. I was allowed to walk the ten feet to the bathroom by myself. What the fuck was happening?

I tried not to question it as I slipped into the bathroom and went about my morning routine as if this were any other vacation in a crap motel with my hot kidnapper.

Exiting the bathroom, I immediately scanned my surroundings for Sasha.

He was standing by the window, peering out through

the sheer curtains like he was looking for something. Or someone. He'd been doing it off and on since we'd been here, which made me wonder if he was as restless as I was.

As soon as he realized I was in the room again, he turned and gave me another head-to-toe. "Sit."

Obediently, I returned to the bed.

Closing the curtain, he followed me and grabbed one of the handcuffs, reattaching it to my wrist. So much for freedom.

The second the cold metal clicked into place, my dick stirred again, woken by the contrasting warmth of Sasha's hands. The fact his face was so close to mine didn't help matters, or that the shower left him smelling clean and woodsy.

"What is that?" Sasha growled. I didn't have to follow his gaze to know what had him pissed off again.

"What the fuck do you think?" I snapped back, bracing for another fist to the face.

"Get rid of it."

I scoffed, rolling my eyes. "Yeah, ok. I'll get right on it." Maybe Russians could control their dicks like that, but I sure as hell couldn't. It had a mind of its own. Clearly.

He seized a handful of hair on the top of my head and twisted my face toward his. "Either you take care of it, or I will."

The threat only made me that much harder, which I'm sure was *not* his intended effect. Or maybe it was.

"You'd like that, wouldn't you?" I hissed as his fingers tightened in my hair. "I saw you yesterday. You couldn't take your fucking eyes off of me."

"You better watch your mouth."

"Or what? You'll hit me again? I told you, just kill me. Because your money's never coming and I'm not fucking scared of you." False. I was terrified of him, but since all of the blood was currently rushing southbound out of my brain, I didn't have the ability to be rational.

"I think you like when I hurt you," Sasha said between his teeth, his big hand palming my dick and squeezing, pulling a whimper out of me. "I think that's why you won't be quiet for two seconds. Why you're always pushing the limit."

My eyes closed as he stroked me harder, almost painfully. "Yeah? I think you've been looking for an excuse to do this."

"Do what?" God, why did he have to growl it like that? It was like every single syllable came from the back of his throat instead of the tip of his tongue.

I forced my eyes open to focus on his, anchoring myself in their icy blueness. "Touch me."

"I don't need an excuse." He withdrew his hand abruptly and handcuffed my free wrist, a dangerous look in his eyes. At that moment, I realized I was in for a world of hurt, especially since both of my hands were useless. He hovered over me again, one knee balancing on the edge of the mattress.

"I can do whatever the fuck I want with you," Sasha continued, his face close to mine. His breath was like a caress, all minty fresh and hot against my skin. "There's no one who can stop me."

"And what is it you want to do with me?" I knew what *I* wanted him to do with me. I wanted him to touch me again, with his rough and unforgiving hands. I wanted to experience what it was like to be the one pursued for a change, to surrender the control to someone else. It made zero sense, but nothing about this fucked up situation made sense.

He nudged my face to the side with his nose, his lips brushing my ear and sending a shiver down my spine. "I want to use you…" He inhaled before he grabbed either side of my jaw and yanked my face toward his so we were nose-to-nose. "To get what I want…" He was glaring, but his pupils were so big I could hardly see the icy blue I was used to. "And then? I never want to see you again."

Rejection stabbed through the middle of my stomach, hot and sickly, followed quickly by embarrassment and anger. He played me and my dumbass set myself up for it.

Letting go of my face roughly, he stood and reached for the duct tape. He made a show of picking it up and pulling off a piece, like he was waiting for me to say something. There wasn't anything left *to* say. This was my fate. Another worthless pawn in the game of life, pushed around the board by other people who didn't give two shits if they sacrificed me along the way.

Sasha slapped the tape over my mouth, his jaw shifting to the side. Standing straight again, he swallowed, like he was going to say something. He didn't. After a minute, he headed for the door. With a backward glance that I swear went straight to my dick, he ducked out the door.

Fuck me.

And fuck him.

And fuck this kidnapping bullshit!

# 20

# SASHA

The Birdcage was loud and smoky as I stepped through the front door, despite the fact it wasn't even dinner time yet. Depravity was a round-the-clock business; perverts didn't seem to care what time they came to satisfy their sinful urges, as long as there was someone to pour them a drink and grind against their crotch. Lada's club gave them all of that and more.

Taking off my sunglasses, I hooked them on the collar of my t-shirt as I made my way to the back.

"Aleksandr," a girl called as I walked by, waving her pink feather boa at me. "Come here."

I ignored her and kept going.

Lada ducked her head out of her office and slid out in front of me, blocking the hallway with her tall, curvy frame. She was one of the few women who was near eye-level with me and that was without her heels. "What are you doing here?"

"Looking for Eduard."

Her fingers wound around mine, lifting my hand for a closer inspection. My knuckles were still bruised from

Yuri's stupid face, but they weren't swollen anymore. "I saw what you two did to Yuri."

I cocked my head, waiting for her to go on.

She let go of my hand and slipped hers into the front pocket of my pants. Pulling out the pack of cigarettes, she helped herself to one. I fished my lighter out and sparked a flame for her, still waiting for her opinion on the ass beating her so-called boyfriend got.

There were times I swore she hated him more than I did, but she knew better than to try and leave him. The bastard forced himself into her business and into her, leaving her trapped with nowhere to go.

Lada took a drag and blew the smoke to the side, looking at me under thick black lashes and piles of eyeliner. "You should have killed him."

"One day I will."

"Promise?"

"Killing is what I do."

"Except now." She picked something off her tongue and flicked it away, giving me a pointed once-over. "Now you're a baby sitter."

I ignored her and the echo of Yuri's taunt. "Can you do me a favor?"

She raised her brows, pulling on the cigarette, the orange glow skittering up the white stick.

"I want to know who he's talking to," I continued, lowering my voice. "Especially about me." Since the line was officially drawn in the sand, I wouldn't put it past him to try and seek some sort of retribution for his wounded pride.

Her gaze raked over me again while she exhaled the smoke. "Whatever you say, Sasha."

Giving her a nod, she stepped to the side and I continued down to the basement.

Vlad stood up from his chair, folding his newspaper. "Aleksandr."

"Is Eduard here?"

He shook his bald head. "He said he'd be back later."

I turned to go when whimpering from the storage room caught my attention. Anger prickled along my skin as I processed the noise. Throwing a glance at Vlad, I walked to the door, pointing at it. "Tell me those aren't the girls Yuri picked up."

Vlad didn't say anything. He didn't have to. I knew. Yuri's dumb ass brought them here for their so-called training instead of taking them somewhere else because he was lazy and this place was close to the warehouse the cops raided. As much as I hated them, cops weren't stupid. They'd be searching all of the Russian-owned businesses in the area and that would lead them straight here.

Shaking my head, I yanked the door open and stalked inside.

A dozen girls were scattered around the room, laying on mattresses or huddled together. Most of them looked strung out, with vacant stares that barely seemed to register my presence. Some had ripped clothing, others none at all.

"Katya?" I asked, scanning the faces for the little blonde Roan was so goddamn concerned about. None of them spoke up or made eye contact.

Vlad stepped up next to me. "Looking for someone?"

"A blonde girl. About, yay high," I replied, holding my hand beneath by chest. "She called herself Katya."

"There." He jerked his chin toward a lump in the corner. "She's a wild one but I think we finally broke her."

I considered her sprawled form, in nothing but a bra and underwear. She stared at the ceiling, empty eyes and slack mouth. If I didn't know better, I'd think she was dead. Well, she *was* dead. The girl named Katya ceased to exist the minute someone snatched her and stuffed her onboard a container ship. That thing laying there was just a shell of a girl who'd been used and drugged and beaten, worse than any animal.

"I didn't realize you liked them so young," Vlad said with a chuckle. "Guess it explains why you haven't married. If you want, I can save one from the next batch for you."

My lip curled. "Get the fuck away from me."

I didn't wait for his reply. Stalking forward, the conscious and coherent girls shrieked and shied away, curling up at the furthest ends of their dirty mattresses.

Katya didn't move.

Dropping to one knee next to her, I scanned her petite form, taking in all of the bruises and bite marks. Her wrists were free now, but they'd been rubbed raw by some sort of restraint. The inside of her elbow was already riddled with track marks and dried blood. There was nothing left to salvage.

"Lord Jesus Christ, have mercy on thy servant," I murmured, dragging a soiled pillow over Katya's face.

"No!" Vlad's footsteps thundered behind me.

I unholstered my gun and jammed it into the pillow, firing off a round to a chorus of screams and Vlad's howling.

"What the fuck?!" Vlad clamped his hands on his head, staring at me as I got to my feet, the gun hanging at my side.

"You have one day to move the rest out of here," I said calmly. It was a miracle Viktor hadn't been arrested yet because of Yuri's idiotic moves. I couldn't wait to tell him about this one. Maybe he'd finally get some sense and let me get rid of him.

"Why the fuck did you kill that one? Yuri—"

"Can go fuck himself! Now you have an hour." I lifted the gun, taking aim at one of the other girls. She sobbed and curled into herself, trying to make herself as small as possible. "Or maybe I should kill the rest and watch Yuri blame everything on you."

"No! I'll move them. Ok? I'll move them."

"Wise choice." I stepped past him, my shoulder narrowly missing his as he scurried out of the way.

"What about the dead one?"

I slid a look over my shoulder. "Do I look like I fucking care?"

Marching up the stairs, I rolled my head from side to side, trying to crack my neck. I didn't re-holster my gun, not because I thought I'd have to use it again, but because it tended to keep people from talking to me and I was *not* in the mood to fucking talk.

"Aleksan—" One of the dancers popped out of the dressing room, took one look at me, and darted back inside.

That's what I thought.

Sliding up onto a barstool, I set the gun on the bar top and retrieved my pack of cigarettes. I texted Viktor about Yuri's brilliant move while Lada stepped in front of me, bracing her palms on the edge of the bar. "Tea or vodka?"

"Vodka."

Nodding, she poured me a glass and left, wisely leaving the bottle behind.

Some time later, Eduard appeared, slapping my back. "What's with you? You look like someone kicked your dog."

"I don't have a dog," I muttered, taking a sip of my drink.

He chuckled and shook his head. From the look on his face, he wasn't buying my non-answer, but he didn't keep pushing either. "Good news and bad news," he said, unzipping his Adidas jacket and waving Lada down for a glass.

"What's the bad?"

"We have a rat." He blew Lada a kiss and took the glass of vodka from her. He took a sip and leaned closer, lowering his voice. "Someone tipped off the police about the girls. Anonymous phone call, according to the records. Gregor said he can't trace it."

"What about your resources?"

"They're working on it."

"So what's the good?" I tapped ash off the end of my cigarette, preparing for more bad news despite what he said.

"The cops didn't find anything." Eduard shrugged and tossed back the rest of the vodka with a grimace, helping himself to my bottle.

First the bank robbery was a fail because of Igor's *bad* information. Now, the warehouse was raided based on *inside* information. Was it one rat, or a whole colony? And what were they ultimately after?

"How long are you going to hang on to the kid?" Eduard asked, interrupting my theorizing.

Roan.

He was going to fucking end me.

After waking up with a little situation of my own, I took a cold shower which did absolutely nothing. Somehow he crawled inside my head and refused to leave, tormenting me with images as blinding as the sun — the way he ran a hand through his hair, the definition in his arms, his fucking smile. Seeing no alternative, I allowed the fantasy to play out in my mind, imagining all the things I wanted to do to him ever since that fucking football game in the park.

Fisting my cock, I jacked off hard and fast, remembering Roan on his knees in the same shower not but twelve hours before. The release was welcome, but the disgust that followed almost made me vomit.

I thought I'd managed to purge him from my mind until I got out of the shower and saw him in bed with an erection clear as day. Ignoring it was the only option until Roan got the best of me. Like usual, he had to open his fucking mouth — test me, bait me, drive me insane. I'm sure he didn't expect me throw it back at him, to push *his* fucking buttons and then leave him with a raging hard-on.

It was a double-edged sword, though. I might have left him flustered, but he resurrected every sinful thought I had in the shower. As it was, I was surrounded by a dozen willing, half-naked women and all I could think about were the long, hard lines of Roan's body. His soft mouth, his stunning eyes. Between the time I spent following him and the time he'd been my captive, I think I memorized every inch of him. Well, almost every inch. But I'd felt enough of his cock to have a pretty good idea of what that looked like too.

"I don't know," I spat out quickly in answer to Eduard's question. "I don't know how long Viktor wants to hold out for his father." It wasn't entirely the truth, but Eduard didn't need to know the particulars.

"I can't believe a man like that wouldn't pay."

"No?" I raised my brows at him. "Do you remember what happened to Dominika?"

Eduard shook his head, sipping his drink.

Of course he remembered. Everyone heard the story.

Dominika's father, Dimitri, arrived to make the exchange. Instead of throwing out a bag of money and whisking her away to safety, he shot her in the head. Why? Because she was weak enough to get caught. He shot her kidnappers, too, and the whole ordeal was over in a matter of seconds. If Dimitri's reputation as a cold motherfucker wasn't known before then, there was zero doubt about it after the fact. And yet they called *me* an animal.

"But he's American," Eduard said after a minute, making a face. "Americans like their children."

I snorted and answered while I lit the last cigarette out of my pack with the dying embers of the other. "You watch too much TV."

Out of nowhere, long, fake nails raked across the back of my neck. A pair of teeth nipped my earlobe and a cloud of candy perfume engulfed me.

I waved the girl away, trying to resume my conversation with Eduard, even though he had a bottle-blonde in a hot pink bikini feeling him up.

The girl behind me circled around to the front, running her hand over my thigh and straight to my crotch. "You look stressed. I can help."

Looking her up and down, my lip curled instinctively. "And what number would I be today? Six? Seven?" It was still early by whore standards, but most managed to rack up double digits by midnight.

She gasped, like she had any virtue left to warrant outrage. Her hand flew toward my face. I caught her wrist and crushed the bones in my grip until she yelped out loud, beating my bicep to try and free herself.

"Get the fuck away from me. You touch me again with those filthy hands and I'll cut them off." Shoving her hand into her chest, I glared at her until she slithered away.

Lada cursed me from the other end the bar and ran off to check on her employee.

Eduard chuckled and shooed his afternoon delight away as well. "You should have taken her up on it. Maybe you wouldn't be such an asshole."

I slammed the rest of my vodka and slid off the

barstool. “Keep me up to date on the rat. The sooner this shit is over, the sooner I’m out of this fucking country.”

“You’re leaving?” Eduard spun on his stool, watching me. “I just got here.”

“He hasn’t eaten all day.”

“Fuck him,” Eduard exclaimed, lighting up his own cigarette and blowing out a stream of smoke. He didn’t mean it literally, but my heart still skipped a beat. “You know they can go weeks without food.”

“All too well.” A phantom pang hit my stomach. I silenced it with another drag, tucking the cigarette between my lips. Shoving my gun back into place, I gave Eduard a parting nod and headed for the door.

# 21

# ROAN

Hour after hour, I laid there.

I counted all the watermarks on the ceiling. Twice. There were forty-seven, which made me deeply concerned about a mold problem in the walls.

I watched a spider weaving their web in the corner of the room. At one point, it descended on a gossamer strand right as the air kicked on. The sudden gust swung the spider like a pendulum and it disappeared.

For the next hour, I waited to feel the whispery brush of spider legs on me. All of my paranoia was for naught. The spider never reappeared, as far as I could tell.

I listened to the cleaning lady in the room next door, having a one-sided conversation in Spanish for an indeterminable amount of time. My attempt to get her attention was fruitless. No matter how hard I threw myself against the headboard, which in turn slammed into the wall, she didn't come investigate.

By the end of the day, I was fucking exhausted. My shoulders were on fire and my wrists were scraped to hell. Plus I had a hair or *something* on my nose I couldn't get to no matter how hard I tried. It was like the time my leg was in a cast and I could only relieve the itch by shoving a wire hanger down the inside, except there were no hangers in sight.

What if he left me here? Sasha'd never been gone this long. Even in the dog cage, I felt like I saw him every couple of hours. How long had it been? All day? It seemed like all day.

I imagined the headline when someone finally found my corpse, shriveled and handcuffed to a bed. BANKER'S WORTHLESS SON, KIDNAPPED AND LEFT FOR DEAD — EVEN THE KIDNAPPERS DIDN'T WANT HIM.

The funeral would be great. Mom would make sure of that. My disgusting remains would be laid to rest in the most expensive casket available, topped with an obnoxiously large headstone. I doubted Dad would even be there, unless Joyce managed to pencil it in his fucking schedule and disguise it as a business meeting.

Frankie was probably the only one actually missing me. Could *she* pay the ransom? I'd reimburse her, for sure, but it was better than waiting on a handout from my dad. If Sasha ever came back or let me talk for more than a second, I'd try and find out.

It was the little balloon of hope I clung to until the door opened at long last.

Sasha's hands were full with a bag of food and more water. I couldn't see his eyes behind his sunglasses, but I knew he was looking at me. It was the same feeling I had before I was kidnapped, a gut feeling I'd stupidly chosen to ignore because "it can't happen to me." How naive. Anything can happen to anybody at anytime. Case in point.

Setting the stuff down on the table, he walked over to

the bed and slipped his sunglasses off. "No talking, or no food."

I lowered my gaze, which he must have taken as a "Yes" because he unlocked both handcuffs. Rubbing one wrist after the other, I peeled the tape off as soon as I had feeling in my hands again.

Sasha, in the meantime, dragged the table closer to the door and planted himself in a chair right in front of it.

Since I wasn't allowed to speak, I didn't ask permission to go to the bathroom. Not that there was anywhere else *to* go. He didn't say anything when I closed the door, nor when I opened it again.

But now I was faced with a new decision. There were only two choices for seating options: the bed, which I didn't want any part of after laying there all damn day; and the chair, at the table. With him. I suppose there was always the floor, but ew. No way in hell.

There was a bag of food and a water bottle at the opposite end of the table, so I assumed that's where I was more or less being told to sit.

Easing into the chair, I avoided eye contact while unpacking the bag. It was a sub, which was fine, along with a bag of chips and a snickerdoodle cookie. I would have eaten pretty much anything he brought, but the cookie made me pause. Did he know, or was it a coincidence he happened to pick my favorite type of cookie? He didn't have one. He didn't have dessert of any kind. Was this an olive branch? Why would you give your hostage an olive branch? God, he was so confusing.

I was nearly through with my sandwich when Sasha scared the shit out of me by speaking.

"Are you still hungry?"

My gaze snapped upward. No surprise, he was watching me, but it was with a mildly curious expression instead of one that looked like he was seconds away from ripping my head off.

I shook my head.

He nodded once and stood, clearing away his trash. I did the same, even though I could have finished the last two bites. The snickerdoodle, however, remained on the table.

His cell phone rang and he answered in Russian. Shooting a look at me, his spine straightened. Snarling his response, he yanked the door open and stepped out, actually leaving me alone and unrestrained.

Now was my chance.

I darted to the nightstand and picked up the phone, frantically dialing 911.

Nothing.

No dial tone. No ringing. Just, nothing.

Slamming the handset down, I grabbed the cord in the back and slid my hand along it until something sharp poked my finger. Wires. Someone cut the fucking phone line, and I'm pretty sure I knew who that someone was.

Hurrying to the window, I pushed the curtain aside a fraction of an inch. It didn't take long to spot Sasha on the balcony, still on the phone.

Could I sneak past him? No. Hell no. He'd fucking beat me just for opening the door. I'd been in a couple of fights over the years, but there was no way I could go toe-to-toe with him.

I could ambush him. When the door opened, I could hit him with something. Like the fucking phone he sabotaged. Or a chair. Except, I'd have to hit him hard enough to knock him out, otherwise he'd probably kill me, even if he was waiting for his ransom.

With no viable option, I shook my head and trudged to the bathroom in defeat. Might as well make the most of my limited freedom, which meant another shower while I was able. The AC started acting up a couple hours ago, so the room was on the toasty side. I was surprised Sasha didn't say anything when he came back.

Turning on the shower, I stripped out of my clothes while I waited for it to heat up. I'd no more than stepped out of my pants when the bathroom door flew open.

Sasha's eyes narrowed and his lips parted, but no sound came out. And then, like I threw ice water in his face, he backed out at warp speed and yanked the door shut.

Being caught buck naked should have been embarrassing. Well, it *was*. But it also gave me an idea. A crazy, suicide-mission idea. Given what happened this morning, I figured it was worth a shot. If I was going to die anyway, at least I'd know I tried everything.

Cracking open the bathroom door, I peeked outside.

Sasha was pacing with his fingers laced together behind his head, eyes closed, lips murmuring. It looked like he was praying or at least chanting some sort of mantra.

Now or never, Roan.

God, this was going to hurt…

I opened the door the rest of the way and walked out, timing my steps with Sasha's. He crashed right into me, his eyes opening to the size of saucers. For one second, I saw something other than contempt or annoyance on his face. In a normal human being, I'd say it was fear. But Sasha didn't strike me as the type of man who feared anything, let alone a naked college kid he'd used as a punching bag for the past several days.

As fast as I saw it, the look was gone, replaced by white-hot fury.

My head bounced off the wall he slammed me into, except instead of using his forearm to pin me in place, he smashed his palm in the center of my chest and stood as far away as possible.

"What the fuck?!" was all he managed to bite out.

I debated answering, but since he wanted me to shut up all the damn time, that's the path I took. Maybe he'd reconsider the ban on talking in the future.

"What do you think you're doing?" he demanded, searching my face for the answer I refused to give. My dick, however, was getting harder by the second, happy to offer whatever explanation Sasha wanted.

His hands slapped the wall on either side of my head, caging me in as he surged forward, his nose a hair away from mine. "You have exactly three seconds to get your ass back in there and put some fucking clothes on or—"

"You'll what?" I smirked, literally risking life and limb by reaching out and grabbing ahold of his dick. Part of me was surprised to find him hard with how angry he was, but then again, there had to be a reason for all that anger. Surprisingly — thankfully — he didn't break my arm, nor did he stop me from rubbing his growing hard-on through his jeans. "What? Tell me, Sasha. Tell me what you're going to do to me."

He didn't answer. The muscles in his throat were so tight he probably couldn't have spoken even if he wanted to. The look in his eyes was indescribable, somewhere between fear and hunger, with more than a touch of anger.

Biting my lower lip, I unbuttoned his jeans. When he didn't stop me, I pulled the zipper down. I slid both hands inside the waistband of his boxer briefs and pushed them down low on his hips, freeing his erection from the restraint of the cloth and denim. We both exhaled at the same time, him in obvious relief and me in surprise.

Given his height and the bulge he sported while he *wasn't* hard, I figured he was fairly well hung. What I hadn't given any thought to was the fact he was uncut. That was a new one for me.

Bracing against the wall with his head hung, Sasha watched as my hand reached out again, caressing him along his length hesitantly. His abs caved inward when I gripped him tighter, like he sucked in a breath and held it. With each stroke, I watched him, waiting for his brain to override his body. He hadn't pummeled me yet, but who knew if or when he'd snap.

When his hands slid down the wall and dropped to my shoulders, I took it as a hint. Kneeling in front of him, I gripped the base of his dick and licked my lips. Rolling the foreskin back, I tentatively swirled my tongue around the head of his cock, mentally preparing for a punch or something equally painful.

Above me, Sasha groaned something in Russian and braced one hand against the wall again. It was the first actual noise he'd made. Since it seemed like he approved, I kept going, taking more and more of his length into my mouth. When my nose brushed the trimmed black patch above his cock, his fingers threaded through my hair and tightened. Another Russian word slipped out of him, but it was more of a sigh.

I pulled back, sucking along the way. His hips chased after me, his fingers splaying along the back of my head. Not shoving or restraining me, just… touching, tangling in the longer part of my hair.

Instead of deep-throating him again, I popped off the end of his cock, trading my mouth for my hand, continuing the steady rhythm. Licking along his smooth skin while I jerked him off, I made my way down to his balls and sucked one into my mouth. He gasped, the muscles in his lower abdomen flexing under my palm like granite.

His breathing was getting shallower and his balls tightened. I traced a line up the underside of his cock with my tongue and sucked on the crown. At the risk of getting hit, I finally allowed myself to look up at his face, to see how I was doing.

Sasha's eyes may have been the color of ice, but all I felt was blazing lust when he looked at me. It radiated from his gaze, the hand in my hair, every thrust of his hips. No one had ever looked at me like that, like the sun rose and fucking set with me. It was thrilling, empowering. He *wanted* this — he wanted *me*. Bad.

As his cock slid further into my mouth and down my throat, my gaze fell, concentrating on the task at hand. Big dicks were nice and all until they cut off your airway, and I wanted to make sure I made this worth his while.

"Look at me," he rasped.

Flicking my gaze upward again, he gritted his teeth before both of his hands slid through my hair, holding me in place. I had a feeling I knew what was coming and that I'd get zero warning.

There were two more thrusts and a groan and I tasted his release on the back of my tongue. I swallowed everything he had, sucking the end of his cock until he jerked his hips out of reach with another ragged breath.

So his dick was the *ultra*-sensitive kind afterward. Good to know.

Good to know? Jesus, Roan! This was hopefully a means to an end and that's it.

My task complete, I stood slowly, licking my lips. His eyes were glued to mine, burning with desire and outright confusion. For someone who was always so in control, it was strange to see him looking at *me* for the answer. But it was also kind of hot, to think I'd been able to make a man like that come completely undone in spite of himself.

While I wished he'd say something, I also knew better. I

could count on one hand the number of things I knew about this man and "not chatty" was at the top of the list. I think I could safely add "closeted" as number two.

At the very least, I proved keeping me alive wasn't an altogether terrible idea. Hopefully, that little gift would buy me some good will. Then when the time was right, I could get the fuck out of here.

## 22

# SASHA

WHAT IN THE FUCK JUST HAPPENED?!

I had no idea. I mean, I *knew*. Jesus. I'd had enough blowjobs in my life to know. But why? Only Roan knew the answer to that and for once he wasn't fucking talking. Why wasn't he talking?!

Roan.

Goddamn it!

Somehow, someway, the kid made me see fucking stars. For that brief moment, the only thing that mattered was his mouth — hot and wet and fucking perfect.

I didn't ask him to. I certainly didn't tell him to. He just… did.

Then he stood up and walked back into the bathroom and took a shower like none of it happened.

What the fuck.

What the fuck?!

Completely dumbfounded, I tucked my dick back where it belonged and zipped up my jeans. All I knew was I had to leave. I didn't know what I was capable of in the moment. I didn't know who I was, but I knew *what* I was.

Disgusting, that's what.

Immoral.

Reprehensible.

I spun away from the wall and headed for the door as fast as my legs would move. There was more vodka in the car, I knew that. And a fresh pack of cigarettes. Those were safe ways to pass the time, instead of having your hostage suck you off while hiding out from the cops.

After I retrieved my emergency provisions, I returned to the second floor and perched on the top step. There was no way I could go back into that room, not while Roan was awake. I'd spend the rest of the night on the step or in the car if I had to. I didn't trust him. I didn't trust myself.

I lit the first cigarette and inhaled deeply, but it did nothing to resolve the sickness inside. Twisting off the bottle cap, I took a long pull of vodka, trying to forget the way he looked at me. Those blue eyes that looked purple in the dim light of the shitty motel room. The way his mouth looked, cheeks hollow, lips wrapped around my—

Heat seared into my forearm. I grimaced, growling through the pain and trying to ignore the smell of my own flesh burning.

When the hissing subsided, I flicked the spent cigarette down the stairs and blew away the residual ash. The black blister on the inside of my forearm was one of many, mostly disguised amongst my tattoos. I needed to remember the *pain*, not the way his golden hair felt as it slipped through my fingers, tousled and messy at the top and faded down the sides, a less severe version of my haircut.

Pain.

Black, empty pain.

What was it he called me? Mr. Black? Perfect. That's

what I would be. Not Sasha. Not Aleksandr. Just black. The Wolf of Verkhoyansk. Cold, unfeeling, merciless.

I had a fucking job to do.

If I really needed to get off, I could go pick up any number of women at the Birdcage. Or some chick in a bar whose name I didn't know. It didn't matter. I had options. Plenty of *female* options — the *natural* option, as God intended. I had a *choice* and I chose *not* to dwell on the fact all I wanted was to march back in there and force Roan to his knees again.

I immediately lit another cigarette and held the smoke in as long as I could, until my lungs burned from the nicotine and the lack of oxygen.

Expelling the smoke in a steady stream, I tipped my head against the bannister and closed my eyes. I knew I needed to leave America for a while, but it was clear I needed to go home, to Russia. As soon as this was done, that's what I was going to do. The West was perverted. It made *me* perverted and that was not ok.

I'd just made my decision when a door creaked next to me. My eyes flew open and shot to our room. Roan didn't appear, yet he clearly opened the door. Not a crack. Full on, open. Was he insane? He had to have been. First the blowjob, now this. That explained everything. He was a fucking lunatic. No wonder gays were sent to psychiatric hospitals.

Getting to my feet, I approached the room carefully, waiting for him or something else to come flying out at me. That's when I caught sight of his foot on the bed. My gaze traveled up his now-clothed leg, over his shirtless midsection, and landed on his face. He was laying on his side with an arm tucked under his head, facing the door, yet his eyes were closed. There was no way he was asleep that fucking quick.

Kicking the door open the rest of the way, I smirked when he jerked upright, eyes wide.

"Why is the door open?" I snapped, leaning against the frame.

"It's hot in here."

"Turn the air on."

"It's busted."

I took a final drag from my cigarette and crushed it under my heel before striding over to the air conditioner.

Sure enough, the AC was blowing hot air instead of cold. There was enough gunk clogging the inside it probably fried the compressor. Or it was out of refrigerant. Either way, it was a problem I couldn't exactly fix at the moment.

The bottom of my stomach fell out the second I realized the door was wide open and there was literally nothing stopping Roan. He could bolt at any time, but so far he hadn't moved. I didn't want to run to it in case it gave him the idea. If he managed to get away from me, I was fucked. I was built for hurting people, not running a goddamn marathon.

Roan cleared his throat quietly before speaking. "Can I ask you something?"

I looked up sharply, moving back to block the doorway as nonchalantly as I could. "Nyet." Not that a "No" ever stopped him before.

"What happens if my dad doesn't give you the money? Can someone else give it to you?"

I cocked my head. "We didn't ask for money."

He pushed himself into a sitting position slowly, his blond brows knitting together. "You kidnapped me for a ransom. Right?"

Resuming my casual lean against the doorframe, I

crossed my arms over my chest. "Currency comes in all forms."

"What did you ask for?"

I chuckled, raising my brows at him. Was he serious? "Why? Are you going to give it to me?"

"Maybe if you tell me what it is..." He looked so innocent, so unassuming, despite his obvious attempt at wheedling information out of me. I needed to shut that shit down. Now.

"Or maybe I'll break your jaw so you stop asking questions."

That damnable smirk was back, along with an impish sparkle in his eyes. "If you break my jaw, I can't give you any more blowjobs."

Unfolding my arms, I took a step toward him, my hands clenched at my sides. "Do not say another fucking word about that. In fact, conversation is over completely."

He blinked once, back to being the picture of innocence, all wide eyes and pouty lips. "Why? I thought you liked it?"

It took three steps to reach the bed.

Two seconds to pull back my fist.

And one punch to the side of his jaw to knock his smart ass out.

Exhaling a deep breath, I scrubbed my hands over my face. This is why I preferred killing to kidnapping. Get in, get out. Done. Now I was stuck with an unconscious hostage, a motel room to pack, and zero insight from the boss as far as what the next step was.

Guess it was time to improvise.

# 23

# ROAN

He broke my jaw.

That fucker actually did it. I couldn't believe it!

I opened and closed my mouth carefully, relieved when the tendons complied. Ok. Not broken. He just bruised the shit out of it. No more blowjobs for him, that was for sure.

How was it so cold in here? And why was it so dark? I couldn't even see my hand in front of my face.

A sliver of light across the room barely illuminated anything, but it wasn't where I remembered the bathroom door being. That was weird. And it smelled different. I should have smelled cigarette smoke and stale, mildewy air, but instead it was… dank.

As soon as I swung my legs down off the bed, there was a rush of heavy metal links dropping to the floor. I didn't know which to be more concerned about — the chain, or the fact the floor itself was concrete again, not the scratchy motel carpeting.

Dropping into a squat, I grabbed my ankle and swore the second I felt a leather cuff attached to a thick chain. There was no escaping that. Following the links upward, I groped along in the dark to see what I was attached to. My hands slid up a rough, metal pole, at least six inches in diameter. Following the pole down again, my fingers scraped along bolts in the cement beneath my feet.

A basement. I was in a basement, chained to a fucking support post like a rabid dog.

"Sasha! Where are you?" I yanked on the chain, metal on metal clanging in my ears. "You son of a bitch! Get down here!"

Footsteps sounded overhead, along with the floorboards squeaking, but I couldn't tell if he was coming or going.

"I know you can hear me, asshole!" I shouted upward, smacking the chain against the pole as hard as I could.

The footsteps clomped off in another direction. The house above me got quiet. Guess the answer was going.

"I'm going to strangle you with this fucking thing," I seethed, sliding the chain between my hands, trying to estimate what sort of range I had.

The answer was not much.

I could reach the cot he'd so graciously dumped me on, along with a random toilet in the middle of the basement that I tripped over. That was it. I had about six feet or so, which meant I wouldn't get anywhere near the stairs or whatever windows might be down here.

It was better than the dog kennel, I suppose, but I was freezing. Shivering against the damp chill, I shuffled back to the cot and slipped under the blanket, grateful it was at least thicker, not to mention cleaner, than the one in the kennel. Apparently Sasha didn't feel the need to put my t-shirt back on before leaving me down here, not like it would have done a whole lot of good.

Sasha. Goddamn it!

I thought I was getting somewhere with him. I mean,

Jesus Christ. The motel door was open! It was right there! And like a moron, I *stayed*, because the scared little voice in my head held me back. I could have outran him, but I didn't even try. And this is what he thinks of me?

I hadn't given him any reason to *not* trust me. Hell, I even offered to get him whatever it was he wanted from my dad. And let us not forget about the blowjob he refused to acknowledge.

Hot, angry tears slipped out of the corners of my eyes. So much for my brilliant plan of winning him over. I was officially out of ideas and I'd lost the one tiny chance I had of escaping because I didn't want to risk getting beaten again. Waiting to die was the only thing I could do and the last thing I wanted.

"What do you want?!" I screamed at the ceiling. I don't know if I was talking to Sasha or God. At the moment Sasha *was* God. He controlled everything in my existence and I fucking hated him for it.

---

THE SOUND OF KEYS JINGLING WOKE ME.

I sat up quickly and tried to assess where the noise was coming from. Everything echoed so strangely down here, it was hard to tell.

A door opened somewhere and someone clomped down the stairs, flicking on a light as they went.

Wincing, I covered my eyes with my hand. They were still burning from my pathetic tears earlier and the light didn't help. "It's about time, you fucking asshole."

I smelled French fries a second before a paper bag landed in my lap. Squinting, I cracked an eye open, surprised to see Ivan standing there and not Sasha.

"Oh, sorry," I said, clearing my throat. "I thought you were the other guy."

Ivan held up a drink and inched closer with it. He set it on the floor a good five feet away from me and scurried back to safety like I was Hannibal Lecter. "He's not here."

Just like before, I made no move for the drink. This guy was too skittish, but he was way chattier than Sasha. Maybe I wasn't entirely out of options after all. I wasn't about to start handing out free blowjobs, but if I could get this guy to sympathize with my situation, maybe I stood a chance. "Where is he?"

Ivan shrugged.

"Something more important than his hostage?" I ventured, surprising myself with how bitter it sounded.

He snorted out a laugh. "You never know with the Wolf of Verkhoyansk. He's very busy. Always someone to kill or—" He stopped talking and cleared his throat.

"The what?" The giant wolf tattoo on Sasha's stomach immediately came to mind. I wondered which came first, the name or the tattoo. Either way, I didn't know if I should be impressed my kidnapper had a criminal nickname or terrified.

"That's what they call him," Ivan said quietly, almost reverently.

"Like a code name?"

"Like a warning."

"Is he supposed to be like the bogeyman?" I chuckled at Ivan's wide-eyed expression.

He shook his head emphatically. "He's worse."

The seriousness with which he answered gave me goosebumps. Terrified. I was officially back to being terrified. "How so?"

Ivan blinked solemnly. "He's real."

I couldn't exactly argue with that. Sasha *was* real and

the pain he doled out was real, too. My thumping jaw was proof of that, along with the bruises on my face and abdomen. "Why a wolf? Is that some Russian thing?"

Ivan shrugged, hooking his thumbs in his pockets. "I heard it was because when he was ten years old, he killed a man twice his age. They said he cut him into little pieces and fed him to his pet wolf."

"That's crazy," I replied with a laugh, hoping it sounded natural. I tried not to picture a pint-size Sasha tossing chunks of human flesh to a wolf and failed miserably. "What ten year old kills someone?"

"Someone from Verkhoyansk." Ivan shook his head at my confused expression. "It's a terrible place. The night makes people..." He twirled a finger at his temple, the universal motion for "crazy." I guess you had to be if you chopped up people to feed to a wolf at the ripe age of ten.

Ignoring the shiver that raced down my spine, I forced a smile to my face and abruptly changed topics. "So where are you from, Ivan?"

"Kazan."

"Huh." Yeah, I had no idea where the hell that was. Right up there with Verk whatever. I looked him over, trying to figure out my next move given the new surroundings and my new jailer. "How are you liking America so far?"

He smiled and nodded. "It's nice. Very different. But good."

"Do you know what they want from me?"

The smile vanished. "I can't say." Damn it!

"You can't say because you don't know or you can't say because they told you not to tell me?"

"I don't know," he replied with a shrug. For some reason, I believed him. He seemed like the kind of guy who wasn't very high up on the totem pole. "All the decisions are coming from Viktor. Sasha does the work."

That was a new name. Ivan, Yuri, Sasha, Viktor. I kept them in the order I learned them, so I could remember as much as possible when I eventually hauled ass to the nearest police station. If I ever got the fucking chance.

"And you work for Sasha?" I asked.

Ivan nodded and then stopped, making a face. "Yes and no. I work for Yuri, but you don't say no to Sasha."

"Uh-huh." Probably because he'd tear your arm off and beat you with it. "So the kidnapping thing. I take it I'm not the first?"

"It's not personal, it's just business," Ivan stated matter-of-factly. Well, to the person being held captive, it was *very* personal, but I understood what he was trying to say.

The more important thing was the chain of command. I thought Sasha was at the top, but there was someone else. That complicated things. If Sasha wasn't the one calling the shots, then the likelihood of him striking some sort of deal with me was probably slim to none.

"Well, thanks for the food, Ivan." I didn't want to press my luck with him. He'd already given up way more information in one conversation than I'd managed to wring out of his boss over the course of… shit, four days? Five? Time was a blur at this point.

He nodded again and ducked up the stairs, thankfully leaving the lights on.

I glanced around the empty basement and sighed. It was as desolate as I imagined in the dark. There were a few cots crunched together and shoved against the far wall. Each support post had a chain attached to it but I was the only one down here. At least for now. If the chains were anything to go by, they could have at least four of us at a time.

Besides the random toilet in the middle of the space, there was also a standing shower. It was just the fiberglass shell and a shower head. No curtain or door, completely open and exposed, like the toilet. If these were normal people, I would assume they were installing a bathroom and, you know, forgot to put up walls or finish it off like a proper bathroom.

But since they were fucking Russian criminals, I knew I was sitting in the middle of what I was fairly certain was an extension of their human trafficking ring, waiting to see what *my* fate would be.

Make the best of it, Roan. Just be patient and wait for the next opportunity. And this time? Don't fucking hesitate.

## 24

## SASHA

ROAN WAS AWAKE WHEN I CAME DOWN THE BASEMENT stairs, laying on his back, with one knee bent and his arms folded beneath his head. I couldn't help but notice the way his whole body tensed the closer I got, each exposed muscle visibly tightening. I should have given him a shirt after I moved him, but I didn't and I certainly wasn't going to now. Didn't want him thinking I was going soft.

"I brought you dinner," I said, holding a plate of lasagna out to him.

He didn't look at it — or me — before he unfolded his arms and rolled away from me.

"Nothing to say?" I quirked a brow at his back. I couldn't believe it. Had I walked into an alternate universe, one where my hostage was quiet for a change? Not challenging everything I said, practically begging me to hurt him?

After a solid minute of staring at the back of his head in total silence, I set the plate on the floor and walked away.

The next morning was more of the same. Roan was

awake, sitting upright this time, watching the stairs with bright eyes. As soon as he saw it was me, his shoulders slumped and he turned his gaze to the floor.

If it wasn't me he was waiting for, then that meant he was expecting Ivan. He was *excited* at the thought it was Ivan and *disappointed* when it wasn't.

"Breakfast," I growled, holding a plate of eggs and bacon out for him. It didn't escape my notice he hadn't eaten any part of dinner from the night before. The plate was where I left it, completely untouched.

Yet again, Roan refused to take the plate. He refused to even look at me no matter how much I glared at him or how hard I willed him to lift his eyes.

I swapped the old plate with the fresh one and marched back upstairs. As soon as I grabbed my cell phone, I dialed Ivan's number.

"What the fuck happened?" I demanded as soon as he picked up.

"What are you talking about?"

"The kid. He hasn't said a word. He hasn't eaten."

"He ate lunch."

"Well he didn't eat dinner and he didn't want breakfast. So what happened? What did you do?"

"Nothing! I swear! He seemed fine."

"Fine? How would you know what 'fine' looks like?"

He sputtered on the other end. "I don't know. He was talking, laughing. Isn't that fine?"

"Laughing?" I gaped at the phone, nearly throwing it at the closest wall. "What the fuck was he *laughing* about?"

"I don't know. I don't know why you're asking me all these questions! I did what you asked, boss. I stayed at the house and I gave him food. That's it."

I stole a glance at the time, trying to ratchet it down a notch. "Come here at one. And bring lunch for him."

"Yes, sir."

Hanging up, I threw the phone on the kitchen table. The kettle screamed on the stove behind me, but instead of making a cup of tea, I threw the whole thing in the sink and stormed outside for some fresh air.

---

IVAN PRACTICALLY TIPTOED INTO THE HOUSE, CLUTCHING A brown paper bag with Chinese characters on it and approached me like you'd approach a wild animal. He held it out with one hand, but I shoved it back at him.

"You take it to him," I snapped.

"Why?"

"Because I fucking said so."

Ivan swallowed and headed for the basement stairs. I trailed after him, but instead of descending all the way, I stopped at the edge of the drywall, out of sight, to eavesdrop.

"I brought you Chinese. I hope that's ok," Ivan said over the bag crinkling.

"Yeah, thank you," Roan replied in a completely normal voice.

"You didn't eat breakfast?" Ivan asked. Anger twisted through me at the news. Not that I expected him to after the stunt with dinner.

"I wasn't hungry."

"Oh, ok."

"Hey, you want some? It looks like you got enough to feed an army." Was he fucking serious? He wanted to have a goddamn picnic with Ivan in the basement?

"Uh…" Ivan switched back to Russian. "*What am I supposed to say?*"

I was fuming, but Roan chuckled. "I have no idea what

you just said, but here." The chain clinked and scraped over the ground.

Enough was enough already.

Storming down the rest of the stairs, I watched Ivan take a carton of food from Roan and nearly drop it at my sudden arrival.

"*Get the fuck out of here,*" I snapped in Russian.

"*What did I do?*" Ivan shrank back, his eyes wide.

"*Go!*"

I stared him down until he walked away and returned upstairs. As soon as he was gone, my gaze slid to Roan. He retreated to the cot and sat, stabbing at the fried rice with his plastic fork. So once again, he would eat what *Ivan* brought but not me.

He talked with Ivan. Laughed with Ivan.

Roan hadn't picked his head up once since I appeared. He kept his gaze turned down, like before, chewing in silence.

"Look at me," I growled.

He refused.

I closed the distance in a few long strides and seized his jaw, forcing his head backward until he had no choice but to look up. "Did you fuck around with him?"

He smirked but didn't say a goddamn word.

Knocking the white carton out of his hand, I dropped my hold to his throat and slammed him backward into the mattress. "Answer me," I snarled through gritted teeth.

"No," he spat back with a glare, the muscles in his neck flexing under my hand.

No he wouldn't tell me? Or no he did *not* fuck around with Ivan? As much as it irritated me to not know, I wasn't going to ask for clarification.

"Do not speak to him again. Is that understood?"

Roan's teeth clenched, his mouth pressing into a hard line.

It didn't look right on him. He should have been smiling, or at least smirking. Not glaring at me like I was the devil himself.

Somewhere along the way, I ended up with most of my torso against his, the rise and fall of our chests mirroring one another. I was suddenly aware of the fact his cock was not only hard, but it was pressing against mine. I didn't even know when *I* got hard, but I was. He felt it too, because his mouth softened and the muscles in his neck relaxed beneath my fingers.

His hips shifted, adding more pressure, more friction. It could have been him trying to find relief from my weight on top of him, or he was purposely antagonizing me. Given his past history, I opted for the latter.

I reached between us and grabbed ahold of him through his sweatpants. God, he was *so* hard. "What did I say about this?"

He didn't answer, just licked his lips and pressed his hips up against my hand, like he was calling my bluff. He should have learned by now not to do that.

Slipping my hand beneath the waist band, I gripped his cock tightly, watching him exhale and squeeze his eyes shut. Using his own pre-cum to add slip to my hand, I jacked him off in long, hard stokes. I couldn't take my eyes off of him. I wanted to memorize every expression he made, every time he gasped or sighed, the way his whole body tightened beneath me.

I wanted to remember it all, because it would never happen again. He could consider this a return favor for the blowjob — something *else* that would never happen again. After this, we were square.

His hand slid up the arm I was bracing on, following the curve of my tricep and slipping beneath the sleeve of my t-shirt to grip my shoulder. Raking his teeth over his lower lip, he groaned and rolled his hips, thrusting up into my grip while his other hand skimmed across his bare chest to toy with his nipple.

"Sasha..." The way he said my name, that breathy sigh... it was so hot. So... wrong. He didn't seem to care. Digging his fingers into my shoulder, it was like he was trying to pull me closer. Or he was fighting an orgasm.

"Look at me." The command came out as a growl, one he immediately obeyed. His lashes parted, revealing the depths of his eyes. Up close, in this light, they were a vibrant cornflower blue. I'd never seen anything like it before and doubted I ever would again. But more than that, he had the same carnal look in his eyes as the day before yesterday when he was on his knees, licking every inch of my cock like it was the greatest thing ever.

"I'm so close," he whispered, holding my gaze, his breathing ragged.

"Come for me."

"Oh God..." He kept his eyes on me until they rolled back in his head.

His whole body shuddered, ropes of cum shooting out of his cock, coating his abdomen. I gave another couple of slow strokes, making sure to wring every bit of his orgasm out of him. There was some on my hand, but he wore the majority of it on his flat stomach. Without even thinking, I licked it off my knuckle. A strangled moan sounded in the back of his throat. He swore softly, his eyes half-hooded as he watched me.

Oh fuck. Fuck. Fuck. Fuck!

Pushing away from him quickly, I retrieved a napkin from the takeout bag and wiped off whatever was left on my hand.

Roan propped himself up on his elbows, watching me

with those bedroom eyes. Lips parted, he was still panting, but not talking. Why wasn't he fucking talking?

Oh my God...

I didn't spare him a backward glance as I made my way toward the stairs as fast as I could. Taking them two at a time, I didn't breathe until I reached the top.

What the fuck did I just do?!

# 25

# ROAN

WHAT THE...?

The way Sasha hauled ass out of the basement, you'd think he was late to a meeting with Putin himself. Meanwhile, I laid there in a state of shock, unable to move or form a coherent thought.

When it was pretty clear he wasn't coming back, I sat up and surveyed the mess in front of me. There went dinner and I was fucking starving. In his pissiness, he sent my fried rice everywhere and Ivan had taken the other carton.

Why *was* Sasha so pissy, anyway? He looked like he was going to rip Ivan's head off when he came downstairs. And he wanted — no, demanded — I look at him while he asked about the guy. What did he even mean by any of that? Just because I sucked his dick, he thought I was suddenly doling out BJs to all of my kidnappers? Even if I was, why the fuck did *he* care?

Shuffling over to the paper bag, I grabbed a handful of napkins and wiped my abs off.

I called his bluff about the whole hard-on thing, and he

delivered. By God, did he deliver. Never in a million years did I think he'd go through with it. I thought for sure he was going to knock me out again, not give me a hand job.

*Come for me.*

His words echoed in my head, just as sexy in my memory as they were the first time around. What was *that* about? Dirty talk with your captive? What kind of kidnapper was he? My God…

It wasn't dirty talk when he licked the cum off the back of his hand, though. Or when he looked at me like he was going to devour me. What would I have done if he tried? Would I have let him? Would I have actually said "No" after throwing myself at him first? *Could* I have said "No"?

Raking both hands through my hair, I sat back on the bed, staring at the brown grains of rice on the floor.

I was still sitting there when the basement door opened again and footsteps jogged down the stairs. My heart stuttered for a minute, waiting to see who it was going to be.

A twinge of disappointment shot through me. It was Ivan, carrying a broom and dustpan.

He frowned at the mess. "Sasha?"

I nodded. Sasha said not to *speak* to him. He didn't say anything about head movements or hand gestures.

Sighing, Ivan set the dustpan down and started sweeping up the rice.

Shifting off the bed, I knelt and grabbed the dustpan. I held it for him while he swept, dumping the garbage into the brown paper bag, along with all of the evidence from whatever the hell it was that happened post-rice throwing.

Glancing up, I watched Ivan carefully as he worked. Did he know what happened? He didn't seem to. But I didn't know him like I knew Sasha. I didn't know what his tells were.

Fuck, Roan. You don't *know* Sasha anymore than you know what the hell is going on!

"Did you even get to eat?" Ivan asked, depositing the last pile of dirty rice into the bag.

I shook my head, getting to my feet again. Two forkfuls hardly counted after being on a hunger strike.

"You're quiet now," Ivan observed, leaning against the broom. "You talked before but now, nothing."

I bit my lower lip and pointed upstairs.

A smile cracked the side of his face. "I get it. It's his way or roadway." Sasha's way or the highway. No shit.

Shaking my head, I lifted my pant leg, pointing to the cuff on my right ankle and over to the shower. Even if I'd wiped my skin clean, I wouldn't object to an actual shower.

Ivan shook his head. "Sasha's the only one with the key." Of course he was…

Sighing, I sank onto the edge of the bed.

"I'll go ask. And see about some more food," Ivan said, sounding way more optimistic than he probably should have. I didn't have high hopes for a positive outcome to either request.

A short while later, the basement door opened again.

I stopped pacing and crossed my arms, waiting to see which Russian jailer I had the pleasure of dealing with this time: Sasha and his confusing-as-fuck ways or Ivan, with bad news.

My stomach plummeted when the person who came into view was neither Sasha nor Ivan.

It was Yuri, still sporting some nasty bruises from Sasha's beating the other day. He was bad enough, but it was what he had in his hand that was more concerning — a pair of bolt cutters.

"What do you want?" I asked as he stepped off the bottom stair.

Swaggering forward without a word, he held up the tool, like I couldn't see it clearly.

"What are you doing?" I backed away from him as far as my metal leash would let me.

He gave me a nasty smile and chucked the bolt cutters at my feet. "Have nice life, pretty boy."

Was this a trick? It had to be a trick. I didn't move. I barely even breathed.

"If you want to stay here and wait for Sasha to kill you…" Yuri gestured around with his bandaged hand, the one Sasha put a bullet through. "Or you can run." Once my options were laid out there, he pivoted on his heel and started for the stairs.

"Wait! Why would you help me?" Shut the fuck up, Roan! For once in your life don't ask fucking questions!

Yuri paused, throwing me a condescending sneer, and continued on his way. The top stair had a distinctive squeak whenever someone stepped on it. Yuri hit that step, but the basement door didn't swing shut. Even if he managed to close it without making a sound, I didn't hear the lock turn either. He really gave me bolt cutters and left the fucking door open.

There was a strong possibility I'd be shot the minute I stepped outside the basement door, but it was a chance I had to take.

Grabbing the bolt cutters as quickly as I could, I snipped the padlock on the cuff and yanked it out. My hands were shaking as I unbuckled the leather from my ankle and tore it free.

Darting up the stairs, I paused near the top. The basement opened up to some sort of a landing with stairs to the left and an exterior door right in front of me.

I plowed through the door to the outside world and

heaved my first breath of free air, sprinting like a madman down the sidewalk.

No one chased me.

No one shot at me.

Nothing.

I was free, and I fucking ran.

A few blocks away, I collapsed against a tree and clung to its rough bark like a buoy in the ocean. Now there was enough distance between me and the house, I needed to figure out where the hell I was. It was a neighborhood, that much was clear. But I had no idea what town. All of the cars parked on the street had Illinois license plates, so I guess that was a good sign.

Could I trust people in this neighborhood? Not gonna chance it.

It was nighttime, but I had no clue what time it was or which direction I should even try to run. The longer I stood around debating, the better chance they had of finding me.

Darting down the driveway of a dark house, I cut through the backyards, ducking every time a car drove by or I heard voices.

It was slow-going, but eventually I made it to a more populated area. There was a crappy little bar on the corner of the intersection, neon signs flashing that they were open. But that wasn't what made me nearly sob in relief. It was the payphone outside.

Jogging across the street, I snatched the handset out of the cradle and nearly had another breakdown when I heard an actual dial tone. Punching in 911, I pressed my back to the building and glanced up and down the street, waiting for one furious Russian to appear and drag me back to the basement. Or put a bullet in my head.

"911, where is your emergency?"

"I don't know. I don't know where I am. I'm outside of a bar called Stan's."

"Ok, what's going on there?"

"I was kidnapped and I just escaped." Did I really just say that? I mean, I knew I had been, but saying it out loud was so bizarre. It still felt like I was in a fucked up dream.

There was a pause, with furious typing on the other end of the line. "Are you injured?"

"No. Not really. No."

"Ok. Stay right there. I have help coming to you, ok? Just keep talking to me."

Squeezing my eyes shut, all I could do was nod like an idiot, knowing she couldn't see me. The stress of everything flooded through me all over again, strangling my vocal cords. Breathing came in short, labored bursts, while I tried to get my lungs to cooperate.

I was relieved.

I was nauseated.

And I could finally admit how fucking scared I was. At this point, I didn't know if I'd ever stop being scared.

# 26

# SASHA

THE MINUTE I PULLED INTO THE DRIVEWAY, I KNEW something was wrong. The side door was open, for starters, and all of the lights on the first floor were on.

Shifting the car into park but keeping it running, I eased out of the driver's seat and crept toward the house. The unsettling feeling deepened the closer I got. Not only was the side door open, the basement door was open too.

I didn't worry about stealth anymore, hurrying down the stairs as fast as I could, praying the entire way.

As soon as I rounded the corner and saw the empty chain, I swore.

He was gone.

Roan was fucking gone!

I took one look at the bolt cutters and saw red.

Flying back up the stairs, I slammed through the kitchen door. "Ivan! Where the fuck are you?!"

He didn't answer.

Storming through the kitchen and into the living room, I found him sprawled out in the hallway to the bathroom, facedown. Blood seeped out of the back of his head. From where I stood, I could see the front door, which showed zero signs of damage.

I planted my boot against his hip and pushed him over. He didn't flop like a dead man, so I kicked him in the stomach. Hard.

Jerking awake with an agonized gasp, Ivan clutched his stomach with both hands, staring up at me with bug eyes.

"What the fuck happened?" I snarled.

"I don't know!" he groaned, rolling onto his side again.

"Where's Roan?"

"What?"

"Roan! He's gone! What the fuck happened?!"

Instead of answering, Ivan covered his head with his arms and brought his knees up to his chest, probably so I couldn't kick him again.

"You're fucking worthless!" I resisted the urge to kick him anyway and stormed back outside.

As soon as I got behind the wheel, I headed down the quiet street at a nice, normal pace even though it fucking killed me. I didn't need to draw suspicion to myself or the house. Rolling all of the windows down, I scanned the yards as I went and listened for anything that might indicate the location of my escapee.

Alright, Sasha, think. He couldn't have gotten far. I'd only been gone… I glanced at the clock and swore, slamming my fist against the steering wheel.

Thirty minutes meant the average person could make it three to five kilometers. Except, Roan wasn't average. He was a goddamn gazelle, which meant he could easily be eight to nine kilometers away. I had two things working in my favor: Roan didn't have shoes and he hadn't been eating. Hopefully that meant he wouldn't be able to max out the distance. But when you factored in adrenaline...

Fuck!

The fact it was already dark would be both a benefit and a hinderance to him. No, he couldn't run as fast, but it also meant I couldn't fucking see him. He could be hiding right next to me and I'd never know it.

As I circled the block for the fourth time, I called Eduard. It was bad enough Ivan knew Roan escaped somehow, but there was no way I could manage this one solo. Eduard was the only person I trusted not to fuck me over.

"We have a big fucking problem," I said when Eduard answered.

"What's wrong?"

"Roan is gone." Nausea slithered through my insides, twisting everything until I didn't know if I wanted to throw up or break something. I'd never failed. *Ever.*

"The kid?! What? How?"

"I don't know. I came back to the house and he was gone. Ivan says he doesn't know what happened."

"Did you call Viktor?"

"Are you fucking crazy? I'm not telling Viktor shit. I'm going to get the kid back and pretend none of this ever happened."

"What do you need me to do?"

"Bring your laptop and your duffel bag. Meet me at the house. And *don't* let Ivan out of your sight."

"I'm on my way."

I swore again and slammed my palm into the steering wheel. Where the fuck was he?

# 27

# ROAN

Waiting at the police department took forever. The interview with the cop dragged on and on and *on*. He was nice enough, but I was exhausted, physically and mentally, and answering the same questions over and over wasn't helping.

"I think that about covers it," the officer said at last. He gave me a small smile and flipped his notepad shut. "I'm sure a detective will be in touch with you tomorrow to go over everything again."

"Yeah, ok. Um, I don't have my phone. It was on me when they grabbed me but I don't know where it is."

"Is there another number we can reach you at?"

"My parents." Ugh. The last place I wanted to be, but the only choice I had at the moment. The lease was up on my townhouse and Frankie didn't answer her damn phone. So when the officer announced dispatch located my parents and called them to come get me, I feigned gratitude, feeling less like a rescued victim and more like a teen busted for underage drinking.

"Ok. Great." The cop held up a finger and tilted his

head to the side slightly, listening to something in his ear piece. "Speaking of, it sounds like they're here. I'll walk you out."

"Thank you." The words stuck in my throat as images of Sasha floated in my brain. Instead of threatening me with bodily harm, the officer smiled again.

In the lobby, Mom burst into tears and ran forward, wrapping her arms around my neck and squeezing until I couldn't breathe. "Sweetie, are you ok? When the police called and said you were here, I was so stunned! What are you doing all the way out here in the suburbs? Where are your shoes? Your shirt?"

"Wait." I pushed away from her like she slapped me. I couldn't have heard her correctly. All of the fucking concussions Sasha gave me must have screwed with my hearing. "Did you just say 'what am I doing here?' Are you serious?"

Mom blinked her weepy eyes, but didn't repeat the question.

Dad already looked bored. "Can we talk about this in the car? I have an early flight."

I ignored him and turned my attention back to Mom. "You didn't know I was missing?"

She brushed the tears from her cheek and looked up at Dad, deferring to him as always.

"You said you were going to leave," my asshole father reminded me with a bitter smile. "And then you did. A little late to be crying wolf, don't you think?"

"I didn't *leave*," I snapped. "I was fucking *kidnapped*! There's a difference!"

"Let's get you home, ok?" Mom wrapped her arm around me and rubbed my arm, leading me out to the car.

Why couldn't Frankie have answered her damn phone?

Maybe then I'd be with someone who actually believed me.

In all of the rescue scenarios I imagined, *not* being believed never even occurred to me. I didn't want a fucking parade, but I couldn't believe my own parents were giving me the side-eye.

I stopped abruptly and faced my father with a glare. "If you thought I up and left without a word, how do you explain the ransom demand?"

He laughed, opening his door. "A ransom?"

"Yeah. They wanted something in exchange for me. I don't know what, but they said it wasn't money."

"Don't be ridiculous. Who kidnaps someone and *doesn't* want money?" He rolled his eyes and slid into the car.

Dropping into the backseat, I propped my elbow on the arm rest and held my forehead in my hand. None of this made *any* sense.

My parents said they didn't know I was kidnapped, and they didn't know anything about a ransom demand.

Sasha clearly kidnapped me and clearly said he was waiting on some sort of payment.

They couldn't both be right.

So who the fuck was lying — and why?

---

The first thing I did when I got home was to call Frankie again. She'd finally gotten the original message from the police station and was in mid-freak out when she answered.

"I'm coming over there right now," she said.

"Yeah, 'cuz that's what he needs after everything he's been through," Freddy said in the background. "You showing up and stressing him out even more."

In the process of hanging up, I heard her shout, "Shut the fuck up, Freddy!"

While I waited for her to make the drive to my house, I took the longest, hottest shower of my life. By the time I got out, she was there, sitting on my bed, practically bouncing in place. Thank God I'd taken a tank top and basketball shorts into the bathroom with me. Not that she hadn't seen me naked, but I didn't need her losing her shit over the giant bruise on my solar plexus from Sasha's homophobic freak out. She was already going to spaz about the bruises on my face and jaw.

As soon as she saw me, Frankie ran and jumped into my arms, wrapping her legs around my waist. "Oh my God! You're ok! I told them I hadn't talked to you! I texted your mom like, everyday, and she said she hadn't seen you and that you were probably 'finding yourself' and not to worry. But I worried, Roan! I knew you weren't ok! Freddy and I looked everywhere for you and we couldn't report you as missing because you're an adult and there wasn't enough evidence to think you were in trouble."

Hugging her tightly, I carried her over to the bed. She hung on like a little spider monkey, so I more or less ended up flopping us both into the center of the mattress.

"Yeah, I was off 'finding myself' with the Russian mob. It was great." I rolled onto my back and glowered at the ceiling. "Thanks for trying, though. It's more than my parents fucking did."

"Do you want to talk about it?" She practically whispered the question, drawing idle circles on my bicep.

"I wouldn't even know where to start..."

"What happened to your hand?" She reached across me and picked up my left hand, examining the scab on my palm with a wrinkled nose.

"Some asshole swung a knife at my face. I just reacted." I shrugged.

She looked like I drop-kicked a cat right in front of her. "Oh my God! Why would he do that?"

"I think it was because I wouldn't give him a blowjob. I don't know. It all happened so fast. But he's the same one who helped me escape, so maybe he's just psycho. I mean, they're all psycho, right? They have to be." I had a sneaking suspicion Yuri's help had more to do with fucking Sasha over than any sudden moral dilemma, but whatever. It got me the hell out of there.

"All? How many were there?"

At one point I felt like I could have described them all, but now? I couldn't get Sasha out of my head long enough to picture anyone else. "I don't know. I only interacted with a few."

She scooted closer to me, touching my jaw lightly. "How did this happen?"

"That's Sasha's handiwork."

"Sasha?"

Shit. I shouldn't have said his name. When the cop asked, I said I didn't know their names. All I told him was that they were Russian, or so I thought. I don't know why. It seemed like the smart thing to do in the moment, like if I kept their secret, they wouldn't come after me again. Besides, it's not like they'd ever be arrested anyway. Guys like that never were.

I cleared my throat, realizing I hadn't answered her. "Uh, yeah. He was like, the main guy. I think. I mean, he had a boss, I guess, but everyone else seemed to do what he said." Even me. Because as Ivan put it, *you don't say no to Sasha.*

"What did they want with you?"

"I don't know. Sasha said they wanted something from my dad, but Dad said he didn't get any ransom."

She made a face. "That's weird."

"Right?! That's the part I don't get. Sasha has no reason to lie to me. I'm literally *nothing* to him." I shook my head, brows furrowed as I tried to sort through the different explanations. "But is my dad that much of a fucking asshole to not only refuse to pay whatever ransom they wanted but then to also blatantly lie to my face?"

"Yes," she answered, completely deadpan.

Sighing, I rubbed my eyes with one hand. I didn't want to believe it, but yeah. He was. It was a bitter pill to swallow, realizing you don't mean jack shit to your family despite your best efforts.

She poked my rib. "Did you tell the police about him?"

"Who?" I opened an eye to glare at her.

"The dude you keep talking about. Sasha."

"Yeah... Why?" Nope. Total lie.

"Because it's a little weird you keep referring to him by name. You know? The guy who kidnapped you, imprisoned you, beat you..." She raised her brows at me, her brown eyes round with worry.

"It's the only name I know." Lie.

"What did he look like?"

Returning my gaze to the ceiling, I sputtered out an awkward noise, complete with a noncommittal shrug. "I don't know. Like a criminal? Big. Lots of tattoos. That sort of thing."

"Is he hot?"

"Ugh, Frankie! Do *you* think everyone with a dick is hot?"

"That wasn't a no…"

"No!" And another lie. It was amazing how easily they rolled off my tongue.

"So no freaky deaky role play with a hot Russian? A little BDSM? Exploring your kinky side?" She shimmied her shoulders, wiggling closer to me and looking pointedly at the red marks visible on my wrists.

"Oh yeah," I grinned at her, nodding emphatically. "He pretended to be a kidnapper and I was his helpless victim. It was *great.* Especially when he handcuffed me to the bed."

"So hot… Did you call him Daddy?"

I shot her an unamused look. "For the love of God, no."

She cackled before snuggling in with a wistful sigh, resting her cheek against my shoulder. "In all seriousness, though. Are you ok? I mean… the robbery. Now this. It's a *lot.* You don't have to pretend to be ok."

"I know…"

"So, *are* you?"

I exhaled a breath, trying to figure out what the fuck I was even feeling. "I don't know," I mumbled, lacing my fingers through hers. "I don't know what to think, what to feel. I'm just… numb. I keep thinking I'm going to wake up and this is all going to be some fucked up dream."

"Just remember I'm here for you, Roan. I'm always here for you."

"I know." I pressed a kiss to her forehead and closed my eyes, hoping tomorrow I'd wake up with amnesia and all would be right in the world.

## 28

## SASHA

I DROVE AROUND FOR HOURS LOOKING FOR ROAN, FEAR and anger squeezing my chest with each minute that ticked by. Eduard monitored the police scanners while he waited at the house with Ivan. All for nothing. Roan was gone. I lost him.

Furious and defeated, I returned to the house to get some fucking answers.

Eduard was down in the basement with Ivan when I arrived. The kid was tied to a chair, bleeding and sweating profusely. Eduard had gotten started without me, which was fine. He hadn't learned anything useful and Ivan was probably safer in Eduard's hands than mine at the moment.

"Start from the beginning," Eduard said when I approached, fists clenched at my sides.

Ivan shook from head to toe. Blood dripped from the corner of his mouth and his eye was swollen shut. "I cleaned up the mess, I came upstairs. I went to tell Sasha the guy wanted a shower and food but I couldn't find him.

His car was gone. So I went to watch TV. That was the last time I saw him."

I folded my arms over my chest. "You didn't call to ask me anything."

"I thought maybe you went to get food yourself. It wasn't important."

"And then what happened?" Eduard prompted.

Ivan swallowed. "I don't know."

"What do you mean you don't know?" I asked, eyes narrowed. "You watched TV and what? He summoned a pair of bolt cutters by magic? The Domovoy crawled out of the walls and handed it to him?" Unfolding my arms, I bent down and picked up the bolt cutters in question. "They seem real. Real enough to cut through the lock and let him escape. I wonder what else they can cut through."

Even though Ivan's wrist was duct taped around the arm of his chair, Eduard threw his weight on top of it, flattening out the kid's left hand.

"No! Sasha, please!" Ivan tried to jerk his hand away. When that failed, he tried curling his fingers, but Edward kept them splayed.

Ignoring Ivan's pleading, I wedged one of the blades between his pinky and his ring finger. With all of his struggling, he started bleeding well before I slammed the handles toward one another.

Ivan screamed. His pinky fell to the floor and rolled like a sausage link; the wound spurted blood all over my boots.

"Who did it? Who helped him? Was it you?" I yelled over his howling and the vigorous shaking of his head. "If it wasn't you, then who was it? Did you let someone in the house? Tell me!"

"I didn't! Sasha, please! I didn't!"

"Who hit you then?" Eduard asked, grabbing a

handful of his sweaty hair and yanking his head backward. "Who betrayed us?"

"I don't know!"

Eduard and I exchanged a glance, getting a read on where the other person stood. He gave a slight nod, in agreement with my assessment. Positioning the bolt cutters on either side of Ivan's ring finger, I raised a dark brow at Ivan.

Beads of sweat rolled into the one eye that was open, making him blink like mad. "God, no. No, please! Sasha! Don't!"

Snip.

Ivan's screaming tapered off into a sob. Choking on his tears, he gasped for air, his remaining fingers clawing at the arm of the chair. "I thought I heard something," he wailed. "I went to go look. Then I saw you. You were standing over me."

I grabbed his jaw, squeezing hard. "Are you saying *I* did it?"

"No! No! I don't know! I never saw anyone else! But I heard them!"

"Why didn't you say any of that before?"

"Because, because I failed you…" Ivan's head slumped forward, held up only by my grip and the tape strapping him down. As soon as I let go, his chin fell to his chest and the sobbing renewed.

Exhaling, I swiped a hand down my face roughly. "Clean him up," I muttered to Eduard. "And get him the fuck out of my sight."

Eduard nodded and wandered over to his open duffel bag, pulling out a small butane torch and a knife.

I dropped the bloody bolt cutters on the floor and gave Ivan one last disgusted look before turning toward the stairs. He failed at guarding Roan. He failed at holding out during interrogation. For all intents and purposes, I should put a bullet in his head and cut my losses. He was lucky I had more important things to do — namely getting Roan back.

The torch sparked behind me. A second later Ivan's scream reverberated through the basement. The smell of sizzling flesh wafted up the stairs.

"Where are you going?" Eduard called after me over the top of Ivan's wailing.

"Taking back what is mine."

I found him once before. I'd find him again. This time I'd make sure he didn't escape.

## 29

# ROAN

THE DAY AFTER MY ESCAPE, I LAID IN BED FOR WHAT seemed like an eternity. Staring at the ceiling while Frankie snored softly next to me, I tried to dredge up the energy to move. I couldn't. Despite being back in my bed, safe in my house, I slept like shit and it wasn't because Frankie flopped around all night or kept touching me with her cold feet. That part was actually comforting, reminding me I was *here* and not *there*, wherever there was.

I'd been picked up in one of the suburbs outside Chicago, about halfway between the university and home. But I didn't know if that's where I'd been the entire time, or if that was merely the last stop on the crazy train.

I had no idea where the warehouse was.

I had no idea where the motel was.

I was no closer to solving anything in the daylight than I had been at the police department.

It was the lack of answers that finally motivated me enough to get out of bed. Stuffing a pillow under Frankie's arm in lieu of me, I padded across the room and down the stairs, making my way into Dad's office.

I didn't want to believe a fucking *criminal* was being more honest with me than my own father, but the whole ransom thing was *not* adding up. Someone was lying. I wanted to know who and I wanted to know why.

Sliding into the chair behind Dad's desk, I turned his computer on and logged in under his profile. Since he auto-saved every password he had, I didn't have to work too hard to get into his email.

There was a shit ton of email in his inbox, but nothing really jumped out at me. Nothing in Russian. Nothing cryptic. No blaring subject line referencing me or any demands. Just stock quotes and investor bullshit and reminders from Joyce about various appointments.

Similarly, there was nothing in his saved emails either.

Clicking on the deleted folder, I scrolled through a ridiculous amount of junk email and advertising.

Still, nothing.

Closing out of his email, I turned my attention to his actual desk, rifling through the drawers. There weren't any odd letters, envelopes, polaroids. Nothing.

I pushed the last drawer shut and stood to leave when something caught my eye. There was a flash drive in one of the USB ports. That, in itself, wasn't earth shattering. The fact my name was written across it *was*.

Sinking back into the chair, I moused through the computer windows, pulling up the information from the USB. There was only one folder and it, too, was labeled ROAN.

Double clicking, I held my breath as dozens of other folders opened, each labeled with a date. There were *hundreds* of photographs of me, if not thousands — at school, at my apartment, performing at my fucking senior showcase, even graduation.

Videos recorded me for days. Weeks! There were clips of me and Frankie, at home and out and about; playing soccer; playing one of any number of instruments; me, just by myself, when I thought I was tucked away in my apartment, in my own happy little bubble. It was like they had cameras everywhere.

Did that mean Sasha was there the *whole* time? Was he the one who'd been stalking me? And how the hell didn't I *see* him? It's not like he blended in easily.

They even took pictures of me *after* I'd been taken. I mean, I guess that was all part of the process. But it was unnerving to see myself like that — unconscious, thrown on a dirty floor in a fucking dog kennel like I was garbage.

Somehow that, *that* picture, cemented the whole experience. It was photographic evidence I wasn't lying, I wasn't crazy, this wasn't some sick ploy for attention. The bruises, the concussion, Sasha — it *all* happened.

In the midst of all of the photos, there was only one document.

My stomach twisted violently as the cursor slid over the icon, opening it.

PHILLIP SINCLAIR —
WE HAVE YOUR SON

Oh, God.

I was going to be sick.

Covering my mouth with one hand, I forced myself to keep reading.

. . .

IF YOU WANT TO SEE HIM AGAIN CALL THIS NUMBER

312-555-5869

He *knew*.

Unequivocally, without a shadow of a fucking doubt, he *knew*.

My father *knew* and he didn't do anything! He just let them keep me. For a week! Doing God knew what. But did he care? Fuck no. He stood outside that police department and *lied* to me!

The world spun suddenly. I pushed away from the desk and put my head between my knees, trying to breathe.

A hand on my back made me jump.

Frankie jumped as well with a squeak. "I'm sorry! Are you ok? I woke up and you were gone. I got scared. What are you doing?"

I shook my head. Words wouldn't leave my throat no matter how hard I tried, so I pointed at the screen instead.

She moved closer to the computer, gasping about every other word, ending with a "Cocksucker!" Whirling to face me, she pulled me into a fierce hug. "I'm so sorry! Oh my God. I don't even know what to say!"

We sat like that for I don't know how long, me hugging her waist from the chair and her holding me while perched on the desk. Technically, I knew Frankie was warm and soft, and I should be *feeling* warm and soft, but I didn't. The numbness I experienced before returned in force. I felt nothing except a strange hollowness.

"What are you going to do?" she asked after a bit, pulling back to look at me.

"I don't know… I mean, what *can* I do? I can't confront him. He'll keep lying. I suppose I could give this to the police, but I'm sure those guys are long gone by now. Besides, it's not them I'm mad at anymore."

She frowned at me. "You should still be mad at the people who kidnapped you. You should be fucking furious."

"It's just business," I said, echoing Ivan's view on the matter. "Which is what I'm sure my asshole sperm donor would say, too. His ROI on the bank is worth a hell of a lot more than me."

"So hit him where it hurts." Frankie beamed, entirely too angelic considering she was advocating something destructive and/or illegal. "You could crash his Porsche. Oo, empty his bank account into one of your own and go travel the world on his dime. Fuck him and fuck Georgetown."

I looked up sharply, an idea sparking in the back of my brain. "Oh my God. That's it."

"What's it? What are you doing?" she asked as I scooted her out of the way, digging around in the center desk drawer like a deranged person. I popped the tiny button for the hidden compartment under the desk and crawled under there to get my treasure. As soon as I had it, I sprang to my feet and charged upstairs, Frankie on my heels. "Um, Earth to Roan! What are you doing?"

"I have to go," I said, ripping my tank top off and grabbing a fresh shirt out of the dresser.

"Go where?"

I ducked into my closet and yanked on a pair of jeans quickly before she barged in on me there, too. "I know how I'm going to get that piece of shit back."

"You are not even making sense right now." She was rubbing circles on her temples when I rushed past her. "What piece of shit? The kidnapper? Or your dad?"

I hurried out of my room and down the stairs again. "Don't worry about me. I have a plan. I think."

It was another stupid, crazy, suicide-mission plan, but a plan nonetheless. And for some reason, those seemed to be turning out ok for me lately.

## 30

## SASHA

I WAS IN THE MIDDLE OF DOWNING MY THIRD CUP OF TEA and going over Roan's dossier for the hundredth time when my phone rang. Swiping it off the table, I answered without even bothering to look at the caller ID.

"Aleksandr Vassiliev?" a male asked, clearly Russian based on the accent alone.

"Speaking."

"My name is Misha Chernyshevsky."

I sat up straighter, paying much closer attention to what he had to say. "I've heard of you."

"And I you, which is why I'm calling. Are you in the city?"

"Why?"

"Meet me at Delirium, in the Ukrainian Village. One hour. Come alone."

He disconnected, leaving me staring at the phone while ice water ran through my veins.

Misha Chernyshevsky worked directly for Sergei Sidorov, the ruling boss of Chicago. By extension, Viktor also worked for Sergei, taking orders and paying tribute, but Misha was different. He was special.

Fresh from Moscow, Misha made quite the stir when he arrived in America. He was a former Spetsnaz operative, yet he proved himself invaluable to Sergei's organization in the few years he'd been here. They forgave him for working for the government and learned to embrace his expert marksmanship and eye for security. Part bodyguard, part hitman, rumor had it Misha was one of the few men Sergei trusted, which made him one of the most dangerous. If Sergei's word was God's, then Misha's was the Holy Spirit's.

So what the fuck did a man like Misha Chernyshevsky want with me?

---

I'D ONLY BEEN TO DELIRIUM A HANDFUL OF TIMES, whenever Viktor was summoned by Sergei to discuss business. Since I wasn't sure what kind of meeting I was walking in to, I stopped by my apartment and changed, swapping the comfort of jeans and a t-shirt for a tailored black suit. I also upgraded my hardware — two guns I knew they'd confiscate, along with a third they'd overlook and a couple knives to round out the arsenal.

The club was technically closed, but when I walked up to the front door, it swung open before I could even knock.

An armed guard patted me down, taking the guns holstered in the small of my back and on my shoulder, as predicted. He turned and set them on a shelf, waving me forward and stupidly leaving me with the one on my ankle as well as all of the blades.

A large, blond man in a gray suit strolled forward, his

sky-blue eyes bright. "You must be Aleksandr." He extended his hand. "I'm Misha."

"Sasha," I replied, shaking it firmly.

He inclined his head and gave me a small smile before gesturing to a curved, black staircase. "Let's talk privately."

I climbed the stairs warily and hung back at the top, letting Misha take the lead.

He pushed open the door to a private room and gestured for me to go first. When I lingered at the threshold, glancing at the interior of what was clearly a VIP room, he chuckled. "It's not a trap. At least, I don't think it is."

Brow furrowed, I continued into the room only to stop dead in my tracks when my gaze landed on the last fucking person I ever thought I would see.

Roan Sinclair.

Sitting casually on the couch like he was waiting for an old friend, Roan sat up straighter when he saw me, his chin tipping up in defiance. I didn't miss the way his gaze raked over me, probably just as confused by my suit as I was by his mere presence.

"*What is going on?*" I asked Misha in Russian.

"*This boy came looking for you.*"

"*What?*" I couldn't help my jaw dropping before I snapped it shut. *Roan* came for *me*? I'd been searching for him all night. Every hospital, police department, public transport. I even drove out to his university and checked his townhouse. Nothing. Yet, here he was, apparently of his own free will.

"*He said he has something to discuss.*"

"*So what am I doing here?*"

"*He only wanted you.*" Misha chuckled softly and I quickly erased any surprise from my face. "*He was very insistent on speaking with the Wolf of Verkhoyansk.*" He glanced between Roan and I, an unsettling smirk lifting one side of his mouth. "*I guess now I can see why.*"

I shot Misha a look, but he was already gone, closing the door behind him on his way out.

"Sasha," Roan said, giving me one of his little smirks.

"Roan," I ground out, hating we were essentially on equal footing. But now he was in my sights, there was no way in hell I was letting him walk out that door unless it was straight into my SUV and back to confinement.

"You look confused," Roan said, patting the arm of the chair kitty-corner from him. "Why don't you have a seat? We need to talk."

Clearing my throat, I moved closer, unbuttoning my suit jacket along the way. My, my, how the tables had turned. I went from calling the shots to having a twenty-two year old order me around in the span of a day.

Angling myself toward him in the chair, I watched his every move, waiting for the attack. He seemed to be studying me with the same wariness, his gaze darting from my face to my hands and back again.

After a prolonged period of silence, I spit out the question that had been festering since yesterday. Unfortunately, it was with none of the control I usually displayed. "How did you escape?!"

A coy smile lit up his face. "Doesn't matter. I'm here to talk about something else."

"It does." I cocked my head, trying to keep my voice steady and not beat the answer out of him. "Ivan lost two fingers because of it."

Roan's brow furrowed, the mischievous spark in his eye diminished. "How?"

I leaned forward, holding his stare to make sure he was paying attention. "I cut them off."

"Jesus Christ!" He recoiled and averted his gaze. For a

split second, he looked at me the same way everyone else did, like I was some sort of monster. But when he looked up again, all I saw was confusion. "Why would you do that?!"

"Because you escaped," I replied with a shrug. "I needed information."

"So you cut someone's fingers off?"

"I would have cut off every piece of him if it meant getting you back." The truth of that statement hit me as hard as a battering ram. I *would* have — and I'd do it again. Roan didn't seem to understand the lengths I'd go to once I dedicated myself to a job. And losing him? Unacceptable.

"Why?" Roan asked quietly. "What is it you want from my dad?" He leaned forward ever so slightly, his blue eyes full of sadness, desperation even. He reminded me so much of Pavel right then. The memory seized my heart and squeezed, to the point I thought it was going to burst.

"It doesn't matter." Shaking my head, I propped my elbows on my knees and laced my fingers together, staring at the glass table in front of us. My lighter was in my pocket, as always, taunting me. If I could burn myself, it would burn away the feelings. But I couldn't exactly do that in front of the kid. Until then, I'd have to visualize a void and throw every useless thing into it, like feelings and memories and unnatural desires.

Black, empty, nothingness. That's what I said I had to be. That's what I was meant to be. A wolf. *Man is wolf to man.* That's what was tattooed across my abdomen, beneath the snapping jaws of my eponym. *That's* what I had to remember, not a blue-eyed boy from twenty years ago who sealed his own fate by making the wrong fucking choice.

"Is it this?" Roan's voice broke through the memories.

He held out his hand and uncurled his fingers, revealing a key. No, *the* key. The master key for the Northern Illinois Bank & Trust security deposit boxes. I swiped for it, but he jerked his hand away, his face suddenly hard. "No. First, you tell me why."

I narrowed my eyes at him, trying to see what his angle was. "Why are you here? Why did you look for me? And how the fuck did you know to ask for the Wolf?"

He licked his lips quickly. "Ivan called you the Wolf. I figured if I asked around for a huge, tattooed guy named Sasha aka: the Wolf, that word would get back to you. And I was right." A soft smile tugged the corner of his mouth. Smart little shit, I'd give him that.

"Why did you come back?" I repeated each word slowly. He had freedom. Somehow, he found a way and he left. And now, eighteen hours later, he purposely sought me out. Me. The one who kidnapped him in the first place.

His blue eyes dropped for a minute and his jaw shifted to the side. I thought he was going to ignore me, but he dragged his gaze back up to mine, all of his earlier cockiness gone. "Because you didn't lie to me."

I furrowed my brows, not understanding what he was really trying to say.

He looked away again with a wince. "My dad lied. He told me he never got a ransom demand, that my parents just thought I left. But I found it on his computer." Shaking his head, he glared at the nothingness in front of him, his hand clenching around the key. "All he had to do was give you this stupid fucking key and he couldn't even do that for me."

"Wouldn't," I corrected. "He *wouldn't* do that for you. He was given many opportunities."

His gaze flicked back to mine, his full lips twitching in thought. As much as I hated to admit, he looked better as a free man. The golden glow I was used to seeing returned, somewhat. His hair was still a tousled mess on top, but he'd shaved and smelled like summertime again. "And then there's you…"

Ready to be insulted, I pushed my shoulders back, molars already grinding together to keep from tearing his head off.

"You said you'd cut a guy into pieces to keep me around. I know, it's all about this" — Roan held the key up for emphasis — "that I'm a means to an end for you, but it's more than I can say about that asshole. He was willing to let me be held hostage and more than likely killed over a fucking key."

"So you came to me for revenge?" His anger was palpable. Not that I blamed him. If I had a father and he treated me the same way, I would want revenge too.

He sucked his lower lip between his teeth, giving a small shrug.

"You want me to kill him?" I clarified, focusing on murder instead of his mouth.

"No!" he replied, his eyes wide.

I spread my hands, equal parts confused and frustrated. "Then what? Why are you here?"

"I want to help you."

"What?" Were we still speaking the same language? I ran through the English dictionary in my head, trying to remember if there was some alternate meaning to the word "help." Nope. None that I could think of.

"I want to help you, Sasha." Roan was practically on the edge of the couch, his body turned toward me so much our knees touched. Hope shone in his eyes, hardly tempered by the angry line of his mouth. "I want to help get whatever is in that bank that's so damn important. I don't care if it's money or nuclear fucking launch codes."

For the second time, I nearly had to pick my jaw up off the ground. "Why?"

Bitter as it was, he forced himself to smile. "My asshole father values the security of his bank more than my life. He knows if he gave you the key and the customer found out, *he* would be dead. I want to watch him sweat. I want him to look over his shoulder, wondering 'Is today the day?'"

Shit… did he know whose deposit box we wanted? I didn't. As far as the operation went, it wasn't important. I was beginning to think I'd been misinformed.

Had this been a test all along? Some fucking game Viktor set up? He obviously had a rat in his brigade, but if my real purpose was to flush them out, why didn't he say that instead of this wild goose chase?

A cold unease crawled into my stomach. I was tired of being tested. I'd proven my worth, my abilities, for over twenty fucking years. It was never enough.

"I know how that bank got started," Roan continued, earnest and irritated all at once. "Prohibition. You think the early investors were good people? They were mobsters. Guys like O'Banion and Capone. They needed a safe place to clean their dirty money and my great-grandfather gave it to them."

What he was saying made sense — more sense than the limited information Viktor revealed along the way.

"I want him to be afraid," Roan concluded, his voice lowering at the same time he turned his face away from me. "Like I was."

Surprise stilled my tongue. From an early age, I had fear beaten out of me. On the rare occasion it flickered, I refused to acknowledge it and I would *never* admit it out loud. But he did — to the person who caused the fear, no less.

One thing kept circling in the back of my head —

Roan came *back*, even after everything I'd done. He didn't tell the police who I was, or I would have been arrested by now. He didn't stay away, locked safely in his father's mansion. No, he wandered the streets of Chicago asking to speak to the man who'd kidnapped him, beaten him, and did disgusting things to his cock.

Springing out of the chair, I put as much distance between us as possible. Exhaling a breath, I kept my back to him and closed my eyes. Despite my efforts, I could still remember how he felt, the sounds he made, how he tasted.

Fucking animal.

Savage.

Filth.

"Sasha?" Turning at the sound of my name, I flinched. He stood right next to me, a small crease between his eyebrows. "Where'd you go?"

"What the fuck are you talking about? I'm right here."

"You don't look ok all of a sudden..."

I grabbed the front of his shirt in both hands and shoved him against the wall. "What the fuck do you know about how I look? You think you can walk in here, making demands? I should snap your fucking neck and take the key from your dead body."

"You're not going to do that," he shot back with that fucking smirk, his previous concern for my welfare gone in the blink of an eye. He might have been afraid once upon a time, but he certainly wasn't now. "You *need* me."

"You think you know what I need, hmm?" We were nose-to-nose, so close I could feel his heartbeat pick up beneath my fist. "You don't know shit about me, boy."

"I know whenever you get close to me, you can't keep your hands off of me. I bet you're hard right now." His chin tipped up a second before he grabbed my cock. It was already halfway to hard, but feeling the heat of his hand through the my pants finished it off. He smiled like the cat that ate the damn canary, adding more pressure.

"Get your fucking hand off of me," I snarled, throwing a cautious glance toward the door.

Grabbing ahold of my wrists, he spun suddenly, pushing me against the wall with surprising strength. "You could have killed me at any point, but you didn't. And you won't. So stop with the bullshit."

I leaned forward, lowering my voice. "What makes you so sure it's bullshit?"

His mouth hovered over mine, his stunning eyes staring right through me, like he knew my dirtiest secret. Then his lips were on mine. Full and soft and so fucking trusting.

Seizing his face between my hands, I dug my fingers into the back of his skull. I could crush it. I *should* crush it and end the twisted feelings snaking their way through my insides.

Perversion. That's what it was. Foul and loathsome perversion.

Roan's lips parted and his tongue slipped out, tracing my bottom lip. My mouth seemed to open by itself. The wickedness in my blood drove my tongue out to meet his, a pitiful moan sounding in the back of my throat. He matched it with one of his own, like kissing me gave him some sort of relief. When his hips pressed against mine, it obliterated any question as to how aroused he was. His hands splayed against my chest, eventually drifting southward, flattening against my abs, lower and lower…

A knock sounded on the door approximately two seconds before it swung open.

I shoved Roan as far away from me as possible, as roughly as possible. "*You're fucking insane! Now get out of here with your lies before I rip out your fucking tongue!*"

Roan stumbled but regained his footing. There was a

flash of hurt in his eyes, but it was gone just as quick, replaced by a scathing glare. His chest rose and fell rapidly, his hands clenched at his sides.

Misha stopped in the doorway, his head cocked. "*Everything ok?*"

"*Stupid American brat,*" I snarled, trying to look disgusted. It wasn't that hard. I *was* disgusted — at myself, my weakness and stupidity. "*Thinks he come in here and make demands from someone like me. He's lucky this is Sergei's club, or I'd beat his ass.*"

Misha's gaze slid to Roan, lingering on his wrinkled t-shirt. "Is your business concluded?"

Roan swallowed thickly and nodded. "Yeah. I'd say so."

"Good." Misha took another step into the room and gestured for Roan to walk through the door.

"Thanks for helping me," he said to Misha on his way by, pausing to shake the man's hand. "I really appreciate it."

Misha inclined his head.

"Oh and another thing," Roan said, slicing a glare at me over his shoulder. "You owe me a new phone." I snorted and rolled my eyes, but at least the demand helped sell my complaint. "You can drop it off at my hotel. I'm staying at the Drake." And then he was gone, leaving the door open behind him.

Misha watched him until he disappeared from view before strolling forward, steepling his fingers together. "*Interesting boy.*"

"*Pain in the ass boy.*"

"*Usually one in the same.*" Misha's eyes narrowed on my face as he leaned closer. Before I knew what he was doing, he lifted his hand and dragged his thumb beneath my bottom lip.

My lungs ceased to function at the touch. My heart stopped when he pulled his thumb away and glanced at it before rubbing it against his other fingers.

"*Sorry, thought I saw something,*" he said, giving me a polite smile. "*Sergei would like a word with you before you go.*"

"*Is Viktor here?*" I asked, trying to sound completely normal after thinking I was seconds away from death. No, not true. I thought I was seconds away from a world of pain and *then* death. The fate that awaited all of the corrupted creatures like me.

Misha's smile remained. "*No. This is between you and Sergei.*"

Fuck me.

# 31

# ROAN

"You are a fucking moron! You know that?" Frankie screeched at me through the laptop. I cringed, but didn't try to interrupt. "I can't believe you went looking for that guy! Why in God's name do you think that was a good idea?"

"Because he's the same one from the bank robbery."

"What?!" Her face zoomed in on the video screen, her brown eyes boring a hole through the technology. "The bank robbers are the ones who kidnapped you?! You need to go to the police! Right now!"

"It's fine."

"No, it's *not* fine! These are dangerous people, Roan! Do you hear me? Dangerous! Did you forget they shot one of their own people during the getaway? You need to get out of there. Right now."

There was a knock at the door that made both of us look to the side sharply.

"What was that?" she asked, but I was already on my way to open it, running my palms down the sides of my legs.

Glancing through the peep hole, I was somewhat relieved it was Sasha and not a Russian hit squad. Unless he *was* the hit squad. I still wasn't quite sure, despite my bold declaration earlier that he wouldn't kill me.

As soon as the door opened a crack, he threw his shoulder into it and barged in.

"Yeah, sure. Come on in," I muttered, scrambling out of his way.

Checking behind the door, he closed and locked it before prowling through the rest of the room, clearing the bathroom, the closet, and finally cutting across to the balcony to snap the drapes shut.

"Oh my God. Is that him?" Frankie shouted from the computer.

"Shit." I darted over to the laptop, hand outstretched to smack the top down. Sasha beat me there, grabbing my wrist while his eyes narrowed on Frankie.

"Francesca Starling," he said, arching a questioning eyebrow at me.

"Oh my God," Frankie gasped, covering her mouth with both hands and staring at the screen. "He knows my name Roan! How does the fucking scary Russian know my name?"

"I'll check in with you later," I said quickly, slapping the computer closed and scowling at Sasha. "Did you have to freak her out?"

He gave me a smug smile.

I folded my arms over my chest, leaning against the desk. "So do we have a deal?"

Sasha closed the distance between us, crowding my personal space like always. At first I thought it was an intimidation tactic, and maybe it was, but Misha did the same thing and he had been nothing but nice to me.

"You give me the key, I take what I want," Sasha said,

his face dipping slightly, "and then what? My boss thinks you're chained in a basement right now. How do I explain your sudden disappearance?"

"Just say you got tired of waiting for my dad, so you made a move. You took me to the house and I got the key for you." I shrugged. Seemed like a believable story.

"And then I'm supposed to eliminate any witnesses." His head tilted to the side after the proclamation, like I expected any different. It was always the same with him. Pain, or death.

"Say I escaped," I answered blithely.

"No one escapes from me," he growled.

I gave him a wry smile. "That's not entirely true."

His face darkened and I swore I heard his molars grinding. "How the fuck did you get bolt cutters?!"

Laughing quietly, I took a moment to enjoy how annoyed he looked. Not knowing was killing him and I loved every second of it. "That's not part of the deal. The deal is you get the key and whatever other inside information you need. Hell, I'll even go into the vault and get it for you. And you promise not to kill me or cut off any body parts."

"Fine." Glowering, he held out his hand and beckoned with two fingers.

I dug the key out of my pocket and held it aloft before dropping it into his palm. "I'm trusting you, Sasha."

"This better work or I *will* kill you," he replied, pocketing the key.

"It'll work. You just have to trust me in return."

"I trust no one."

"Not even your family?"

"I don't have a family."

"That's sad." It also explained a hell of a lot…

He made a face at me. "Why?"

"I don't know. Seems like a lonely way to go through life."

"Americans are so sentimental," he huffed, rolling his eyes. "*You* have a family. They did nothing for you."

"Wow." I blinked, reeling from his blunt-as-fuck observation. "I guess Russians really are cold-hearted bastards."

His expression remained surprisingly calm. "Is that supposed to offend me?"

"Just stating the obvious."

"I'd rather be a cold-hearted bastard than have people think I'm soft." By the way he gave me a once-over, I assumed he was referring to me as the soft one. Or maybe Americans in general, since it seemed we settled into our own mini Cold War.

"I don't think there's anything soft about you," I threw back, dragging my gaze up and down his body. It was to prove a point, but also... damn, he looked good in a suit. Somewhere along the way he lost the black tie from earlier, so now it was just the crisp white shirt, partially unbuttoned, beneath the black jacket.

He leaned forward, answering through his teeth. "Good."

Unfolding my arms, I reached for him. "So just how hard are you? Do you need to throw me around first, or is the verbal banter enough?"

"Don't touch me," he snapped, jerking away and retreating several steps.

"You didn't seem to mind earlier," I challenged, taking a step in his direction. Why was it ok for him to get in *my* face, but not the other way around? Hypocrite.

"Earlier?" His dark brows slanted sharply, his shoulders and spine so rigid you could probably bend metal against them. "You're lucky no one saw!"

"Why? Is it such a crime?"

"Yes!" Danger flashed in his pale eyes, tinged with another emotion. Hatred? Fear? "It is the worst sin! Worse than murder or adultery or theft. The only cure is death."

"Maybe that's how it is in the Old World, but not here."

He barked out a laugh. "No? Let me tell you a story. When I was fifteen, I met a man. A boy, really, like me. We worked for the same man, lived in the same house, pulled the same jobs. Two years later they caught him with another man." He swallowed thickly, the muscles in his neck visibly tense.

"It was an American. They beat the American senseless and brought Pavel to our boss. They tortured him for days." His gaze clouded over, dropping from my face. I wanted to reach out to him, but I was frozen in place by his story and its underlying message. I knew where it was headed before he even said the words.

"Everyone in the brigade came and watched as a group of us beat him to death," Sasha continued, rubbing his knuckles as he spoke. He didn't even seem to be aware he was doing it. "I broke my hand I hit him so hard."

Silence pressed around us. The weight of his past was suffocating, but he seemed unaffected by it. Maybe because he'd lived with it for so long already.

"Sasha, I—"

"Don't," he growled, his eyes clear and hard, like ice again. "You think I'm sad because I killed my friend? I'm not. I'd do it again. He deserved it. He made the wrong choice."

I shook my head, refusing to believe his bravado. "You don't mean that."

"You know nothing." His lip curled into a sneer.

"I know you're not heartless."

"Heart has nothing to do with it. There is right and

there is wrong. Queers are wrong. They are sick." He tapped his temple with two fingers. "Killing them is the most merciful thing you can do."

"No, Sasha. Whoever told you that is the one who is wrong." I moved forward another step, trying to get him to listen — really listen. He wasn't in the fucking Soviet Union anymore. "You can't help who you love any more than you can help how tall you are or what color your skin is. It's not a fucking choice, it just *is*."

Shaking his head, he looked away sharply, his hands balled into fists.

"What do you see when you look at me?" I asked, spreading my hands to the sides. "Do I look sick? Do I look like someone you should torture and kill because I'm gay? How about when you look in the mirror?"

Shit. Too far, Roan...

His head whipped toward me and he lunged forward, his hand wrapping around my throat in an instant. "You better watch your fucking mouth!"

"Go on, kill me," I spat with what little air I had left. "It doesn't change a goddamn thing about either of us."

Breathing hard, his fingers tightened. I was convinced he was going to do it — he was finally going to kill me. With one quick jerk, he pulled me forward. My mouth crashed against his, teeth and tongues colliding. I wasn't kissing him so much as *being* kissed, with anger and need and desperation. The hand on my throat slipped around to the back, threading through my hair to cradle the back of my head.

Unbuttoning his jacket, I ran my hands around his waist, pulling his hips against me. Groaning against my lips, his other hand palmed my jaw, holding me in place while he ravaged my mouth with his.

I pushed against his hips with mine and shifted my

foot forward, getting him to back up. We kept going until we reached the bed and broke apart, gasping. My lips and chin already felt raw from his five o'clock shadow, but I didn't care. I could spend hours kissing him and not care.

Grabbing his belt, I unbuckled it and shoved his pants down past his hips. They crashed to the floor with a heavy clunk and I glimpsed a gun on the carpet. Ignoring that, I pushed against his abdomen. He took the hint and sat, kicking off his shoes and pants while simultaneously unbuttoning his shirt and shrugging out of all of the fabric on his upper body. Two more heavy thunks accompanied his clothes. Not one but three guns were now scattered on the floor.

In a matter of seconds, he was completely naked, reclining on his elbows. As much as I wanted to pounce on him, I forced myself to take a moment and look at him, really look at him, to marvel at the magnificence in front of me. The tattoos didn't stop on his arms and torso, he had them on his legs too. I could have spent hours studying each of them, trying to decipher their meaning. And then there were his muscles…

"What are you looking at?" he asked, his voice tight.

"You. All of you." The sudden desire for skin-on-skin contact was overwhelming. I pulled my shirt off and cast it aside. He sat up so quickly I thought he was going to run, but he didn't. He grabbed my waist with both hands and pulled me forward, pressing kisses to my abdomen.

Fumbling with my jeans, I finally managed to push them down. As soon as I did, Sasha yanked me onto his lap. We didn't stay like that for long. He rolled quickly so he was laying on top of me, reclaiming my mouth with his.

I reached between us, gripping his dick and stroking him with long, slow movements. Moaning into my mouth, he deepened the kiss while his hand skimmed across my chest, down my stomach, and straight to my hard-on.

The roughness of his palm, the heat, the weight of his body against mine, it was just as good as the first time — no, better, because I was free to touch him, *really* touch him, in return. And I did. The hand that wasn't stroking his cock was off exploring other areas; the silkiness of his hair, the tightness of his traps, the sculpted wave of his abs.

He explored me too, with his hands *and* his mouth. Working down my throat to my chest, he caressed and kissed as he went, moving lower and lower until his breath swept over my dick and the inside of my thighs. He ran the tip of his finger down the V in my lower abs, still avoiding the one place I wanted his attention more than any other.

Pressing kisses along the inside of my thigh, his fingers continued tracing different muscles, dropping down to my balls for a bit. No matter how much I squirmed or tried to make contact with his hand, he kept avoiding it until I actually whined.

"Please," I exhaled. "You're killing me."

"Please what?" He dragged the tip of his tongue along my thigh before biting it and sucking the sensitive skin.

I gasped before spitting out the answer. "Touch me. I want you to touch me."

His hand gripped the base of my cock and his mouth came down on the crown. I don't know what kind of noise I made, a groan or a sigh. Hell, probably both because it felt fucking fantastic.

His tongue swirled around the head, while he jerked the length of me. Watching him, his black hair and his tattooed hand moving up and down in tandem, was a thing of beauty, but I still wanted more.

"Sasha..." I ran my hand through the longer hair at the top of his head and tugged. He glanced up before pulling his mouth away, brows dipping. "I want to taste you." When he quirked a brow at me, I smiled and tossed my head to the pillow behind me. "Come here."

He crawled up my body slowly, like a predator stalking its prey. I still didn't know why they called him the Wolf, but at that moment, with the way his pale eyes were locked on me, the moniker fit perfectly. Pausing only to kiss my lips roughly, he kept going. Once he was situated above my head, he lowered his torso and picked up where he left off.

Wrapping my arms around his thighs, I pulled myself up, licking the underside of his cock. A shiver rippled through him and I smiled to myself, swallowing as much of him as I could. His moan reverberated through my dick, spurring me on. It was the best kind of competition there was — who could out-do whom, who could make the other twitch or shudder, who would make the other lose it first.

Breathing hard, he popped off the end of my dick, swearing in Russian. "Roan…"

He was so close, I could see it, feel it. Squeezing his firm ass, I sucked harder. His hips jerked forward, shoving his cock further down the back of my throat. His head dropped to my leg, grunting something I didn't understand. I ignored what was probably a warning and kept going. A second later, his cum coated the inside of my mouth.

As I swallowed the lot of it, his lips wrapped around my dick again. He sucked me hard and jerked even harder, like he was punishing me for "winning" our so-called race. Warm pressure built below my stomach; I wasn't going to hold out much longer.

"Oh God, you're going to make me come," I said, thrusting into his hand and mouth.

Just like me, he ignored the warning. The orgasm

ripped out of me and straight into his mouth, an act in and of itself that magnified the blissful haze I was floating in.

Struggling to catch my breath, I forced my eyes open when he climbed off of me. I thought he was leaving like last time, but he didn't. He flipped positions so his head was up by mine and we were laying side by side, our forearms resting against one another. It was probably the closest thing to snuggling in his fucked up world, but it still made me smile.

He tucked his other arm behind his head and exhaled a deep breath, ending with a soft "Fuck." Staring at the ceiling, his mouth pressed into a hard line. I didn't have the foggiest idea what he was thinking about, if the swearing was meant for me, what we did, or the situation in general.

"Thank you," I murmured, turning my face toward him and trying not to laugh. Apparently playing with fire was my new past time and I couldn't get enough of it.

His gaze snapped to mine, flashing with irritation, but the slight curve to his mouth gave him away. I discovered the impossible — his armor had a chink in it. "What the fuck did I say about that?"

I shrugged innocently. "I guess I don't listen."

He snorted. "Yeah. No shit…"

I couldn't help but laugh that time. Naturally, he didn't. The annoyed look he sent my way made me laugh even harder.

"I should have brought the duct tape," he sighed.

"Should have brought the handcuffs." I rolled over and grabbed his face, kissing him again.

## 32

## SASHA

"What's that?" Roan asked, his fingers skimming across one of the tattoos on my ribcage.

I managed not to laugh by grinding my teeth together, but I squirmed away from the sensation. "Don't do that."

"Do what? Ask about your tattoos or this?" He grazed his fingertips along my ribs again.

Jerking away, I sliced a warning glare at him.

"Are you ticklish?" His eyes lit up with a mischievous spark.

"I will break your fucking hand if you touch me like that again. Understood?"

Chuckling, he went back to looking at the black ink all over my body. He'd been inspecting them for I don't know how long, perched on top of me and moving my limbs like a mannequin to see whatever he wanted. I had no idea why I let him.

He touched the same spot as before, but much harder. "Do you like cats?"

"What?" I glanced down to see what he was talking

about. It was a black cartoon cat in a top hat. "No. I mean, I don't care about them. They're just cats."

"Then why'd you get it?"

"Because I'm a thief." I arched a brow, waiting for his moral outrage. He didn't even blink.

"What does this one mean?" He tapped the skull on my chest.

"That I'm a murderer." I held his gaze as I replied. To his credit, he didn't look away or show any sort of emotion. It's not like he should have been shocked, considering I killed two cops in front of him not even a week ago. "And this one," I continued, pointing to the giant dagger through my sternum, "means I'll do it if you pay me."

He shifted closer, propping himself up on his elbow and studying the snarling wolf in the middle of my abdomen. "Is this why they call you the Wolf?"

"No." I didn't necessarily mean to answer so tersely, but I wasn't going to apologize after the fact.

He wasn't fazed by the brevity of the answer *or* my tone, like he'd come to expect both. "Then why do they call you that?"

"Which story would you like to hear? The one where I was raised by wolves, or the one where I use them to tear people apart?"

"Ivan said you cut someone up and fed them to a wolf."

I chuckled. "Ivan is an idiot."

"So you didn't kill someone when you were ten?"

"Oh, no, that part is true." He pushed himself up into a sitting position, his gaze locked on mine, like he was trying to tell if I was joking. Unfortunately for him, I wasn't. "It was self-defense," I added. "Life is not kind in Verkhoyansk."

"That's where you're from?"

I nodded.

"So how did you end up here?"

"Do ever stop talking?" I shot back. Did he really expect me to pour out my life story to him? To tell him great tales of growing up in the brutal wilderness of Siberia before touring the slums of Moscow, New York, and Chicago?

"No," he replied with a grin, turning his attention back to the tattoos, tracing the outline of the script beneath the wolf head. "Do you have a favorite?"

"Do you have a favorite piercing?" I huffed, flexing my abs to stop myself from squirming again beneath his hand.

"This one." He touched the silver hoop in his nostril. "I thought my dad's head was going to explode the first time he saw it."

I couldn't help but chuckle again. At least he was a pain in the ass to everyone and not just me.

"These," I answered at last, bending one of my legs to show him one of the giant eight-point stars on my kneecap. They matched the smaller ones on either side of my chest.

"Oh my God. Didn't that hurt?" he asked with a grimace, running his thumb over the center. "It's all bone there."

I shrugged, lowering my leg again. "No. Nothing hurts."

"Nothing?"

"No, not anymore."

"What does that mean?"

Shaking my head, I sat up, swiping my suit jacket off the floor. I fished my cigarettes out of the pocket and slipped one between my lips, lighting it to Roan's objection, as desperate for the nicotine as I was for the interrogation to end.

"This is a non-smoking room," he pointed out.

"Do I look like I give a fuck?"

"At least go by the balcony. Jesus."

Obliging him, I stood and pushed the sliding glass door open, blowing the smoke outside.

"You know those will give you cancer, right?" he asked, rolling onto his side and propping his head up.

"I'll be dead before I get cancer." I inhaled and held it a moment, exhaling through my nose and adjusting my lean against the doorframe to a more comfortable position.

"Does anything bother you?"

"Yeah." I flicked some ash off the end, squinting at him. "You."

"Funny." He sat up, raking a hand through his disheveled hair. "I'm going to go take a shower." He didn't wait for a reply before he slipped off the bed and padded to the bathroom.

Staying right where I was, I finished my cigarette, trying to figure out what the fuck I was supposed to do now. I had the key and technically I still had Roan. It wouldn't take much to knock him out and drag him back to the safe house. Or, I could leave. Get dressed, walk out the door, and never see him again. That would have been the smarter thing to do.

Roan was worried about cancer; I was worried about an even darker disease. It already claimed Pavel and now it was poised to take me too. No matter how much I screamed at myself internally or punished my body for reacting the way it did, I couldn't stop it.

But if Viktor wanted him dead, Roan didn't stand a chance. Since my boss had yet to make that decision, I didn't want to let Roan out of my sight, even if it meant I had to go back to stalking him. It would probably be easier now that he'd graduated and was presumably back at his father's house. I wouldn't have to chase him all over campus or follow him to his lessons after class, forced to listen to children absolutely butchering the violin. How he remained so patient and encouraging was a mystery. I would have broken the instrument in half and cursed the brats for disgracing music.

No, I couldn't let him go only to keep stalking him. Seeing him, even from a distance, was a reminder I didn't need.

I could always fake his death. Find a guy with his build, his hair. If I mangled the face enough, Viktor would never know. Roan could move on with his life and I could pretend like none of this ever fucking happened. Glancing at the rumpled bedsheets, I took a drag off my cigarette and looked away just as quickly.

Squeezing my eyes shut, I rubbed my forehead with one hand. It was easier to blame Pavel for everything, to say it was a stupid indiscretion in my youth, dumb curiosity and nothing more. But twenty years later? I couldn't use that excuse again.

"Sasha?"

Dropping my hand, I opened my eyes. Roan stood in the doorway of the bathroom, his head cocked to one side. "Are you coming?"

Taking a final puff, I flicked my cigarette over the balcony and closed the door.

"Are you ok?" he asked, watching me approach with a frown.

"I'm normal."

"Ok…"

"Why? Something wrong with my face again?"

A smile softened his worry and he looked away, a faint pink in his cheeks. "No, that's not what I meant. Now, or earlier. You looked… sad."

"It's how I look." I shrugged at him. "I don't waste my time smiling at every little thing."

"Yeah, I know." I caught him rolling his eyes before he turned, stepping into the shower and wetting his hair.

I followed, lingering outside the shower door to watch him. His eyes were closed while he shampooed his hair, fragrant suds dripping down his body. He rinsed his hair clean, dashing water out of his eyes right as I stepped in and pushed him backward against the tile.

"Fuck that's cold," he gasped, arching his back. My chest pressed against his, pinning him against the wall he was trying to get away from, and I slanted my mouth over his. He groaned softly, slipping his arms around me, holding on tightly.

My hands rested on his hips while I kissed him slowly. I nipped at his lower lip and kissed his chin, making my way along his jaw and down to his throat. Sinking my teeth into the side of his neck, I sucked his skin, relishing the taste and the way he whimpered. His lips were already dark and swollen, but it could have passed as natural. I wanted to mark him for the world to see, to know he was taken.

His hand slipped between us, rubbing his cock against mine. No, not just rubbing, he was stroking them *together,* his long fingers sliding up and down easily. Horizontally, vertically, swirling around each other. It was such a foreign sensation, but it was fucking incredible.

I kissed him again, matching the tempo of the kiss to what his hand was doing. Long, slow, twisty strokes got a soft, languid kiss. Hard and fast got hard and fast, teeth and tongues, until we ripped apart only for the sake of air.

His hips flicked forward with his hand, his breathing increasing. I caught his face between my palms, kissing him hard, and deep. When he was close, I let one hand fall to his chest, my thumb grazing across his nipple in random patterns. He moaned into me, his grip on our cocks tightening right before he came all over me.

"Fuck," he panted. He dropped his cock entirely and gripped mine, smearing his cum around like lube. With the way he was going, I wasn't going to be very far behind him.

He bent forward, kissing and licking my chest. When he flicked his tongue over my nipple, a shot of electricity went straight to my balls. I caught the underside of his jaw between my thumb and forefinger and pushed his face upward, crushing my lips against his as my orgasm rushed out, all over his hand and his cock.

"*Fuck me,*" I grunted as the last bit of cum rolled out, dripping to the shower floor.

"You're so sexy when you speak Russian," Roan murmured, stepping closer and kissing the tattooed date on my collar bone.

"*Is that a fact?*" I asked with a smirk.

He pulled back, meeting my gaze with a wry grin. "Smart ass."

"Look who's talking." I took a step backward so the water hit my chest, washing most of the semen away before I grabbed the body wash and took care of the rest.

"Are you hungry?"

I quirked a brow at him, shampooing my hair. "What?"

"Food. You know, that stuff you kept barking at me to consume?" He took the bottle of body wash and nudged me out of the way to wet the rest of his skin. "I'd like to get some. I haven't eaten at all today."

"Order room service."

"There's this place around the—"

"We shouldn't be seen together." I ducked my head

beneath the sprayer and rinsed off completely, exiting the shower as fast as possible without slipping on the wet tile.

He turned the shower off and followed me out. "What are you talking about?"

I tossed him a towel and kept going.

It didn't slow him in the slightest, but at least he wrapped it around his waist, removing some of the temptation.

I had to get away from him. Now. Being this close to him made me want things I shouldn't want. It made *him* want things he shouldn't want. Staying was a bad idea. I saw that now.

"Where are you going?" he asked, hot on my heels.

I ignored him.

"You can drop the broody bullshit now," he snapped. "I've seen behind the curtain."

"Curtain?" I whipped around, advancing on him. "Another fucking Communist joke?"

He held his ground, brows furrowed. "What? No. Wizard of Oz." I stopped short and he flinched, resuming his glare a second later. "If this thing is going to work between us, we need some fucking ground rules. For starters, you don't get to hit me anymore. Understood?"

"There is no thing." I turned away and stalked back to the bed, grabbing my pants off the ground.

"Pretty sure that wasn't the deal."

"I have the key. You're free. Deal is done." I pulled my shirt on and tucked it in roughly before shoving my holsters back into place. Yanking my suit jacket on to hide them, I marched toward the door.

"Deal is *not* done." Roan stepped in front of me, blocking my exit. I could have moved him, one way or the other, but I kept my hands to myself by clenching them at my sides.

"Move."

He crossed his arms over his bare chest, still glistening from the shower. "No."

"You think you can stop me from leaving?"

"I don't know why you're leaving to begin with. One minute you're all over me and the next you're back to being a dick."

Why did he have to be so goddamn stubborn? "Get the fuck out of my way."

"Rule two, you don't get to bark orders at me anymore."

"Fuck you and fuck your rules. I'm leaving. Now."

"Sucks being trapped somewhere, huh? Lucky you, you're not stuffed in a fucking dog crate or handcuffed to a bed."

I matched his scathing glare. "Unless you want to go back to the fucking dog crate, get out of my way."

"Not until you tell me what the fuck your problem is. We agreed — I'd help you get what you need out of the vault and you put the fear of God into my dad. And now you're, what? Up and leaving without having some sort of a plan?"

"The plan? You want to know the plan? The plan is to walk into that bank, open that fucking box, and get what my boss wants. Then I'm going to find someone who looks like you and put a bullet in their head. *That* is the plan. Happy?"

"No!" He stared at me, aghast. "You can't just kill someone because they look like me."

I snorted, shaking my head. "You're so naive."

"Enlighten me, then. Please. Tell me why I should be perfectly ok with you running off to kill someone."

"Because it's what I do."

"Not good enough."

My fists clenched so hard the bones felt like they were about to snap. "Someone has to die. That's how it goes. So it will either be you or someone who looks like you."

"It doesn't have to be that way."

His optimism was cute. Misplaced, but cute. So very American of him. "It does," I said quietly.

The lines of his face softened, his shoulders drooping. "Are you going to come back?"

I swallowed and stared at the door behind his head. I couldn't look at the sadness replacing his anger. He knew the answer the moment he asked the question.

"Stay away from your father," I said, still not looking at him. "He's not a good man and he will not protect you when people come for him."

"Are you the one coming for him?"

Reaching past him, I turned the door handle and opened it a crack, despite the fact he was still standing in front of it. "Don't look for me again. And never go back to that club. Those men are dangerous."

"I can't believe they're any more dangerous than you."

"I'm serious," I snapped, meeting his dejected gaze with mine, hoping he saw every bit of my frustration. "For once, fucking listen to what I say."

"Or what?" Always pushing…

Shaking my head, I opened the door wider. It pressed into his shoulder, but he was rooted in place by his stubborn pride. I didn't let up on the pressure. With each passing second, I questioned my decision to not forcibly remove him from my path.

Finally, he stepped to the side.

The door swung open the rest of the way and I walked out, staring straight ahead. I hadn't looked back at Pavel's corpse and I wouldn't let myself look back to see the cracks in Roan's golden shell.

No, I made my choice. I may have succumbed to a moment of weakness, but I knew I was stronger than the corruption in my blood. I would finish this job and I would never think of Roan Sinclair ever again.

## 33

# ROAN

THE SUN FELT LIKE IT WAS A FOOT AWAY, BAKING ME WITH its invisible rays. Sweat gathered along the nape of my neck, but I refused to seek out shade. After days of not seeing the sun, I was more appreciative of its blistering warmth than I'd ever been. Plus, I was hoping a tan would help hide the giant fucking hickey Sasha left on me, along with whatever was left of my bruises.

Dipping a hand into the pool, I splashed some water on my torso and kept floating, eyes closed behind my sunglasses. A thousand different things ran through my head — Sasha, mainly, and trying to figure out what spooked him; the uncertainty of my future, whether it was here or in D.C.; and trying to figure out a new way to make my asshole father suffer since Option A was clearly out.

"You better not be napping," Freddy's voice spoke up over my music. "I brought snacks."

"And I brought booze!" Frankie chimed in.

I cracked an eye, squinting at them. "How did you get in here?" Ever since Sasha's grim warning about people coming for my dad, I made sure the alarm was set 24/7. Not for him, for me. I knew an alarm wasn't going to stop anyone intent on murder, but it would give *me* enough time to make myself scarce. He was on his own.

"Your mom was on her way out," Freddy replied, arranging the food on a floating tray.

Figured. While Dad had a strange case of amnesia regarding the abduction of his only child, Mom was in the throes of retail therapy to deal with *her* stress over the ordeal. After I came back from meeting Sasha — and subsequently spending the whole evening with Sasha until he freaked and bolted for the second time — she sat me down with a cup of herbal tea and asked if I was ok.

I lied. There was no point in being totally honest with her, since we'd just end up circling back around to *her* and whatever new spiritual journey she was on.

"I'm fine," was the only answer I offered.

"Are you being safe?" she asked, pointblank. "Sexually, I mean."

I almost choked on a dandelion or whatever weed was floating in the cup. "What?"

She touched her own neck, indicating the spot where Sasha left his mark. "I want to make sure you're using protection."

I slapped a hand over it, too little too late. "Yeah, Mom. Jesus." Aside from the fact I hadn't actually been on the receiving end of anal, it was a topic I would never, *ever* discuss with my mother. Ever. It was bad enough she knew Frankie and I did it. I found pamphlets on teenage pregnancy and various methods of birth control in my room for weeks afterward.

"Is that where you were this past week?" Mom leaned in, asking in a whisper. "It's ok, you can tell me. I'll understand."

My jaw almost hit the floor. "Are you serious?"

"I still don't think your dad knows that you came out. I mean, not that it's a big deal. Everyone is gay these days, but I can understand if you and your boyfri—"

"I don't have a boyfriend, Mom! And I wasn't lying about being fucking kidnapped. Unlike your husband, I don't make a habit of lying, especially about something as serious as that!"

She sniffed and swept a blonde strand behind her ear. "Your father and I tell each other everything."

"Oh, ok. So you knew I'd been taken and Dad was refusing to pay the ransom?"

She sighed and pulled on her earlobes, eyes closing to meditate or whatever the fuck she did. "Roan..."

"No, either you tell each other everything, or he lies to you as much as he lies to me. Which is it?"

She didn't say anything else. Not that I expected her to. She'd defend him until the death even though he treated her like shit, too. As long as she had a working credit card and a sympathetic therapist, she'd stick by him.

Shaking my head, I pushed the cup of nasty green water away from me and stood. "Thanks for the tea. Oh, and if you're curious about how my senior showcase went, you should check out Dad's computer. Yeah, my kidnappers got some excellent footage for you."

That was three days ago. She'd been hitting the Magnificent Mile hard since then. I could picture Dad screaming as soon as he got the credit card bill. Hell, maybe I should ask her to pick up some stuff for me, just to prove a point.

"Earth to Roan!" Frankie yelled, beaning me in the head with a koosh ball.

Shaking the water out of my hair, I frowned at her. "What?"

"What do you want to drink? Beer or margos?"

Freddy pushed the floating tray toward me and eased himself into the pool. He'd brought a variety of fruit, chips, and my personal favorite — mini tacos.

"Beer," I replied, snagging a taco.

"Me too," Freddy added.

"Get your own," Frankie snapped, digging around in the cooler. She popped the top on a Corona and stuffed a lime wedge into it while I paddled over to the side to take it from her.

"Thank you."

"No, thank *you*," Freddy said, snatching it out of my hand and swimming away with it.

"Asshole!" Frankie grabbed a chunk of ice and lobbed it at his head. Luckily, he was halfway to the other side of the pool, so it sank harmlessly to the bottom.

"I think the day you two get along, Hell might actually freeze over," I said with a laugh, taking the second beer from her.

"Not likely. Cheers." She smirked and held her margarita aloft before downing half of it.

Freddy hauled himself out of the pool, muttering.

"What's up?" I asked.

"Forgot the damn salsa verde in the car."

"Consuela's salsa verde?" I perked up, watching him swagger across the pool deck. The Starlings' longtime cook made the best salsa verde known to man. I'd grown up eating so much of her food over the years that when I thought of comfort food, it was her cooking that usually came to mind. My parents, on the other hand, changed cooks as often as people changed their underwear. Between Mom's crazy cleanses and Dad's overall demeanor, I didn't blame any of them for leaving.

Freddy grinned and waggled his brows.

"Wait, did she make tamales too?" I asked, practically salivating at the thought.

His paced quickened noticeably and I scrambled back to the edge of the pool.

"You guys," Frankie groaned.

We both ignored her.

He was already to the patio door by the time I got out of the water. Freddy threw a glance over his shoulder and I walked forward casually, like I was headed to one of the lounge chairs. As soon as he turned his back, I sprinted after him.

"At least save me one!" Frankie yelled after us.

Freddy and I raced through the house, slipping and sliding on the tile as we went. As soon as I gained ground on him, he shoved me in the shoulder, sending me toward one of the couches.

I jumped up on the cushion and leapt over the back, happy my high school track skills were still sharp. Landing right behind him, I hip-checked him out of the way and into the wall.

He recovered quickly. We reached the front door at the same time, fighting each other as well as the handle with our wet hands. Freddy got it open, but I darted out first and hurried down the front steps toward his car.

"No! Those are mine!" He grabbed my arm and tried to slow me down, but it was hard to keep a solid grip with the sunscreen I'd put on.

I dragged him along in my wake, reaching out for his car door. "Bullshit! You can have them whenever you want! You know she made them for me!"

As soon as I got my fingers on the door handle, Freddy slammed into me from behind, using our joint weight to keep the door closed. He snaked his arms around my waist, flattening his palms against the window while I tried to shrug him off enough to get the door open.

With a startled yelp, Freddy was gone.

I turned in time to see him get slammed onto the hood of his own car by one very pissed off Russian.

"Sasha!" I tried to shove him off, but it was like trying to move a mountain. He pinned Freddy to the car by his throat, completely unconcerned by the fact my friend was already turning purple under his large hand. "Get off him!"

"Who the fuck is this?" The question was more of a growl, Sasha's pupils narrowed to pinpricks.

"None of your business!"

"Should I kill him?"

"No!" My indignation turned to real fear since I knew Sasha gave zero fucks about doing it. "Let him go! Now!"

Sasha retracted his hand slowly, his mouth settling in a hard line of disappointment.

Freddy sucked in a breath and grabbed my arm. I helped him stand up straight and pulled him to my side, out of Sasha's reach.

"Are you ok?" I asked quietly, praying to God there wasn't any real damage.

Freddy nodded, rubbing his throat and throwing a death glare at Sasha. "Who the fuck is that?"

"No one," I answered quickly, ignoring the tic in Sasha's jaw. His black brows dipped, eyes narrowed as always. "Why don't you go get some ice for that? Ask Patricia for some Advil or something."

Even after nearly being strangled to death, Freddy hesitated, glancing between Sasha and I with questions in his warm brown eyes. He didn't want to leave me alone with a Neanderthal, which I appreciated, but I also had questions

I knew Sasha would never answer with someone else nearby.

"I'll be in in a minute," I said with the most reassuring smile I could muster.

Nodding, Freddy headed back toward the house, giving Sasha a wide berth.

Sasha watched him go, his gaze simmering with a murderous rage that turned on me as soon as I shoved him in the chest as hard as I could. I was pleased when he actually took a step back to keep his balance.

"What the fuck is wrong with you?" I snapped. He cocked his head, but didn't say anything. He stood there, arms crossed, watching me with an infuriatingly blank expression. "You can't go around strangling people!"

He still didn't seem fazed. Probably because strangling them was nothing compared to shooting them in the face. Or feeding them to wolves — I never did get a clear explanation of his origin story…

"What are you doing here?" I mimicked his pose, hoping it pissed him off as much as his stance was pissing *me* off.

Stooping, he snagged a white box off the ground and held it out to me. It was a brand new phone.

"I pay my debts," he said. As soon as I lifted the box from his fingers, he started down the driveway toward his Mercedes.

"Wait!" I tossed the box on the roof of Freddy's car and hurried after him. "That's it?"

"What else is there?"

"What about that thing?"

"I told you, there is no thing."

"So you didn't kill anyone lately?"

He spun quickly, getting in my face. "You ask too many

questions, you know that? One day you're going to ask the wrong person the wrong question."

I heard his vague threat and promptly dismissed it. If there was one thing our forced time together taught me, it was how to ignore his snappy non-answers. He was the type of guy used to getting his way the first time around. Unfortunately for him, I was the type who didn't let shit go.

"You could have mailed the phone," I said, crossing my arms over my chest again. "What are you really doing here?"

He made a face like it was the dumbest question ever. "Why would I mail it when I have your address? That is a waste of time and postage."

"Because the last time I saw you, you basically said I'd never see you again. And now here you are, bringing me expensive electronics and giving my friends brain damage."

"Well, *now* it's the last time." He turned to go, but I grabbed his elbow. When he jerked back around, his other hand was clenched in a fist. I flinched, but it didn't come flying at my head. Surprisingly. Guess that was progress.

"I think you're lying," I said, sounding way more confident than I felt. "I think you'll find another excuse to come see me."

"Trust me — I won't."

"What if I come see you?"

He took a step forward, his teeth on edge. "What did I say? Don't ever go back there. Don't ask about me. Forget I exist."

"I can't," I admitted quietly. As much as I may have wanted to, there was no way I could forget about him. Not just the kidnapping, or the bank robbery, but everything else that had happened — the burning looks he gave me, the way his hands touched me, so powerful but so uncertain. Memories of him were seared into my skin as permanently as the tattoos were in his. I didn't know what any of it meant, but I knew I'd regret just walking away without trying to figure it out.

"You have to," he replied, peeling my fingers off his elbow.

"I still want to help you."

Recoiling, he made a face, either because he was insulted or because he smelled the desperation on me. "I don't need your help." Without waiting for a reply, he pivoted on the ball of his foot and strode away.

I didn't let him get far. "Security isn't going to let you get anywhere near that vault," I called out, smirking when he paused, head tilted, but still refusing to look at me. Seemed I had the upper hand again. "Oh, yeah. The bank has armed security now. There's also a temporary moratorium on opening new safety deposit boxes. Dad might not know what you're after, but he knows it's in one of those boxes. So now, only vetted box holders have access."

Sasha turned slowly, processing the new information and looking less than happy about it. A muscle twitched along his freshly-shaven jaw every now and again. I don't know which version I preferred — the clean shaven or the slightly scruffy. Both looked good on him.

"You can get to it?" he asked, strolling forward until he was right in front of me. The familiar warmth of his gaze raked over me the closer he got, lingering where my swim trunks hung low on my hips, exposing the V muscles he'd spent so much time torturing the other day.

"I've had my own box since I was thirteen," I replied, trying to ignore the fact the heat from his gaze made my dick sit up and take notice.

He still seemed irritated, so I was surprised when he

lifted his hand to my throat, brushing the pad of his thumb over the remnants of his hickey. The barest hint of a smile pulled up one side of his mouth, pleased by only God knew what.

My fingers skimmed along the the top of his jeans. Even though his t-shirt was in the way, heat radiated into my hand. Despite his icy exterior, I'd come to associate Sasha with fire — a fiery touch, a fiery temper, and fiery passion when he let his guard down.

With his thumb pressing the center of the mark, the rest of his hand wrapped around the side of my neck, jerking me forward. Rule #1 aside, I didn't mind when he manhandled me like *this*. Sasha took what he wanted, when he wanted it. And by the look in his eye, he wanted me, regardless of what his inner voice was telling him.

His lips were a breath away from mine when Frankie's voice screeched through the air.

"Are you fucking kidding me?!"

She was down the stairs in a flash, dripping water, and looking like a swamp creature with her long brown hair plastered to her body. Freddy hung back on the porch, a bag of frozen peas pressed to his throat.

Sasha straightened, pulling his mouth away from mine in the process. He didn't, however, take his hand away from my neck, even when Frankie marched up to him and attempted to get in his face.

"Who the hell do you think you are? Trying to kill my brother and now my best friend? Get your hands off of him!" She swatted Sasha's hand away from me at the same time she slipped her arm around my waist and pulled me closer to her. As if her impressive five feet and four inches was at all intimidating to someone who was a foot taller than her.

Instead of crushing her like a bug, Sasha watched her

with an amused expression.

"Frankie, it's ok," I said quickly. She actually tried to hit him again, but I yanked her hand back to safety before Sasha decided to rip it off.

"What is the scary Russian doing at your house?" Frankie hissed at me, shooting a glance at Sasha out of the corner of her eye.

"He was dropping off my phone."

"So why did he bodyslam Freddy into a car?"

I didn't really have a good answer, so I turned it back on her. "What's up? Do you need something?"

"Yeah, I just came out to make sure I could get one tamale before you heifers ate them all," she replied with a brilliant smile and a chipper tone. Dropping the nice act immediately, she punched my shoulder. Hard. "I came out here to make sure he didn't decide to kidnap you again, you idiot!"

"That was a..." I glanced at Sasha, looking for the right word. "Misunderstanding."

"Misunderstanding my ass! Was this a 'misunderstanding'?" She picked up my left hand and bent it back, all but shoving it in my face. "How about the bruises all over your face? You told me *he* did that!"

"Ow, Jesus!" I ripped my hand away from her and rubbed my elbow. "You made your point!"

Sasha took a step forward and Frankie jumped about a foot in the air, circling behind me and shrieking. "Oh my God! I'm sorry! Please don't kill me!"

"He's not going to kill you," I said, giving Sasha a pointed look.

"Is she always like this?" he asked.

I made a noncommittal noise.

Frankie jabbed me in the ribs with a scowl.

Rolling his eyes, Sasha reached for his wallet and

pulled out a business card for a Russian restaurant. "Meet me tomorrow at one. We'll discuss the rest of the plan." He emphasized the last word by arching an eyebrow.

I took the card, trying not to grin like a goddamn idiot. "See you at one."

With a curt nod, Sasha turned and headed for his SUV.

Frankie and I watched him walk away in silence. She tilted her head and crossed her arms, while I bit my lip and tried to subtly adjust my hard-on.

"I hope you know what you're doing," Frankie muttered.

I expelled a breath and looked down at the card. "Me too."

## 34

# SASHA

CIGARETTE SMOKE DRIFTED UP INTO THE AIR, MELDING with the rest of the pollution floating through the streets of Chicago. I shifted my lean against the building, scanning the other end of the street for a while. Tucking the cigarette between my lips, I pulled my phone out and double checked the time. It was ten to one.

I'd just slipped my phone back into my pocket when an Audi SUV pulled up in front of the restaurant and stopped. Pinching the cigarette between my thumb and forefinger, I took one last drag and flicked the butt to the sidewalk, crushing it under my heel. At least he was punctual.

Popping a piece of gum in my mouth, I waited while Roan climbed out of the car, staring up at the building. His gaze dropped from the sign above the restaurant, landing on me, and a smile spread across his face. It was so infectious, I almost smiled back. Almost.

I made my way to the front door and opened it for him, throwing a glance up and down the street to make sure no one was paying us any attention. "This way."

"Always such a gentleman," Roan said, brushing past me.

My only response was an irritated noise. Once we were inside, I stepped around him and led the way through the restaurant. There was a brown paper bag set out on the pass through between the kitchen and the server's area that I grabbed before pushing through another door in the back.

"Where are we going?" Roan asked, following me up the back stairs. Technically it was an emergency exit, but I preferred this way as opposed to using the regular entrance.

"To my apartment."

"You live here?"

"Not all of us live in mansions." I dug my key out of my pocket and shoved it in the lock.

Down the hall, the other apartment door opened and Bohdana stuck her gray head out, glaring at me and muttering away.

"Hi!" Roan chirped, actually waving to the old bat.

I smacked his hand down. "Don't talk to her."

He frowned. "Why not?"

"She's not nice."

"*You're* not nice," Roan countered.

Before I could answer him, I caught a slur in Ukrainian. I turned toward the old woman, pointing at her apartment and answering in Russian. "*Get back inside before you say something you'll regret, you deranged hag.*"

The busybody shook her fist at me, her thumb tucked between her index and middle fingers.

Rolling my gum into a ball with my tongue, I spit it in an arc down the hall, watching it bounce along the floor toward her apartment. "Suka." Shouldering open my door,

I pushed Roan inside, ignoring her doubly-offended screeching.

"Fucking Ukrainians," I muttered, setting the bag of food on the table and unpacking the hot containers.

Roan took it upon himself to wander around the living room, not that there was anything to look at. It was sparsely furnished, ready for me to leave at a moment's notice. Other than my clothes, there was nothing personal. Everything I owned could be stuffed into a duffel bag in under a minute, and that included my weapons.

"What's with the Ukrainians?" he asked, circling back to the table in the kitchen and bracing against the back of a chair. "You guys don't like each other or something?"

"Or something." Grabbing two plates out of the cabinet and a handful of silverware, I set the table quickly. "Thirsty?"

"Sure." Roan slid into the chair, looking at the table curiously. "Why aren't we eating downstairs?"

"I told you, we should not be seen together." I poured two glasses of kompot and set the drink in front of him.

"Does your boss still want me dead?" he asked, eyeing the drink and poking a floating chunk of cherry.

"No." I sat across from him and served up the kotleti and mashed potatoes.

"Why not?"

"Because he thinks you already are." I met his gaze across the table, waiting for the next question, the next burst of moral outrage. Surprisingly, he kept quiet, sipping his drink tentatively.

As soon as I found a suitable stand-in for Roan, I told Viktor I had the key, using Roan's half-concocted idea that I somehow coerced him into getting it for me and he tried to "escape," so I had no choice but to shoot him. Three times. In the face. As far as retrieving the emeralds from the bank box, I told Viktor Eduard and I were going to take care of it the following week.

Hence, why it wouldn't be very smart to be seen wandering around with a guy who looked like the one whose body I dismembered and chucked out into Lake Michigan.

Roan nodded, pushing the fried meat patties around with his fork. A small crease formed between his eyebrows and he drew in a breath. "But—"

"No," I cut him off with a wave of my hand. "No 'but'. I told you. It was you or him. Do not make me regret my decision."

He dropped his fork, leaning back in his chair. "On the one hand, I'm grateful. But—"

"No 'but!'"

"God, you're frustrating!" he growled, pushing away from the table and stalking into the living room.

"*You're one to talk*," I muttered to myself. Sipping my drink, I chewed on a cherry piece, watching him march back into the kitchen, on the verge of a profound declaration. I could already feel him building up to it.

He stopped in front of me, his eyes narrowed, and shoved the table backward.

"*What the*—" The rest of my question was smothered by his mouth against mine. Straddling my lap, he held my face between his hands and kissed me, angrily. It was the best sort of punishment I'd ever had in the thirty-five years of my bleak existence and the last thing I expected.

My hands slipped beneath his t-shirt, skimming over his smooth skin, pushing the fabric upward. He broke away to tear it off, flinging it behind him. He resumed his attack on my mouth, his tongue lashing mine. As soon as he felt my cock harden beneath him, he ground against me, groaning into our kiss.

I grabbed his ass and rocked against him, increasing the friction for both of us. One of his hands cupped the back of my neck while the other gripped my shoulder.

Roan broke away, hissing between his teeth. "Fuck, Sasha. What are you doing to me?"

Running my hands up his back, I let my fingers dive into his hair, twisting in the longest part of it. As soon as he tipped his head back, I kissed his throat and nipped the side of his neck.

"*I don't know, but you're making me fucking crazy*," I growled, pushing his head back toward my mouth and reclaiming his lips. My cock strained beneath him, as desperate as I was for release.

"I hope that means 'bedroom now' in Russian." Breathing hard, his gaze practically melted me to my core.

Grabbing his ass again, I kept ahold of him as I stood swiftly. He wrapped his legs around my waist and kissed me as I carried him across the living room. More or less slamming him against the bedroom door, I kissed him back while he groped behind him for the door handle. As soon as he found it, the door swung open. It was only a few more steps before we crashed onto the bed.

I peeled my t-shirt off while he undid the front of my jeans and pushed them down, stopping only to yank the holster off my belt. He rolled his eyes and dropped the gun on the floor, ripping my pants off the rest of the way.

"If I didn't know better, I'd say you were compensating," he murmured, his fingertips inching down the trail of dark hair from my naval to my groin.

"Good thing you know better." I held the back of his head and punished his sarcasm with a bruising kiss as he dragged his fingers along the length of my cock teasingly.

Breaking apart, he smiled against my lips. "I don't know if I'll ever get over this."

"What?"

"How amazing you are." He fisted my cock and gave it a few lazy strokes, glancing between his hand and my eyes.

I groaned and leaned forward, kissing him as deeply as I could. He let go of me briefly, slipping out of his jeans and kicking them off. As soon as his dick sprang free, it rubbed against mine, sending a rush of warmth through me.

"*Fuck.*" Rolling my hips against his, I pressed my palm against his chest. His muscles flexed beneath it, but I was more mesmerized by the rapid rhythm of his heartbeat. Replacing my hand with my lips, I kissed his chest, flicking my tongue over his nipples on my way down.

He gasped and ran his hands through my hair, his back arching. Before he got too comfortable, I took his cock in my mouth, swirling my tongue around the head while sliding my hand up and down his length.

"*This* is amazing," I murmured, licking the pre-cum off the tip. "And these." I dropped down further, dragging my tongue from his balls up the underside of his cock. "And this." With the barest amount of pressure, I slipped my finger between his ass cheeks, tracing his hole. "I can't wait to see what this is like."

"Don't tease me," he panted.

"Or what?" I tossed back with a smirk before sucking as much of his cock into my mouth as possible.

He swore softly, his lids dropping as he watched me with rapt attention. Licking and sucking his cock lazily, I moved down to his balls, ignoring his whining and the occasional jerk of his hips. When my finger was coated with enough saliva from the blowjob, I drew circles around his hole again, pushing in carefully.

"Oh, God, yes." He pressed back against my hand, taking more of my finger. Returning to his cock, I teased the head while working my finger in and out of his ass slowly, adding more saliva when necessary.

The noises he made were like music to my ears, swearing and groaning and occasionally my name. He may have been fascinated by me for whatever reason, but I was enraptured with him. I loved touching him, tasting him, making him feel pleasure after I'd inflicted so much pain. I couldn't take any of that back, but I could give him this, if only for a moment.

Encouraged by the rocking of his hips and his fingers scraping along my scalp, I added a second finger. He swore again, breathing hard, but it didn't take long for him to relax. Soon both fingers were all the way in, stroking him on the inside, while I continued to lick and suck his cock.

"Sasha?"

"Hmm?" I made sure to hum the acknowledgment around his dick, taking pride in the appreciative noise he made.

"Get my wallet."

I furrowed my brows but did as he requested. He practically snatched it out of my hand and flipped through it, handing me a small blue rectangle. Not a condom — a sachet of lube.

"Do you have a condom?" he asked.

"What?" Did he really just ask me that? Did that mean he wanted to...? I swallowed thickly, buying time, trying to calm the irrational flutter in my chest.

"A condom. Unless, you don't want—" Uncertainty flashed in his eyes. Strangely, it was *his* apprehension that silenced the dozens of questions streaming through my head. If it was what he wanted, I'd give it to him. I'd give him anything.

I reassured him with a soft kiss. "I want to."

"Ok..." He didn't seem all that convinced, but he nodded anyway.

I leaned over and opened the top drawer in the nightstand, grabbing one of the foil packets I kept around for those times when my hand just wouldn't cut it. Tearing it open with my teeth, I tossed the package aside and rolled it on.

Roan opened the packet of lube and rubbed it all over my cock, kissing me as he worked. I held my hand out to him, taking the remainder of the slippery substance and coating my fingers again.

He turned away from me and settled on his hands and knees, presenting me with his perfect ass. I touched the curve of his backside, exhaling a steadying breath as I positioned myself behind him. Slipping my fingers inside of him again, I worked them in and out, spreading the lubrication around until he felt more relaxed.

"Ready?" I asked, trying to ignore the way my voice wavered.

"I think so..."

The voices in my head, cursing me for wanting this — for wanting *him* — screamed at me as I nudged my cock up against his entrance. A shiver ripple through him, or maybe it was my hand trembling. I couldn't tell. To stop it, I gripped his hip and pushed into him as gently as I could.

His fingers dug into the sheets and he sucked in a breath through his teeth. As soon as I breached the tight ring of muscles, he groaned and I swore. My cock wasn't even all the way in, but it already felt amazing. Being inside of him was everything I'd ever dreamed about, and everything that was going send me straight to Hell.

"Fuck..." Roan rocked back slightly, helping more of my cock slip inside. Slowly, steadily, it went further, until my hips were flush with his ass. A shudder went through him before his body relaxed again.

"Oh my God. You're so fucking tight." The feeling was so euphoric, I could barely breathe. I held on to either side of his hips and pulled back slightly before thrusting in again. He moaned, meeting each of my tentative thrusts with a flick of his hips.

I tried to take it slow, to draw out the pleasure for us both. But as soon as we fell into a steady rhythm, I couldn't help but thrust a little harder, a little quicker. Roan matched the pace, groaning and whimpering.

Slipping an arm beneath his, I wrapped it around his chest and pulled him back against me. Now that we were both up on our knees, he turned and kissed me over his shoulder.

"I love the way you fuck me," Roan panted, his head tipped back against me while he stroked himself, hard and fast, in time to my thrusting from behind.

"You feel so fucking good." My fingers curled around his throat, keeping his head pulled to the side so I could bite and suck the tender skin at the juncture of his neck and his shoulder.

"God, don't stop, Sasha. Please don't fucking stop."

"I'm so close. I don't—"

"Harder. I'm right there."

I fucked him as hard as I could, for as long as I could, until stars burst behind my eyelids and an orgasm rocked through me. He came at nearly the same time, clenching around me so hard it stole my breath.

Collapsing against his back, I held him tightly, panting into his damp neck. He reached behind him and stroked my hair, nuzzling the side of my head.

"That was fucking amazing," he breathed.

"Yeah," I murmured, trying to remember how to speak — in any language.

For the first time in my life, the reproaching voice in my head was silent. But the stain of my repugnance would always be there, marring me as much as the cigarette burns on my forearm, or the tattoos over the rest of my skin. I could never escape it, I knew that now, especially now that I'd disgraced myself by giving in. The only hope was to distance myself from it, from Roan, before the degeneracy ruined me completely.

## 35

# ROAN

After cleaning up, we fell back into bed again. I was sore, but all in all, the first time bottoming — especially for a guy Sasha's size — wasn't as bad as I'd expected. Even now, I don't know why I went as far as I did. Rather, why I went as far as I did with *him*. I'd been the top in my previous relationships, but for Sasha, I was consumed with the need to have him — *all* of him. Maybe one day we'd switch, just to try it out, but for now I was happy letting him more or less lead.

"I think I have a problem," I said, staring at the ceiling above his bed.

Sasha propped himself on his elbow, frowning. "What problem? Tell me. I'll fix it."

"Not that kind of a problem." Moving closer to him, I slid my arm under his pillow and immediately jerked it back out. "What the fuck?"

Picking up the pillow, Sasha blinked at the handgun laying there. "What? What's wrong?"

"I heard about this guy who shot his wife one night while he was dreaming. Aren't you afraid you're going to shoot yourself in your sleep? Or, I don't know, someone else who might be here..." It might not have been the best way to ask if I was the only bed partner in his life, but it was worth a shot. I figured it was safe to assume I was the only guy, but who knew if he was into women too.

"No." He grabbed the gun and set it on the nightstand, completely oblivious to the underlying question. Laying down again, he folded an arm behind his head, still frowning at me. "What is the problem?"

Shaking my head, I tried to resume by train of thought before it had been derailed by picturing my Russian Rambo rolling around with a blonde supermodel. "I know I shouldn't be here. You've made that part crystal clear. But—"

"But?"

"Would you stop interrupting? Not every 'but' is bad."

"I know." He slid one hand over my hip and squeezed my ass, biting his lower lip and looking sexy as fuck doing it.

I swatted his hand away on principle, despite the fact I liked seeing this playful side of him. "Oh, look who's a jokester now. I'm trying to talk to you and you're cracking jokes."

He smirked up at me.

"As I was saying" — I stared at him for a beat, waiting for an interruption — "I don't want this to all be over next week."

"What are you talking about?"

"After I get whatever's in that safety deposit box, I still... want to see you." He inhaled a deep breath and folded his arms over his chest, turning his attention to the corner of the room while I continued. "Don't act like I'm the only one who feels this way."

"I don't feel any way," he said, completely monotone.

"Bullshit."

His gaze snapped back to mine, as hard and unreadable as his voice.

"In case you haven't noticed, you don't have to pretend with me," I added quietly. I wanted to touch him, or hold his hand, but the way his arms were crossed told me he was *not* up for that sort of intimacy. "You're human. It's ok to *be* human."

He sat up, brushing the hair off my forehead and running his thumb over the scar near my temple. Did he remember how I got it? It wasn't that long ago, but his brain had to be so compartmentalized to deal with the shit he saw — the shit he *did*. I wouldn't be surprised if his memory virtually erased itself everyday, like a computer rebooting.

"I'm more myself with you than anyone else," he said at last, returning his gaze to mine. "But—"

"But?" I interrupted with a wry grin, trying to keep the mood light. Despite the fact he was usually serious, I didn't like the look in his eyes. It wasn't annoyance, which I'd come to expect. It was more along the lines of grief or sorrow — like he knew something devastating and I didn't.

"But," he repeated, rolling his eyes. Instead of looking at me again, he went back to staring at the corner. I didn't know what was so fascinating about a black duffel bag sitting on top of a chair, but he couldn't tear his eyes away. "It doesn't matter... You'll get the emeralds for Viktor and that is all. We'll say goodbye. You will go back to your mansion and I'll be on the first plane to Russia."

"You're going to Russia?" I jerked away from him. Now I knew why he was staring at the bag — it was already fucking packed! He wasn't kidding. That was his plan all along. Use me for as long as he wanted and then hightail it to another fucking country. "Why are you going to Russia?"

"I've been here for too long. I need..." He muttered under his breath in Russian, his eyes darting skyward like he was searching for the right words. "The West is not good for me. I need to go back for discipline."

"Discipline?" I stared at him, trying to follow his logic. "That sounds like the exact reason you *shouldn't* go back."

"You don't understand."

"You told me this was a crime," I said, gesturing between the two of us. "You said they killed your friend because of it and that was *here*. Why would you go someplace where they *can* and *will* kill you if they find out?"

"They won't find out."

"How can you be so sure?"

"I'll get married." He said the words and immediately swallowed. His gaze finally left the bag, only because it dropped to his clenched hand. "Once you have a wife, no one asks questions."

I was sick and angry all at once. I had no right to this man, no right to his future, but what he was saying made my stomach roil. It felt... wrong. *He* knew it was wrong. That's why he wouldn't look me in the eye, why his jaw was tight and his breathing quickened. It was one thing to stay in the closet, like he seemed hellbent on doing. But to actually go through with a marriage when it was all a lie?

Even though I knew it was ridiculous to be mad, I was. I felt like a cheap plaything, something to amuse yourself with before ultimately tossing in the trash — and worst of all, I practically begged him to do it. The fault was entirely mine for how far things went, I accepted that, but there was no way I was going to keep subjecting myself to *more* pain, physical or otherwise.

Swallowing all of my questions, along with my need for

understanding, I slipped off the bed. Grabbing my jeans from the floor, I pulled them on quickly, before he had time to put two and two together.

"What are you doing?" Sasha asked.

"I gotta go," I mumbled, heading for the kitchen.

"What?"

By the time I located my shirt and tugged it on, Sasha was in the kitchen with me, wearing nothing but a pair of black boxer-briefs.

I avoided looking at him as much as I could, but it was almost impossible. His big frame filled up the tiny space and his eyes followed me everywhere, his disappointment almost palpable. Too bad he couldn't sense mine the same way.

"Tuesday at three. Meet me at the coffee shop across from the bank," I said, hoping he didn't hear the tremor in my voice.

"Roan."

Ignoring him, I yanked the door open and stepped out, closing it behind me as he said my name a second time.

I didn't want to go through the restaurant again, so I followed the exit signs to the main staircase, moving as quickly as I could in case he decided to follow me.

At the top of the stairs, I nearly crashed into a little old lady with a kerchief on her head, a paper sack in each arm.

"I'm so sorry! Here, let me help," I said quickly, taking the bags from her while she yelled at me in another language. It was then that I realized it was the Ukrainian woman Sasha exchanged words with earlier.

She might have been mad, but she didn't take the bags back as she stomped down the hallway, shaking her fist at Sasha's door. I felt a surge of kinship with her in that moment, except I wanted to do more than shake my fist at him. I wanted to beat the bigotry out of him until he saw reason.

"Where would you like them?" I asked as the old lady shooed me into her apartment with a flap of her hand, untying the kerchief with the other.

She kept shooing toward the kitchen, so that's where I went.

Unlike Sasha's cold, empty apartment, hers was warm and homey, stuffed with knickknacks and crocheted blankets. It smelled like dill, which was strangely pleasant.

I set the bags on the countertop and started unpacking them out of habit. She shuffled around behind me, pulling out a stock pot from one cabinet and setting it on the stove before moving over to the fridge. Apparently she didn't mind help from a complete stranger since she didn't even look twice at me.

"You hungry?" she asked, pouring water into the pot. In truth, I was starving. Whatever meal Sasha had tried to serve went completely uneaten once we got... distracted. I didn't even get a chance to answer before she poked my arm with a frown. "Sit down. I cook."

"You really don't have to do that, ma'am."

"Sit!" She pointed a wooden spoon at me like a weapon and I obeyed, immediately. "How you know the Moskal?" she asked, dumping something into the pot.

"The what?" I blinked.

She whipped the spoon in the direction of Sasha's apartment.

"Sasha?" I clarified.

She 'hmphed' and turned her back to me.

"It's a long story," I replied with a sigh, studying the collection of brightly colored, patterned eggs that lined the half-wall between the kitchen and the living room.

"He bad man." She plunked a plate down in front of me. "You nice boy. You stay away."

"He's not that—" I stopped abruptly at the look she gave me, the lie dying on my tongue. How could I say he wasn't a bad person? He was a murderer. An unapologetic murderer, at that. A career criminal who worked for some very dangerous people. He was everything society taught you to fear — to hate, even — and I had more reason than most, considering our introduction to one another. So why didn't I hate him? Why was I so fucking drawn to him? And why was the thought of never seeing him again so damn depressing?

The old lady didn't speak again until she flopped a couple of giant crescent-ravioli looking things on the plate with a scoop of sour cream.

"Are these pierogies?" I ventured, vaguely recalling one of our Polish cooks from my childhood. She'd made piles of food with names I couldn't pronounce, but it was all delicious.

"Varenyky." The little old lady sat down across from me and spread a napkin over her lap. "I'm Ukrainian. No Polish. No Russian. Ukrainian."

"American mutt," I said, pointing at myself with the fork before diving into the doughy pillows.

She laughed and snapped her fingers suddenly, shuffling over to the fridge, muttering to herself in Ukrainian. Pulling a large, purple berry pie out of the fridge and a jar of pickles, she returned to the table with a smile. "I have plenty," she said, spearing two pickles and dumping them on my plate before I could politely decline.

"I'm good, thank you."

"Eat up. I have ice cream."

"I'm fine, ma'am. Thank you. You should sit and eat."

She scoffed and waved me off but finally eased into her

chair. "My name is Bohdana Melnyk. 'Ma'am' is old." Her wrinkly face twisted as she shuddered.

I blinked before cracking a smile. She had to have been at least eighty, but who was I to argue? "Nice to meet you Mrs. Melnyk. My name is Roan. Roan Sinclair."

"Do you want more, Roan?" She was out of her chair again and back in the fridge, pulling out another sour cream container with a red liquid sloshing inside. "I have borscht."

"I..." I sighed, seeing absolutely no point in arguing. Ukrainians and Russians may have had issues with each other, but the two representatives of their respective cultures were just as bullheaded as the other one. No wonder they didn't get along. "I'd love some," I said with a smile.

# 36

# SASHA

"More tea?" The girl appeared once again, smiling brightly and holding up a carafe of hot water.

Nodding, I shoved my mug in her direction. She filled it to the top, glancing at me more than the mug. I envisioned second degree burns on my lap; I was pretty sure she was envisioning my lap, too, and how she could get on it.

"I'll get you another scone," she announced with a wink, sauntering away.

Rolling my eyes, I scooped a spoonful of something claiming to be triple berry jam into the cup before dunking another tea bag inside.

There was still plenty of time before Roan was supposed to be at the coffee shop, but my stomach twisted with every minute that passed. I needed a cigarette, or two, but this fucking country and their no-smoking policies made it such a hassle.

My cell phone rang and I snatched it off the table.

It was Eduard. "*What are you doing?*"

"*Just grabbing a tea,*" I replied in Russian, stirring the tea and jam again. In lieu of a cigarette, it was the next best thing to keep my hand busy.

"*Oh, where? I'll meet you.*"

The server returned with a scone, brushing against my thigh as she set it on the table. "Let me know if you need anything," she murmured, touching my shoulder.

I leaned away from her, not even bothering to respond. "*I've already left. Sorry.*" I ducked my face, hoping he couldn't hear the noise of the coffee shop behind me. "*Why are you calling?*"

"*Viktor wants an update. What should I tell him?*"

"*What did you tell him?*"

"*That we're working on it. He should have his shit soon.*"

"*You don't think he believed you?*"

"*Does Viktor believe anyone?*"

Good point. "*I should have something soon. Ok?*"

"*Do you need me for anything?*" Eduard asked. While he might have been privy to the fact Roan somehow escaped, he didn't know I'd continued to see him or that he was helping in any capacity. As far as Eduard knew, I devised another plan to get the emeralds. Friend that he was, he helped me dismember and transport Roan's body double and didn't ask any questions. He fed Viktor whatever I wanted him to and made sure to keep Yuri from poking around in our business as much as possible.

"Nyet," I answered Eduard distractedly, scanning the faces of the people walking by the storefront.

"*I have a lead on our rat problem. We should meet for dinner and discuss it.*"

The bells above the door chimed. Roan stepped in, pausing inside the threshold. He glanced around before spotting me near the window. I didn't get a smile like before. I barely got any sort of acknowledgement. Shoving his hands in his pockets, he walked over, almost reluctantly, and slid into the opposite chair with a chilly expression.

"*Call you later,*" I said quickly.

Hanging up, I set the phone on the table, trying to decipher Roan's non-verbal cues. As someone who was thrust into this country as a child, unable to speak the language for three years, I had no choice but to learn how to read people. It was the only way I survived. And everything about Roan's stiff posture told me he was pissed. "What's wrong?"

"Nothing." That was a lie, but he kept going. "Do you have the keys?"

Pulling them out of my pocket, I held them out to him by the bits. He pinched the circular bows, but I didn't let go. "Don't lie to me."

"*I'm* not the liar, Sasha." He took advantage of my surprise to rip the keys out of my hand. "Wait here."

In a flash he was gone, jogging across the busy street to the bank.

My leg bounced uncontrollably beneath the table. Sitting was killing me. I peeled off a couple bills and threw them on the table, heading outside quickly.

I didn't go far, just far enough from the door to light a cigarette and not get harassed by every bleach-blonde suburban mom carting their organic smoothie around. The buzz of the nicotine hit me, but did nothing to calm my nerves. Standing here, doing *nothing*, was worse than the initial robbery. Inaction was not something I was accustomed to; it was torture.

I was almost done with my third cigarette when Roan appeared. He stopped in the doorway of the bank, looking over his shoulder, obviously talking to someone.

My stomach flipped the moment I saw him put his hands up, in the "I surrender" motion.

Flinging the cigarette to the ground, I managed to take two steps before he dropped his hands and waved, his smile blinding even from a distance. If I tried hard enough, I was sure I could hear his laugh before he turned his back to the bank completely and set off in my direction. The laugh and the smile stopped abruptly as he crossed the parking lot.

Security didn't follow him.

Police didn't come screaming down the road.

He went in. He came out, according to plan.

Fuck me. It worked.

I exhaled a breath and swallowed the bile creeping up the back of my throat. Shaking out another cigarette, I lit it quickly and inhaled as deeply as I could.

As he approached, Roan tossed his head to the side of the building. I let him go first, smoking more of my cigarette, before wandering after him.

"Well?" I surveyed him from head-to-toe. If he had a bag of emeralds on him, I had no idea where he stashed them.

He scratched the back of his head. "I don't know."

"What do you mean you don't know?"

"You said it was gemstones. Right?"

I nodded, flicking ash off the cigarette and watching him closely. He wouldn't try to fuck me over, but I had no idea why he was being so cagey right now.

"This was the only thing in there." He held up something small and black. A flash drive. I reached for it, but he jerked it away. "Deal's done, right? I don't have to look over my shoulder for the rest of my life?"

"Deal's done." The words stuck in my throat. By the time I spit them out, they sounded foreign to my ears.

"Great. Have a nice life." Roan shoved the flash drive into my chest and walked away.

I stuffed it into my pocket, striding after him. "Roan!"

"We're done, Sasha. You said so yourself. Thanks for not killing me," he said, not once slowing his steps or looking back.

"Would you stop?"

Stubborn ass that he was, he kept walking, fishing his car keys out of his pocket and unlocking his Audi remotely.

Flinging the cigarette away, I darted forward and spun him by the shoulder.

"What?" he snapped, his blue eyes darkening. "What do you want from me? You have what you came for. You don't need me anymore. And *you* were the one who said after this, we'd say goodbye. So why the fuck won't you leave me alone?"

Each question was like a slap, sharp and stinging and completely unexpected. I *had* been the one to say after this we'd no longer see each other. After this was done, I was supposed to get on a plane and exile myself back to Siberia until the cold froze all indecent thoughts of this exasperating boy and cooled the desires he provoked.

Walk away, Sasha. Just walk the fuck away. It was what I told myself time and again, and time and again I came right back to him, like a magnet.

"I can't." The admission was barely audible.

"I'm not doing this with you again. *I* can't," he said, the muscles tensing along his shoulders. "Do you understand? *I* can't play this game with you anymore. Will I see him again or won't I? Will he stay or is he going back to Russia? You're so fucking confusing!"

As soon as I was sure he quit talking, I closed the gap between us and took his face between my hands, pressing my lips against his.

Initially, he stiffened against me, upholding his angry declaration. But the more I kissed him, the more I pressed my body against his, trapping him between myself and his car, the more he relaxed. His hands slipped around my waist and up my back, pulling me closer, if it was possible.

The fact we were out in public made my heart stutter, but I didn't stop. I couldn't. He was like a drug I couldn't kick. I tried, and failed. I didn't want to try anymore. I didn't care if I went straight to Hell. Roan was the first good thing in my life and I wasn't going to give him up.

As much as it pained me, I broke away from his mouth to give my lungs the oxygen they needed. Resting my forehead against his, I closed my eyes, keeping my hands on either side of his face. "I'm not going anywhere, Solnyshko."

"Do I want to know what you just called me?" The sparkle was back in his eyes, my little sun once more. Hopefully the storm clouds were gone for good.

Chuckling, I kissed his lips gently. "Probably not."

"Is it bad?"

"No."

"Then I don't care." He grinned, kissing me again while his hand slipped into my front pocket. A second too late, I felt the flash drive move. Pulling back with a smirk, he held it up between two fingers. "I *do* want to know what's on this, though."

"You and me both."

"Come back to the house with me. We can look at it there." I made a face, but he melted my defenses with a bright smile. "Trust me."

I nodded, despite the knot in the pit of my stomach.

# 37

# ROAN

For the first time, I actually saw Sasha hesitate. It happened in the garage when I got out of the car. Again, in the mud room when he kicked off his boots, and a third time when we cut through the house for my dad's office.

"I don't know about this," he said, hanging back in the hallway.

"It's fine. Patricia is the only one here," I replied. When he didn't start walking again, I slipped my hand into his and tugged him forward.

"Why don't we go back to my place? I have a laptop."

"Trust me on this one," I murmured, dropping into Dad's oversized leather chair and scooting closer to his computer. "We can go there as soon as we see what's on here."

Once the jump drive was in and formatted, the files popped up on the screen. I couldn't read shit — it was all in Cyrillic. With a shrug, I clicked one, unleashing a series of documents and photographs onto the screen.

Sasha said something in Russian and leaned forward, bracing one hand on the desk next to me and staring at the screen. He looked more pissed than usual, which I didn't realize was possible until that moment.

"What is it?" I asked.

"That one." He pointed at another folder.

I obliged and opened the file, surprised when Sasha's face popped up. It was a series of booking photos, but definitely ones from Russia. In addition to capturing the angles of his face, they catalogued all of his tattoos. He didn't have the wolf's head yet, or the stars on his chest. "When was this?"

"Ten years ago," he answered flatly, pointing to another folder.

I opened that as well. It was Sasha again, but this one was definitely *not* a booking photo. It might have been the one that led to a booking photo for all I knew.

Instead of wearing a striped prison uniform, he was dressed in a dark shirt, partially unbuttoned, and white pants. Even in a photograph, I could tell they were tight as hell. It reminded me of what you'd wear to a club. He looked amazing, all except for the gun he had pointed at someone's head.

The man in the picture was kneeling on the ground in what looked like an alley. It was hard to tell since the photo was black and white and on the grainier side.

Without being told to, I clicked the arrow on the right, bringing up the next photo. It was essentially the same picture, except for a large flash of light next to the man's head.

Holding my breath, I clicked again. I only caught a glimpse of the man careening sideways before Sasha pushed the chair back and blocked my view of the screen.

"Don't look at that," he said, his voice tight.

"Who was that?" I asked quietly.

"A bad man."

"Says the other bad man." I winced after the words left my mouth. "I'm sorry. I didn't—"

He held up a hand, cutting me off. "Let me look at the rest."

Nodding, I slipped out of the chair and traded places with him.

He clicked through a couple more folders at warp speed. From what I could tell, they were mostly photos: mangled bodies, charred cars, dismembered limbs. Just as my mind processed what it was seeing, he was on to the next, muttering to himself until he closed out of his own file and moved on. The next one, thankfully, looked like bank documents and scanned sheets of a hand-written finance ledger.

"What is all of this?" I asked amidst the quiet, Russian snarling right next to me.

"You've heard of KGB?"

"Yeah. Who hasn't?"

Sasha tipped his chin toward the screen. "These are KGB and FSB files. SVR too. They have information on everyone in the Bratva, the vory."

"That's like the mob, right?"

He nodded. "This information is very dangerous. Men kill for this sort of thing. To keep it *and* to get it. If it goes into the wrong hands, everyone on here is a target."

I leaned across him and yanked the jump drive out of the USB port. "Then we need to get rid of it."

"No!" He was on his feet in a flash. His hand closed around mine, trapping the jump drive in my palm. "We need to find out who this belongs to."

"And what? Give it back?"

"*Put* it back, yes. Before they know we have it."

"No! *You're* on this file."

He checked his watch, apparently ignoring me. "We have time to go back to the bank. Let's go."

I shrugged his hand off my shoulder. "I'm not putting this back until we know who has all this dirt on you."

"How do you propose finding out?"

"Joyce." I snapped and pointed at him, grabbing the phone and dialing the main branch. It rang three times before Cindy answered.

"Hey, Cindy, it's Roan. Is Joyce around?"

"Roanie Bologne!" Cindy cried. I cringed, immediately glad I hadn't put her on speaker phone. "Umm, yeah. You just caught her. Hold on, sweetie."

"Thanks."

The phone rang again and Joyce picked up. "Hi honey, what's wrong?"

"Nothing." I smiled brightly to help sell the lie. "Hey, um, I found this key in the parking lot by the coffee shop and I think it's for one of our safety deposit boxes. Can you look up the number and see who it belongs to so I can give it back?"

"Oh, honey. You don't have to do that. Just drop it off here and we'll contact them."

"No, it's ok. I don't mind."

"Roan..." I knew that tone. She was getting ready to tell me "No."

I cleared my throat and forced another smile to my face. "Yes?"

"Is this about a boy?"

Closing my eyes, I exhaled silently. "You got me."

"Is it that boy at the coffee shop with the black eyeliner? You know I think he works at the flower shop down the street."

I only vaguely recalled who she was talking about, but I

went with it. "Yeah. I think I saw him drop it while he was leaving the other day."

Sasha's eyes narrowed the more I spoke, his head tilting to the side slowly. I was pretty sure he could hear the other half of the conversation based on the look on his face and the fact his jaw was practically welded shut.

I reached out and ran my fingers along the tiger tattoo on the side of his neck, shaking my head at his completely unfounded jealousy. It didn't work, since he kept glaring.

Joyce chuckled and I could hear typing. "There are easier ways to find out his name, you know."

"I know," I sighed theatrically. Frankie would be so proud. "But he still needs his key back."

"What's the number?"

"346."

"And his name is... oh. Well, that can't be right."

"What? What is it?" I swallowed the lump in my throat.

She huffed. "Well, it says box 346 belongs to an Alina Sidorova. That's not a boy name these days, is it? I can't keep up."

"Alina Sidorova?" I looked at Sasha for the answer.

He, on the other hand, blanched visibly and looked like he was a second away from throwing up.

"That's what it says here," Joyce said. "It's been the same renter since 1998."

"Ok. Well, thanks for checking. I'll drop the key off tomorrow."

"Ok, honey. Hey, go buy some flowers and while you're there, just ask his name."

I hung up with an awkward laugh, my attention solely focused on the sickly-looking Sasha. It was better when he was acting jealous. Jealous made sense. I could handle jealous. What I couldn't handle was Sasha, a force of nature, looking nervous. "Who is Alina Sidorova?"

"The daughter of the most powerful boss in Chicago." He swallowed thickly and nudged me toward the door. "We need to go. Now."

## 38

## SASHA

My mind churned through a dozen scenarios as I sped down the roadway. Roan was seated beside me, abnormally quiet for a change. Whilst I appreciated the silence, it was also unnerving. I wanted the distraction. I wanted him to brighten the mood in that effortless way of his. But I knew I needed to think, and fast.

What the fuck was Viktor playing at? He told me the box had fucking emeralds in it. I got a whole story about missing Imperial emeralds and the millions they'd bring. What a load of bullshit!

There were only two possible explanations.

One, Viktor had gotten bad intel. Highly probable since Igor had bad intel.

Or two, Viktor lied to me.

"Eduard," I snapped into the phone the second he picked up. "*Meet me at the fountain as soon as you can.*"

"*What's wrong?*"

"*Not on the phone. Just be there.*" I hung up and threw the phone on the dash.

"Who was that?" Roan asked. He didn't sound mad,

like I'd been when I heard the old woman discussing some boy with eyeliner. Eyeliner? What kind of a man wore eyeliner?

"A friend," I replied, tamping down the desire to drive to the flower shop and see this boy with eyeliner for myself. It would have to wait — at least until I got my current issue squared away.

"You're really freaked, huh?"

"You have no idea who Sergei Sidorov is, what he can do. You think I'm not a good person?" I scoffed, shaking my head. "With one phone call, he can have your entire family eliminated. Just like that." I snapped my fingers right under his nose.

"So why would your boss want to mess with this guy?"

"That is what I am going to find out."

We drove the rest of the way in silence. As soon as I put the car in park, Roan undid his seat belt.

"No," I said, grabbing the belt and shoving the clip back in. "You stay here."

"No, I don't think so."

Ignoring him, I leaned across his lap and opened the glove box. I snagged the pistol inside and pulled the slide back a bit, making sure there was a bullet in the chamber.

"What are you doing?" Roan asked, pushing back into his seat, eyes wide.

Holding the gun by the barrel, I held it out to him so he could take the grip. "Take this."

"What? No."

I grabbed his hand and slapped it against the grip, forcibly curling his fingers around it. "If anyone but me comes to the car, shoot them."

"Sasha!"

"You have fifteen rounds. There's no safety. Just pull

the trigger." I squeezed his hand briefly and got out of the car.

Throwing a glance over my shoulder every so often, I cut through Grant Park, headed toward Buckingham Fountain. Lighting a cigarette along the way, I tried to look unhurried, like I hadn't just stumbled across a little electronic death sentence.

I spied Eduard in the distance, smoking his own cigarette. His hand was shoved in his coat pocket, despite the warm evening temperature. Tugging up the back of my t-shirt nonchalantly, I tucked the fabric behind my pistol, giving me easier access to the grip.

"Sasha," Eduard said, exhaling a stream of smoke as I approached. "What the fuck is going on?"

"When's the last time you talked to Viktor?" I asked as I stepped in closer, keeping my gaze moving between his face, his hands, and the people walking near us.

He shrugged, taking another puff. "Whenever I got off the phone with you? So, what? Couple hours ago?"

"What, exactly, do you know about the box?"

He made a face and shrugged again. "Nothing. You think Viktor would tell *me* anything? All I know, I got from Igor, same as you."

"Does Yuri know?"

"How the fuck should I know?"

"Get him on the phone."

Eduard muttered under his breath. When he pulled his hand out of his pocket, it was with a phone, not a weapon. Relaxing a bit, I tugged my shirt back down over the gun. We smoked in silence while the phone rang through the speaker.

"What the fuck do you want?" Yuri snapped.

Eduard looked at me and gestured with the phone, waiting for me to speak.

I pushed it back at him and shook my head, purposely inhaling as much smoke as I could so I didn't have to talk.

"Well..." Eduard cleared his throat. "I was wondering what you knew about the bank box. I want all the facts before we hit it."

"Why the fuck would I tell you anything?"

"Because if you don't, your uncle won't get the shit inside."

"Why? Did that dog fuck up again?" Yuri laughed. "I heard about what happened, that little bitch getting away from him. Pathetic!"

My jaw clenched tighter with each word. I spiked the cigarette on the cement and ground it to dust beneath my heel, wishing it was Yuri's fucking face.

"You don't know what you're fucking talking about," Eduard snapped.

"Don't I?" I could practically see Yuri's sneering face.

"No, you don't." Eduard shot me a warning look. I clamped my mouth shut before I blew the whole reason for calling.

"So Sasha really tracked him down after he escaped? How *did* he escape anyway?"

"What's it matter to you?"

Yuri laughed. "It doesn't. It's just too bad we didn't get to have fun with the little bitch first. Hell, who knows. Maybe Sasha did it anyway. Sick fuck couldn't stay away from that pretty face. Do you think he shot him before, or after? During?"

Rage exploded inside me. I lunged at Eduard and his damn phone. "You goddamn lying motherfucker! The next time I see you, I'm going to rip your fucking face off!"

Eduard took a couple steps back, holding his hand up to try and ward me off.

Yuri's twisted laugh echoed through the phone. "Oh,

Sasha. I knew you were there! So predictable! And *so* sensitive!"

"Name a time and place and I'll show you how fucking sensitive I am, you piece of shit! You can't hide behind your uncle forever. Even he'll admit you crossed the goddamn line."

"We'll see about that." Yuri hung up.

"I'm going to fucking kill him!" I shouted at the phone, ignoring the pair of gasping women as they bicycled past us. Unless they spoke Russian, I wasn't the least bit concerned about what they heard.

"You can't!" Eduard smacked my shoulder. "He's protected."

"I don't care!"

"Just take a — fuck!" Eduard shoved me to the side, yanking his gun out from behind his back and taking aim at something behind me.

It was Roan, standing on the other side of the fountain, his eyes wide and his chest heaving, like he'd sprinted from the car.

"No!" I threw my arm out, knocking Eduard's gun arm down. "Don't!"

"It's the fucking kid!" Eduard yelled back at me, his eyes as wide as Roan's.

"I know."

Eduard searched the surrounding area frantically. "What if there are cops?"

"There aren't." I ducked my head, ignoring his bewildered expression, and angled myself toward Roan, waving him over. Now the cat was out of the bag, it would be better to have an ally. Hopefully.

"I thought you killed him?" Eduard stared at me like I had two heads. I still couldn't bring myself to look at him directly, to answer the dozens of questions he undoubtedly had.

Roan jogged the rest of the way, slowing down and eyeing Eduard warily the closer he got. "Adidas," he said with a curt nod.

Eduard made a face before turning his attention to me, still speaking in Russian. "*If he's still alive, then who the fuck did we get rid of last week?*"

I ignored Eduard's questions and stepped closer to Roan, lowering my voice. "What are you doing? I told you to stay in the car."

Worry marred every part of Roan's face, from his eyes to the downward curve of his mouth. His hand lifted, like he was going to touch me, but he clenched it into a fist and dropped it again, flicking a cautious glance at Eduard. "It looked like something was wrong."

Sighing, I leaned forward, resting my forehead against his. So brave and so fucking stupid. He didn't even bring the gun with him. I didn't know what his brilliant plan had been, but I appreciated the gesture all the same.

Roan gripped my bicep gently, exhaling his own steadying breath.

"*What the fuck are you doing?*" Eduard asked, his arms spread wide, his gun still in his hand. "*Why the fuck is he here and what the… fucking fuck, Sasha?!*"

I pulled away from Roan and faced Eduard, squaring my shoulders. I had *a lot* of explaining to do, I knew that. My only hope was that he listened to it all before making up his mind. "Roan got into the box today. It wasn't emeralds," I replied in English, for Roan's benefit.

"Then what was it?" Eduard took the cue and switched to English as well, tossing a suspicious glare at Roan every now and again.

Roan fished the flash drive out of his pocket and held it up.

"What the fuck is that?" Eduard asked, stepping forward and squinting at it.

"Sergei Sidorov's files," I replied.

Eduard's dark gaze snapped up to mine, widening again. "The fuck you just say?"

I nodded, imploring him to believe me, if not by my words, than by my grim expression.

"Get rid of it!" Eduard lunged for the flash drive. Roan made no move to stop him.

"No!" I snatched it from Roan's palm a second before Eduard. "It's leverage."

"It's a death sentence! Besides whatever the hell this is," Eduard said, gesturing between Roan and I with his gun. "If Sergei finds out you have that, he'll kill *all* of us."

Roan flinched. I slid in front of him, grabbing the barrel of Eduard's gun and shoving it down before he shot someone. Namely, me. "You don't think I know that?"

"*Then what the fuck are we still doing here? Kill the kid, burn the drive, and lay low for a while.*"

"*I can't.*" Saying those two words out loud to someone like Eduard, someone from my world, was excruciating. Failure, weakness — it wasn't tolerated. Even if I said it in Russian, so Roan couldn't hear hear how pathetic I was, my stomach still seized.

"*Why not?*"

"*I just... can't.*" Admitting I couldn't stay away from him almost gutted me, but *actually* staying away would have been a far worse pain. There were no words to explain it, it was just a feeling I had, the need to be near him. The only thing I could liken it to was the feeling you got in the dead of winter, when sunlight washed over you and held the cold at bay. I didn't want to go back to the cold now that I knew I could feel something else, something better.

Roan's fingers grazed the small of my back. I couldn't tell if it was silent questioning or an attempt at reassurance, but I shifted my weight to my back foot so his hand laid flat against me.

"Fuck, Sasha!" Eduard spun away, swearing even more in Russian. He whipped back around and stormed up to me, shoving his finger in my face instead of the gun. "*How could you do this? You're so goddamn stupid! You know what happened to Pavel!*"

"*Of course I know,*" I hissed back at him.

"*Then why?*"

"*Don't you think I tried? I tried to stop, to stay away.*" I brandished my left forearm, riddled with the cigarette burns, marks of my shame. "*I tried, Eduard!*"

"*Not hard enough!*"

I took a step forward and snatched his gun hand, forcing the barrel to my forehead. "*Then do what you know is right. Put me out of my misery.*"

"Sasha!" Roan moved toward me, but I pushed him back.

"Go, Roan. Now." I pointed at the car, keeping my gaze fixed on Eduard. "Do not look back."

Defiant as always, Roan stayed exactly where he was.

Eduard exhaled a shaky breath, gritting his teeth. He glanced at Roan, but I smacked his cheek so he'd look at me. When his gaze snapped back to mine, he pushed harder with the gun, his lip curling.

"*Come on, Eduard. Do it. I understand. Kill the disease before it spreads. It's not murder, it's mercy. You know that. End my suffering.*" I tried to keep my breathing even, but my heart was racing so fast I thought it might explode. I wasn't afraid for myself

— I was afraid for Roan. If Eduard shot me, there was nothing stopping him from killing Roan in the next breath.

Eduard swore again, shaking his head and tightening his grip on the gun. "*You're fucking crazy!*"

"*Probably. Now either pull the trigger or put your fucking gun away.*"

Time stopped.

I kept my gaze locked on Eduard's, refusing to blink, refusing to breathe.

At last, he lowered the gun, releasing another ragged breath. "*You better hope Viktor doesn't find out.*"

"*I know...*"

Roan crashed into me from the side, his arms around my neck. "What the fuck were you thinking?!" I barely had a chance to hug him in return before he whirled on Eduard, stepping nose-to-nose with him. "And you? You're supposed to be his friend and you *actually* thought about shooting him? What the fuck is wrong with you?!" Eduard opened his mouth to speak, but Roan kept going. "While we're on the topic of what a fucking asshole you are — where is Katya? What did you do with her?"

"*Who the fuck is Katya?*" Eduard asked, glancing at me for clarification.

I gripped the back of Roan's neck and pulled him away before Eduard reconsidered his decision not to shoot me. "She's dead. And no, he didn't do it."

"What happened?" Roan asked, whirling on me.

"I shot her."

His jaw dropped, eyes widening like I sucker punched him. "You what?! Why? Why would you do that?"

"Because I wish someone would have shot me." My spine straightened, reaffirming my belief in my own decision, despite his horror. "She's better off."

Mouth agape and brows furrowed, Roan continued to

stare at me, like he couldn't comprehend anything I said. In truth, he probably couldn't. He didn't know the kind of life I had, the life Katya *would have* had. He'd merely glimpsed our world and was revolted by it. I didn't want to imagine what would happen if he was immersed in the nightmare for the rest of his life.

"What's the plan now?" Eduard asked in the wake of Roan's shocked silence.

I smiled bitterly. "I'm going to arrange a meeting with Viktor and see what he has to say for himself."

## 39

# ROAN

THE RIDE BACK TO MY HOUSE WAS COMPLETELY SILENT. Sasha was never in the mood to talk but, for once, I wasn't either.

I might have only known Katya for a day or so, but trapped in that fucking dog kennel, it felt like a lifetime. We bonded in our fear, both held captive by people we didn't know, for reasons we didn't understand. I made it out of my ordeal alive. She didn't.

Anger and sadness battled inside of me. Her death was senseless. No, her *murder* was senseless. By none other than the asshole sitting next to me, his chin propped on his fist, driving casually with one hand as if it were another ordinary day. Well, to him it probably was.

How could he be so calm? So fucking blasé about the whole thing? He shot a girl! Not some rival gang member or dickhead who got off on beating people, or even cops trying to arrest him — a scared, helpless *girl*. He *murdered* her and for what? What did that prove? What did that fucking accomplish?

*She's better off.*

Who the fuck was he to make that call? No, I wasn't naive enough to think she'd grow up to be an au pair and go to college and live the American dream. But she *could* have. She could have escaped the hell these sick pricks had in store for her and maybe, just *maybe*, carved out a decent life for herself.

But Sasha took that all away. With zero remorse, apparently.

*Because I wish someone would have shot me.*

Sasha exhaled softly and leaned back in his seat, switching which hand he had on the wheel.

I slid a glance at him out of the corner of my eye. His face, as usual, gave no indication as to what he was thinking. My gaze dropped to his arm, the one he'd shown Eduard — at least, I think that was Adidas' real name — right before he made his so-called friend put a goddamn gun to his forehead.

There were several blistered circles on the inside of his forearm, scattered amongst the various tattoos. They looked like they were healing, but there were plenty of pink, circular scars to indicate he'd been at it a while.

"What are those?" The question came out bluntly, but I really didn't give a shit about being tactful at the moment. I wanted answers.

Sasha's brows lifted when he glanced at me. "What is what?"

"Those blisters on your arm."

"None of your business." He dropped the arm in question into his lap, taking the wheel again with his right.

"So Eduard gets to know, but not me. Got it. Maybe you should fuck him from now on." I shook my head and turned my glare out the passenger window, not caring that I sounded petulant. Given what I just learned, he was lucky I was talking to him at all. I should have told him to get bent and found my own way home. I should have stayed away in the first place, instead of drifting back to him time and again. I should have done a lot of things differently. Hindsight was a bitch.

The leather steering wheel creaked a second before it jerked to the right. The Mercedes screeched to a halt on the side of the road.

"You want to know?" Sasha snapped, throwing the car into park. "I have them because I couldn't stop thinking about *you*. From the moment I saw you. Every impure thought I had, I tried to burn out. At first I told myself it was part of the research, all the thoughts. But then I had you and I *still* couldn't stop."

Well, now *I* felt like the asshole.

"I'm sorry," I said quietly. "I didn't mean—"

"Save your pity. You wanted the truth — now you have it." With that, he shifted the car into gear and pulled out onto the road again. So much for a heart-to-heart.

"You know, it's ok to have an actual conversation sometimes. I won't think less of you if you express an emotion other than anger every once in a while."

"If there's another emotion to express, I'll be sure to let you know," he shot back, adding an icy glare to his barbed words.

"Ooo, sarcasm. That's a new one for you. Already making progress I see." I rolled my eyes and looked out the window again.

"You're a pain in my ass," he muttered, turning onto my street.

"We all have our talents. Mine is annoying you." He snorted, prompting me to turn and look at him. "What?"

"It's true, but it's not your only talent."

"If you're about to make a dick joke, I'm not in the mood."

It was his turn to roll his eyes. "Your music, idiot."

"What do *you* know about my music?"

He shrugged one shoulder, keeping his eyes on the road. "I heard you."

"When? Where?"

"Everywhere." He threw a glance my way before pulling into the driveway. "Your house, mostly, but that big performance before graduation. The coffee shop. Ugh, and with those children."

"You were at the showcase?" I mean, I knew they had footage from that night, but I still couldn't believe Sasha was there. That seemed like the sort of thing he'd pawn off on some other poor bastard.

He nodded, shifting the car into park. "You're very good. You will go places."

Scoffing, I looked away. "Yeah. We'll see." Straight to Georgetown, more likely.

"I know—" He cut himself off and in the next instant he was unholstering the gun from the small of his back. "Stay here. I *mean* it this time."

"What's wrong?" I tried to see what he was seeing, but the house looked fine. There weren't any flashing "Danger ahead" signs as far as I could tell.

"Your house keeper leaves at five, every day, without fail."

"It's only five thirty."

"So why is her car still here?"

I glanced over my right shoulder. Sure enough Patricia's Toyota was parked on the far side of the drive, as usual. "Maybe she stayed late for some reason."

Sasha didn't hear me because he was out of the car and moving toward the house at a surprisingly casual pace, the gun hanging at his side.

Climbing out of the car, I chased after him. "You need

the alarm code," I hissed as soon as he gave me a furious look.

He snarled something in Russian and we both stopped short, looking at the front door. It was closed, but the jamb was busted and there was a black boot print next to the handle.

"We can get in through the garage," I said.

He nodded and set off in that direction.

I punched in the code on the door and followed him when he ducked inside. My car was the only one in the garage, which meant Patricia should have been the only one in the house.

I had visions of the poor woman tied up in the broom closet with one of her cleaning rags in her mouth. Or maybe she heard the front door and went and hid somewhere.

"Watch the blood," Sasha whispered as soon as we turned the corner for the kitchen. He stepped over a giant red puddle and carried on.

It streaked and smeared along the tile, a trail of bloody handprints clinging to doorways and swiping the wall.

There was a loud crash on the second floor that made both of us jump. Sasha started for the stairs, but I kept going down the hallway toward Dad's office. Other than the electronics, he had at least one safe in there. If someone was going to burgle anything, it would be the master bedroom for the jewelry and the office for the safe. And besides, that's where the trail of blood led.

As soon as I saw a wrinkled hand laying on the floor near the doorway, I ran the rest of the way. It was Patricia without a doubt. I reached for her and pulled back with a gasp. It was the *only* part of Patricia. Where the fuck was the rest of her body?

A heavy fist connected with the side of my face out of nowhere.

I stumbled away from the blow before a second one made contact.

A guy rushed out of Dad's office and slammed me into the wall, squeezing all the air out of my lungs and rattling my brain. I had just enough sense left to shove him out at arm's length before he could hit me again. Grabbing the back of his neck, I yanked his head down while driving my knee upward into bone. When he bounced back up, holding his bleeding nose, I returned the favor and threw a punch into his face as hard as I could.

He spun away, staggering, and collapsed against the wall.

That was my cue to fucking run.

I sprinted up the stairs, listening for anything that would point me to where Sasha was. It wasn't all that hard — I just followed the sound of Russians swearing and shit breaking.

Turning the corner into *my* room, of all places, I watched from the doorway as Sasha and another guy traded vicious blows. Not surprisingly, Sasha's size worked to his advantage, but the other guy wasn't tiny by any means. When he landed a kick in the center of Sasha's abdomen, it sent Sasha flying backward against my dresser.

He hit hard, grimacing and holding his stomach. Dodging another attempted kick, Sasha flung himself to the side and swatted shit out of his way as he groped the floor. He finally found what he was looking for, a gun laying in the corner of the room beneath the shattered remnants of my desk chair. The guy lunged for the gun at the same time. Sasha rolled onto his back and fired. Two rounds went straight into the other guy's chest. He fell limp, bleeding all over the area rug.

I jumped, the concussion ringing in my ears. My whole body froze, watching Sasha rise to his feet and walk forward, planting a third one in the back of his opponent's head.

Now that he'd stopped moving around so much, I tried to take stock of Sasha's condition. Blotches of blood and sweat stained his dark blue t-shirt, but I couldn't tell if it was all his, or the other guy's. Probably both. There was a bright red mark on his jaw, along with a streak of blood near his mouth. More blood dripped down his left forearm.

Unable to move, I at least forced my vocal cords to work. "Sasha, are—"

Sasha jerked the gun up again, level with my face.

At almost the same time, cold metal pressed into my temple and a hand clamped on the back of my neck.

Sasha snarled something in Russian and took a step forward.

The guy behind me snapped back, digging the gun into my head.

I squeezed my eyes shut, trying to think of some way out of this. Other than Sasha, there weren't any options available. The second I moved, the guy behind me would blast a hole through my brain.

Then, I heard something I never expected in a situation like this — Sasha laughed.

My eyes flew open, narrowing on him in disbelief.

Still laughing, Sasha kept talking in Russian, relaxing his stance and gesturing to me every once in a while, his gun still in hand. The look on his face was a mix of amusement and disgust. Somehow I felt like I should be offended by whatever he was saying.

The guy behind me shifted, the pressure on my temple lifting slightly while he replied.

"Da." Sasha smiled brightly. It was a beautiful sight to behold — and terrifying. Like his laugh, his smile was so uncharacteristic and so out of place in the middle of a fucking *standoff*, I didn't know how to feel about it.

Without warning, Sasha's gun snapped up, firing a round at me.

The guy behind me yelled and shoved away from me, saving himself.

The next round from Sasha's gun went into the middle of the guy's torso. Just like his partner, Sasha shot him twice and strolled over, depositing a third bullet right between the eyes.

Completely immobilized by shock, I stood there and shook, trying to calculate the minuscule distance between my shoulder and the wall where the bullet lodged. Had he missed, or was that on purpose? Even if it was on purpose, who's to say he couldn't have fucking missed?!

"Are you ok?" Sasha appeared in my field of vision, cupping my cheek gently. "Solnyshko?"

"What in the actual fuck?!" I gaped at him, still trying to process what just happened.

"Are you hurt?"

"You shot at me!"

"We have to go." Grabbing my wrist, he dragged me down the stairs and right out the front door.

"No, *you* need to go." I screeched to a halt like a stubborn mule, wrenching myself out of his vice grip. "*I* need to call the police!"

"Never call the police. You have a problem? I'll take care of it."

"You can't 'take care of it,'" I snapped, mimicking his accent and adding dickish air quotes for good measure. He glared at me and reclaimed my wrist, dragging me the rest of the way to the car. "You just left two dead bodies in the house! The police will definitely be looking for me this time around and they're going to have a lot of fucking questions!"

Sasha opened the passenger door of his SUV and shoved me in with a growl before hurrying around to the driver's side. He floored it away from the house without ever addressing the fact he fucking shot at me or killed two other people without even blinking. Again! Couldn't he go a week without murdering someone?

"Where are you taking me now?" I demanded.

"Back to my place."

"Oh, fuck no. Let me out."

"What's wrong?"

"What's wrong? Are you serious right now?!" I stared at him. "You fucking shot at me! Not to mention the fact whoever those people were trashed my house, tried to kill *both* of us, and cut Patricia's fucking hand off! Who does that?!"

"They needed her fingerprints for something," he replied with a shrug.

"No! You don't get to downplay this!"

"You want the truth, yes? All the time, demanding the truth. Here it is. Those were Sergei Sidorov's men. They were looking for the flash drive. They were looking for *you*. I knew what I was doing when I shot at you. Now, until I can figure out how to fix this problem, I'm not letting you out of my sight."

"So you're kidnapping me again?"

He shot me a look out of the corner of his eye, smirking. "Think of it as… sleepover."

"You're not funny," I huffed, slinking down in my seat and crossing my arms.

# 40

# SASHA

As soon as we were safely in my apartment, I allowed myself a moment to pause and breathe. Standing in front of the fridge, I leaned into the open freezer and closed my eyes, letting the cold air rush over me. It chilled the sweat on my skin, but provided little clarity to my current predicament.

Grabbing two ice packs, I swatted the freezer door shut and made my way into the living room. Roan was sitting on the couch, arms still crossed, staring at the carpet with a scowl.

Tossing an ice pack in his lap, I kept moving, easing myself onto the other end of the couch. I definitely pulled something in the fight. My back was screaming, not to mention the fact I couldn't even close my right hand into a fist. It better not be broken again.

"Thank you," Roan muttered, pressing the ice pack to his jaw.

"You're welcome." Laying my own ice pack on my swollen knuckles, I tipped my head back and closed my eyes.

What a fucking mess. I had *no* idea where to even start to fix this.

"How did they know you were at the bank?" I wondered out loud, trying to work it all out in my head. It had only been a few hours since Roan cleared out the bank box. Unless they had an employee on the inside, there's no way Sidorov could have known the flash drive was missing.

"I bet it was the jump drive." When I shot him a look, Roan kept going. "Why do you think I opened it on my dad's computer? If someone went through all the trouble to get a safety deposit box for *one* jump drive and nothing else, then you know it's important. They probably encoded it with tracking software, so whenever it gets plugged in, it activates a signal."

"You knew that and you opened it at home? Are you crazy or just have a death wish?"

He shrugged. "Someone has to teach my dad a lesson. Might as well be the client he values more than his son."

"You don't mean that."

His jaw shifted and he looked away, throwing the ice pack onto the coffee table. "What was it you said? 'You don't know shit about me'? Right back at you. You don't know the first thing about me or what I want."

"I've watched a lot of people over the years when they think no one is looking. You learn people that way. I learned *you* that way," I said quietly. His head swiveled toward me, suspicion tightening the corners of his eyes. "You don't want revenge. You want understanding."

"I thought you don't 'do' emotions?" He rolled his eyes. "When did you become a shrink?"

"About two minutes ago." I cracked my neck on each side and stood, refusing to get sucked into a touchy-feely conversation. "I'm taking a shower."

"Don't worry, I'm not going anywhere," he said glumly, returning his scowl to the floor.

"No, you're not." I wrapped the fingers of my left hand in his t-shirt and hauled him to his feet. "Get your ass in the shower. Now."

He didn't budge, fixing me with a defiant glare. "What happened to Rule #2?"

"The same thing as Rule #1." I slapped my hand against his cheek and gripped his face, none too gently. When he didn't move on his own, I shoved him by the hold I had, walking him backward toward the bathroom.

He shook his head, his blue eyes darkening. Nevertheless, he kept moving. "No, *this* isn't happening again."

"No?" I arched an eyebrow at him, sliding my fingers down to grasp his throat.

"No." He may have *looked* defiant. He may have *sounded* defiant. But there was no disguising the fact his breathing was shallow and his jeans did jack shit to hide his growing hard-on.

"Too bad." I shoved him into the bathroom and let go, peeling my shirt off. He gasped as I dropped it on the floor.

"Shit!" Roan rushed forward, pressing his hands against my abs. The beginning of a wicked bruise spread across my skin, dark and hot to the touch. "And your arm." He turned my left arm over, inspecting the long gash on the backside of my forearm.

I glanced down and shrugged. "It's nothing."

"It's not nothing." Shaking his head, he grabbed the hand towel and wet it in the sink before wiping my arm.

While he was still investigating, I threaded my fingers through his hair and held the back of his head. Before I knew it, I tilted his face up and pressed my lips to his. For all his earlier bitching, he didn't hesitate to open his mouth, swirling his tongue with mine. One hand gripped the back of my neck while the other slid around my waist to the small of my back. As soon as his hand latched onto my pistol, I pulled back.

Withdrawing it from the holster, he held it up with an exasperated sigh and set it on the bathroom counter. "Rule #3. No weapons in the bedroom."

"This isn't the bedroom," I countered.

"Wherever you're getting your dick sucked is the bedroom from now on." He grabbed my hips with both hands and shoved me against the counter before tearing open the front of my jeans.

"You don't seem to realize how many guns I actually have." I slumped against the counter as he dropped to his knees and my head hit the mirror when he sucked my cock into his mouth. "Fuck, Roan."

Working my jeans down, he tugged a pant leg off one at a time, giving himself more room to maneuver.

Seeing him on his knees in front of me again, his perfect mouth sliding up and down my length, his tongue massaging me, was still like something out of a dream. At times I couldn't believe it was real, but then he'd squeeze my balls or graze his teeth along my dick and I was reminded it was, indeed, reality.

He kept his eyes upward, watching me intently. That look, the lust in his eyes, was somehow better than the things he was actually doing, because it was for *me* — *I* was the reason for that desire.

Slipping both hands on either side of his throat, I pulled him up by his jaw and kissed him hard before forcing myself to tear away. "I need you. Now."

"So what are you waiting for?" He smirked, kissing me again and nipping my bottom lip.

Before I could punish him for that smart ass remark, someone pounded on the front door.

We both turned, eyes wide, toward the sound.

"Are you expecting someone?" he asked, his voice barely above a whisper.

"Stay here," I said, grabbing my jeans and yanking them on quickly. Shoving the gun back into place, I closed the bathroom door and cleared my throat, heading toward the pounding.

"*Who is it?*" I asked in Russian.

"Misha Chernyshevsky."

Fuck.

Steeling myself for the worst-case scenario, I opened the door and gestured for him to come in. "*What can I do for you?*"

"*I'm here for business,*" he replied, shaking my hand once he was inside. "*There's been some trouble lately and I'm following up with all of our contacts.*" Smoothing down the front of his blue suit, he wandered further into the apartment, looking over every inch with a curious expression.

"*What kind of trouble?*" Shit.shit.shit.

He spun on his heel and turned toward me, his sky-blue eyes narrowing on my abdomen. "*Is everything alright?*"

"Mhmm." I should have put my shirt back on. Damn it. In my defense, I wasn't expecting it to be Misha, or anyone else whose questions I was compelled to answer.

"*What happened here?*" He took a step closer, his splayed fingers hovering over the fresh bruise, like he was measuring the size. About a twelve US, if I had to guess. When his eyes flicked up again, I held his curious gaze for a minute before answering.

"*Street fight.*"

"*Did you win?*" He dropped his gaze and picked up my right hand, studying my swollen knuckles.

"*I always win.*" I yanked my hand out of his and folded my arms over my chest. "*Why are you here, exactly?*"

"*Someone killed two of our associates today. I wanted to make sure you were alright. And to see if you have heard anything?*"

I shook my head. "*As you can see, I'm fine.*"

"*I do see. I also see a pretty nasty cut. Was it a knife?*" Misha's gaze swept over me again, his finger skimming along the length of my left forearm.

"*Glass,*" I answered flatly. There was no point in lying about that. A man with Misha's experience would be able to tell the difference between a clean cut and the jagged mess on my arm.

His eyes narrowed briefly, but then he blinked and smiled, clasping his hands behind his back. "*Did you know your boss called my boss today?*"

"*How would I know that?*" I cocked my head.

He shrugged. "*He heard you and Sergei had a meeting… Have you talked to Viktor lately?*"

"*I've been busy.*" The fact Viktor heard I had a one-on-one with Sergei wasn't good, but I had bigger issues to worry about than his precious ego. The meeting sure as shit wasn't *my* idea; I'd been ambushed by Sergei as much as I'd been ambushed by Roan. Besides, when the boss asks for a sit down, you don't say "No." I still had no idea why Sergei wanted to see me that day, seeing as we didn't talk about anything important, so Viktor could fuck right off if he thought I was anything but loyal.

"*With the street fight?*"

"*Among other things.*"

"*Aren't you curious?*"

"*About?*"

"*Who was killed.*" Shit… Before I could come up with a reasonable reply, Misha took a step closer. "*Some friendly advice?*" He gave me a chilling smile, his voice lowering. "*Be careful, Sasha. I'm a wolf too and I smell betrayal in the air.*"

"*Man is wolf to man,*" I quoted with a tight smile.

"*Indeed.*" He shook my hand politely and stepped past me. "*Enjoy your evening.*"

As soon as Misha was gone, I darted across to the bathroom and stepped inside. I pressed a finger to Roan's lips before he could speak and turned on the faucet.

"We have to be careful," I whispered.

"What did Misha want?" Roan asked, matching my volume.

"I'm not exactly sure. I need to find Viktor and get to the bottom of this." I took a step toward the door, but Roan snagged my belt loops and tugged me back.

"Tomorrow?" he asked, both brows lifting.

I considered him for a moment before nodding. "Tomorrow."

A soft smile spread across his face. He peeled his shirt off and turned on the shower, biting his lower lip. "Now, about that shower..."

# 41

# ROAN

Somehow we made it through a shower without tearing each other to pieces. I got the blood scrubbed off of Sasha, but that was as much nursing as he'd allow on his arm. It seemed to be the only open wound, aside from the cut inside his mouth. I only knew about that one because he kissed me much more gently than before.

Or it could have been his concern that Misha may have planted a bug. Given what was on that jump drive, it was an entirely justifiable fear. So, either water was constantly running or he had music playing, anything to distort the sound of people listening — or at least that's what he said.

Needless to say I was a bit surprised when he led me into the bedroom and started kissing me again. Unwrapping the towel from my waist, he tossed it to the side, but instead of pouncing, he stood there with his head cocked. His gaze moved over me at a languid pace, so intense I was sure he was actually touching me.

"What are you looking at?" I asked quietly, brows furrowed. It was the hotel room all over again, except he was the one who appeared mesmerized. Why, I had no idea. He was a work of art — I was a blank, boring canvas.

My question propelled him forward, his warm hands spreading up along both sides of my ribcage. "You." Pressing his lips to mine, he guided me backward until I hit the bed.

I scooted back to make room for him, slipping a hand beneath the pillow I was laying on to make sure I wasn't in danger of accidentally discharging anything. Although it wouldn't have been the worst way in the world to die, given what we were about to do.

Sasha's whole body covered mine as he left trails of kisses down my shoulder, across my chest, up my neck. His skin was practically scorching, rivaling the warmth that bloomed inside of me wherever he touched me.

It was surreal. No, it was *real*. Somehow, I was more connected to him in that moment than in any that preceded it. He was tender — an adjective I would have never thought possible the first time I saw him. Hell, I wouldn't have thought a lot of things were possible back then. It might have only been weeks, but I'd glimpsed so many sides of Sasha, it felt like we'd known each other longer.

He continued to surprise me — like when I got on my knees for him while he was putting on a condom. Shaking his head, he tipped his chin toward the pillow. "Lay down."

Doing as I was told, I resumed my position and watched him crawl on top of me again, nudging my thighs open wider with his.

"I want to see you," he said, brushing a kiss to my lips before leaning back.

I swallowed, trying to remain stoic while he pressed his dick between my ass cheeks. The beginning was the worst.

It didn't help that he was long, and thick, and this was only my second time bottoming.

Relax, Roan… Just fucking relax…

Slowly, the head of his cock pushed inside, generating the burning sensation. It wasn't pain, per se, but it walked a very fine line. Inch by inch, he pressed deeper, one hand guiding himself in while the other rested on my abs, caressing my muscles as they flexed. Biting my lower lip, I reminded myself to breathe and focus on the hungry gleam in Sasha's eyes.

"My God," he breathed when he was fully seated inside of me. He gave me a minute to adjust before shifting his hips, rocking in and out slowly. "You feel incredible. So fucking incredible." He bent his upper body over mine and kissed me, as gently as he was thrusting.

He pulled back enough to look at me again, his eyes hooded. For some reason, I could tell he was holding back. I trailed my fingertips along his cheekbone and down his jaw, pushing my hips against him in encouragement.

Gritting his teeth, he stubbornly refused to let go.

"Stop fighting it," I whispered.

"Nyet." His face dipped down so he could bite my shoulder, relieving the sting by dragging his tongue across the mark. "I want this to last."

Capturing his face between my hands, I kissed him, gently at first. When he didn't up the ante, I parted his lips with my tongue and took what I wanted for a change. Groaning against me, he started to pull away, but I didn't let him. Making him look at me the same way he forced me look at him in that basement, I issued my command with a growl of my own. "And I want you to fuck me."

I thought he was going to combust right there. A Russian word slipped out, followed by my name. His mouth slanted over mine greedily, and all bets were off.

Without warning, he thrust into me so hard, sparks of electricity jolted through me.

"Oh, fuck, that's deep," I gasped. It was worth the discomfort — every time he plunged in, he hit that magical bundle of nerves, pushing me closer and closer to the edge.

Once he had permission, Sasha kissed me harder, fucked me harder, and made it that much harder to imagine *not* having him around. Sweat shone across his muscles, making his tattoos even more vibrant. I ran my hand up his bicep and over his shoulder, holding onto him.

"I'm so fucking close," I panted, squeezing my eyes shut.

"Fuck yes. Do it. I need to see you come."

The pressure inside of me grew with each thrust against my prostate, each stroke I gave my dick, Sasha's hands touching me everywhere. He kept whispering, begging me to finish. I chased the feeling, every muscle in my body tensing until I plummeted into rapture.

Sasha's mouth crashed against mine, muffling the sounds of his own release. After a few, slow thrusts, he eased out of me carefully and moved downward on the bed. Dragging his tongue over my abs, he cleaned up the evidence of my orgasm with a methodical precision.

"That's so fucking hot." I watched him with the utmost attention, running my fingers through his hair.

Swiping his index finger through the last drop, he shifted upward and held it out to me.

I leaned forward and sucked his finger into my mouth, tasting myself along with the saltiness from his skin. He pulled his finger free and replaced it with his tongue, kissing me hard and deep.

"You're mine, Solnyshko," Sasha said, tearing his mouth from mine and fixing me with one of his piercing looks, the kind that saw straight to my soul. "Yes?"

I blinked and nodded, despite the fact I was still trying to work out what, exactly, he was saying.

"From now on, you are *mine,*" he repeated in a growl. The words reverberated from his chest into mine, solidifying that they were real and not just my imagination. "No one else's. Do you understand?"

"I'm yours," I agreed in a stunned whisper.

He rewarded me with a dazzling smile, one so genuine it nearly stopped my heart. He cemented our agreement, or whatever it was, with another earth-shattering kiss.

I had no idea what it meant to "be" Sasha's, but the thought was thrilling, another display of his primal possessiveness. To be wanted with such intensity was intoxicating. Infuriating at times, but intoxicating nonetheless. It might have been crazy — no, it *was* crazy and probably unhealthy and toxic and all the things I shouldn't want… but I did. I wanted Sasha and even if he never admitted it, I knew he wanted me just as much.

---

THERE WERE WORSE WAYS TO HIDE FROM A PISSED OFF Russian mob boss than with another hot-as-fuck Russian acting as your personal bodyguard. Between the food, the language, and a card game called Durak, it was like a crash course in Russian 101.

The drawback? That same hot-as-fuck Russian who didn't let you get more than two feet out of his sight. Going into another room? Nope. He came with. Calling Frankie? Nope. He took away the cell phone. Forget even trying to go anywhere in the outside world. My suggestion to go pick up dinner? He laughed for a couple seconds before stopping abruptly and growling out a "Nyet" with a completely serious expression.

I didn't realize a mundane task, like taking out the trash, would actually lead to an argument. *I* thought I was being helpful — he, however, had a differing opinion on the matter.

"Where the fuck do you think you're going?" he snapped as soon as I opened the door, garbage bag in hand.

"Throwing this away."

"Give it to me."

"I can't even walk to the end of the hall?"

"Nyet."

"Stop being ridiculous." I rolled my eyes and walked out.

He swore in Russian and stomped after me. "Ridiculous? For wanting to keep you safe?"

"You mean keep me prisoner?" I tossed over my shoulder. "Unless these guys are hiding next to the recycling bin, I think I'm good."

"You don't know where they're hiding! That's the point! You didn't see *me* and I followed you for weeks."

"It's so creepy when you say that..."

"You should learn to be more observant!"

Mrs. Melnyk opened her door, scowling. As soon as she saw Sasha, she started muttering, probably in Ukrainian. It was hard to tell the difference between the two languages. Both speakers sounded like they were pissed off all the time but since they seemed to understand each other, I couldn't ever be sure what language it actually was.

Sasha pivoted sharply and strode toward her, towering over the old woman and barking back in what I could safely say was Russian.

Stuffing the garbage bag in the trash chute, I hurried back down the hall, not exactly sure who I was rescuing from whom. Mrs. Melnyk didn't seem the least bit fazed by Sasha's size or his temper.

"Mrs. Melnyk," I said with a smile, nudging Sasha out of the way. "Do you have anything you need carried to the garbage?"

"Such a nice boy." She smiled at me before sneering at Sasha. "Not like this filthy Moskal."

"You forget, I know where you sleep, you crazy old woman," Sasha snapped.

She shot back something in Ukrainian and held up her hands, like she was weighing grapefruits — or Sasha's balls.

Seeing Mrs. Melnyk's life flash before my eyes, I spit out a hasty goodbye and shoved Sasha back across the hall, while he continued to shout at her.

"Oh my God," I exclaimed, pushing him through the door to his apartment. "She's, like, ninety years old! Leave her alone."

"You don't know what she said."

"Sticks and stones, man."

"You're saying I should stone her to death or beat her with a stick?"

"What? No! That is *not* what I'm saying! Jesus! It's an expression." I raked a hand through my hair and walked a couple steps away before spinning around again. "Why does everything with you end in killing people? No, don't answer."

He grunted his annoyance and headed for the bedroom. A couple minutes later, he came out in tailored black suit that made me do a literal double take. Obviously, he looked good in his regular clothes, or none as the case may be, but I forgot how sexy he was all polished up.

"Are we going somewhere?" I asked, though it was

doubtful considering the fit he threw less than five minutes ago.

"*You're* not going anywhere," he muttered, walking over to a cabinet in the living room and rifling around in it.

"Fine. Where are *you* going?"

"To talk to Viktor."

"Are you going to tell him about the jump drive?"

Sasha didn't answer. He was more concerned with messing around with three handguns of varying sizes, checking their ammunition and strapping them to his body.

"If you have to take that many guns to a meeting with your boss, maybe you need a new boss," I remarked, leaning against the kitchen counter.

Tucking his ankle gun out of view, he straightened and met my gaze. Something akin to worry flickered across his face as he came closer. "On second thought, maybe you should come with me."

I couldn't help but grimace. "If he thinks I'm dead, it's probably not a good idea to roll up in the car with you. And I'm not hiding in the backseat. I already feel like your dirty little secret."

His mouth twisted into a frown, but he didn't say anything. It would have been the perfect time to tell me a lie and assure me I *wasn't* his dirty secret, that by claiming me as "his" I was more to him than a piece of ass. But, that would require *feelings*, which he refused to acknowledge as much as his sexuality, whatever the hell it was.

"I'll be fine." I clapped a hand on either side of his biceps and squeezed lightly, pepping myself up as much as him. "Go."

"Do *not* leave." My eyes had barely rolled when he grabbed my jaw and forced me to look at him again, his stare borderline hostile. "Do you understand?"

"Yes, I understand." God, I felt like I was fifteen, being grounded all over again for scratching my dad's stupid car.

He nodded and let go of my jaw to pull me in for a tight hug. Giving me a chaste kiss, he pushed away from me quickly and disappeared out the door.

Alone, I exhaled and looked around the empty apartment, trying to figure out what the hell I was supposed to do with myself now.

# 42

# SASHA

VIKTOR CHOSE A POPULAR TEA ROOM FOR OUR MEETING, which was just as well. I knew the place and I knew I had at least three different exit routes if I needed them.

As expected, most of the crew was there, grouped around different tables. Viktor sat alone, in the center, eating a pastry and sipping his tea like a fucking king. By the look of things, they'd chased out anyone not connected to the organization, save for the wait staff.

I was about to walk in when my cell phone rang.

It was Lada.

Frowning, I took a step back, out of view of the front window and answered.

"I have something," Lada said, almost breathless. The sound of her voice made the hair on the back of my neck stand up.

"What is it?"

"Is it safe to talk?"

I took another step away from the door, turning my back on it in case someone came out. "Spit it out, woman!"

"Yuri." I could hear the tremble in her voice, even through the phone. "He's planning something. Something big."

"How do you know?"

"He met up with Ivan, Kolya, and Gregor. I heard them say 'wolf.' It can only be you, Sasha. I didn't hear what, exactly, but they loaded up with weapons and left."

I checked my watch before throwing a cautious glance inside the restaurant. None of those four were in Viktor's entourage. That couldn't have been good.

Eduard caught sight of me through the window and frowned, a silent question on his face.

"When?" I asked, turning my back on him.

"Just now. I called you straight away."

If they were coming to ambush me, I had at least twenty minutes for them to get here from the Birdcage. It would have to be a short meeting, then.

"Don't tell anyone we spoke," I said before hanging up.

Exhaling a steadying breath, I cracked my neck and walked into the tea room as if nothing had happened. Eduard's gaze followed me the entire way, a dozen silent questions drifting through the air like smoke.

"Sasha," Viktor said with a smile, gesturing to the seat next to him. "Good news, I hope?"

Easing onto the edge of the chair, I pushed it back, giving myself a better view of the front door and the kitchen. "Where's Yuri?"

Viktor chuckled. "Off with his whores, snorting a mountain of cocaine, I imagine. That's why you're the one here discussing business instead of him."

I wasn't in the mood to be flattered. It was uncharacteristic of Viktor and a waste of my time. "When Yuri proposed this idea, did you know whose safety deposit box that was?"

Viktor blinked, either at my abruptness or the question. "Why?"

"Because it belongs to Sergei Sidorov." I watched his expression carefully. He gave nothing away, except, perhaps, annoyance. "And there weren't emeralds, as you said. It was information — on all of us."

"Did you get it?"

"Get what?" I cocked my head at him.

A flash of irritation crossed his face, crinkling the corners of his eyes. "The thumb drive."

My stomach twisted into knots. Lying piece of shit… "I never said anything about a flash drive."

He chuckled again and spread his hands. "You said information, Sasha. What else would it be? Polaroids like in the old days? Calm down."

I slid a glance at Eduard. He was at the next table, sitting up as straight as a board, his index finger tapping on the white tablecloth as he watched us. Other than Roan, he was the only other person who knew I had the flash drive. What was it Misha said last night? *I smell betrayal in the air.*

"So did you get it?" Viktor prompted again.

"Of course," I replied, trying to keep the snarl out of my voice.

"Where is it, then?"

"Not here."

Viktor raised his eyebrows, momentarily stunned into silence. "Why not?"

"What do I look like to you?" I shot back. "My payment just tripled. Between cleaning up after Yuri and ripping off Sergei, this job is worth more than the original price."

"Except you fucked up too. You let the hostage escape."

"I got the key and I killed the kid. Unlike your fucking nephew, I keep my word."

Viktor was about to reply when a black Escalade pulled up in front of the tea room and parked, bringing our conversation to a screeching halt. When the passenger door opened, Misha stepped out. Buttoning his burgundy suit jacket as he walked, his gaze met mine through the front window. Arching a brow, I swear there was a smirk before he opened the door and strode over to Viktor's table.

"Viktor," Misha said with none of his usual pleasantness. He didn't wait for Viktor's acknowledgement before turning to me. "And you are?"

I stood slowly, offering my hand and masking my confusion behind a scowl. "Aleksandr Vassiliev."

"The Wolf of Verkhoyansk in the flesh." Misha smiled and shook my hand firmly, like we weren't already acquainted. "Misha Chernyshevsky."

Viktor was on his feet as well, holding his hand out. "Good to see you again, Misha."

Misha looked at Viktor's hand and sat without touching it. "It's Mikhail to you. Sit."

You could have heard a pin drop.

Resuming his seat, Viktor held his head high, despite the profound insult.

Excusing myself, I turned to leave, but Misha laid a hand on my forearm. "No, Sasha. Stay. I won't be long."

I glanced at Viktor as I lowered myself back into the chair. His smile looked more like a grimace. I'm sure he was already thinking of ways for Misha to have a terrible "accident" in the coming weeks. And from the suspicious glance he sent my way, I'm sure I was also on the list.

Folding his hands on the table, Misha stared at the old man across from him for a moment. The silence ticked on until he spoke at last. "Sergei missed you at the meeting last night."

Viktor stiffened. "On such short notice, it is hard to get away from prior commitments."

"When Sergei calls, you answer. If you cannot do that, then what good are you as a captain?"

"I am a faithfu—"

Misha raised his hand, cutting him off. "We have been betrayed, Viktor. Someone took something from Sergei, something very important. I have been tasked with getting it back."

I pictured the flash drive, tucked away in a place only I knew. Sergei's men had been close to finding it once before, which led me to believe Roan was right. It was only traceable when it was plugged in, otherwise they would have hunted it down by now.

"Who?" Viktor asked, surprisingly convincing in his disbelief. "Who would dare do such a thing?"

"That is what I will find out. And when I do, it will not be very pleasant for him. I promise you that." Misha turned to me, a blond brow arched. "You haven't heard anything, have you, Wolf?"

I shook my head slowly, keeping my teeth clenched.

"Be sure to let me know if you do." Misha stood abruptly and buttoned his jacket again. "Walk me out."

Viktor was on his feet in a flash. "That's it?"

Misha ignored him and kept walking.

I glanced at my watch. The twenty minutes was up. I didn't want to be "predictable" like Yuri said and walk out the front door into an ambush. But then again, I hardly ever used the same door twice, which meant he was probably set up in the back, waiting for me in the alley. Besides, walking out with Misha gave me a very powerful human shield.

Glancing up and down the street, I pushed the door open for Misha.

He stepped through and paused on the sidewalk while his driver walked around the back of the SUV to open the rear passenger door.

"You know Viktor will have more questions now," I said.

Misha smiled, a bright, boyish smile complete with a dimple. "Where's the flash drive, Sasha?"

I blinked, feigning surprise. "What?"

"Sergei's flash drive. Where is it?" The smile never left his face.

"I don't know what you're talking about." Making sure my expression was as severe as ever, I refused to look away first. I didn't even blink.

"Sergei doesn't know. Sergei doesn't *have* to know. Just give it to me and then it is done." Misha brushed his hands together, like he was dusting them off. "No one has to get hurt."

"You can't hurt me any more than the others who have tried, but do what you must," I replied blithely, hoping to call his bluff.

Misha inched closer, his eyes narrowed at my shoulder before he picked something off. One of Roan's blond strands came away, pinched between his fingers. I could have tried to pass it off as one of Misha's, except his hair was stick-straight and perfectly gelled; Roan's was an adorable, wavy mess. "I wasn't talking about *you*."

The blood drained from my face.

I didn't bother saying goodbye. I turned on my heel and sprinted down the block for my car. Fuck Yuri and whatever he was doing. I had to get to Roan before Misha's men did.

# 43

# ROAN

"Oh my God. Are you peeing?" Frankie huffed into the phone.

"No, I am *not* peeing. It's a long story," I replied, shifting my weight on the edge of the tub. I might have thought Sasha was going a bit overboard with the security measures, and yet I was hiding in the bathroom with the sink running just to make a phone call.

"Where are you, anyway? The police were at your house for hours yesterday. Your mom is *freaking*."

Groaning, I raked a hand through my hair, messing it up even more. "That's another long story."

"It's that guy, isn't it?"

"Did Mom tell you what the police said?"

She huffed again, only answering after a prolonged silence. "I don't think they told her anything. Freddy said he saw FBI agents over there, but he's an idiot, so I don't know if I believe that." Dead Russian criminals? I'd believe it. Sasha probably had his own agent tracking him as we spoke. "Why don't you come over?" she continued, sounding peppier than a minute ago. "I'll order food. We can have a *Lord of the Rings* marathon."

My stomach rumbled at the thought of dinner, but Sasha's direct order put the brakes on that plan. "Maybe tomorrow night," I lied.

"It *is* that guy! You're blowing me off for him!"

"It's not like that."

"Then what's it like?"

I didn't have an answer because *I* had no idea. My relationship with Sasha was… complicated, to say the least. Well, it was for me. He, like usual, knew what he wanted and declared it in the most uncomplicated terms possible.

*From now on, you are mine.*

Whatever that meant.

"I'm worried about you," Frankie said quietly. "You went through a lot, Roan. And since you seem to have forgotten, this guy was the reason."

"No, my *dad* was the reason."

"No, Roan. *Sasha* was. He brainwashed you and now you have Stockholm or some shit. You need to get the fuck away from him and go talk to someone."

"I gotta go."

"Roan, wait!"

I hung up on her. Smacking the faucet handle into the off position, I stalked out of the bathroom. I paused long enough to shove my wallet in my back pocket and marched straight out the front door.

In addition to being hungry I was now pissed off thanks to Frankie's lecture. I knew she meant well, but I also didn't want to fucking hear it. I'd had enough of people dictating what I should and shouldn't do. Even if Sasha was the worst decision of my life, it was mine to make.

Since I wasn't in the mood for vodka or the leftover

cabbage roll thingies Sasha made, I headed down the main set of stairs, emerging onto the sidewalk. There was a brewery right around the corner that had my name written all over it.

I was almost to my intended destination when I spotted a familiar face walking down the sidewalk, headed straight for me.

Ivan.

He saw me at almost the same time, despite the fact I did an about-face and lengthened my strides to get away from him.

"You," Ivan spat. "Stop right there or I'll shoot you." He sounded pissed. If his aim was half as good as Sasha's, I didn't want to chance it.

Cringing, I turned slowly, trying to force a smile. "Hey man. Small world." I steadfastly refused to look at his hand, to see which fingers Sasha lopped off.

"Fuck you!" He shoved me hard.

I held up my hands, backing away from him. "I'm not going to fight you, Ivan. Sorry Sasha did what he did, but I had nothing to do with it."

"Nothing? Nothing!" He looked deranged, eyes bugged out and spittle flying. "You *infected* him! You twisted his mind with your perversion. It's sick. *You're* sick. Nothing but pedophiles and rapists."

Shaking my head, I made a face at him, trying to follow the bouncing ball of his logic. "What the fuck are you talking about?"

He said something in Russian, but from the way his gaze was directed he wasn't speaking to me.

I turned in time to see a short, black stick flying at me, wielded by none other than Yuri. It caught me on the side of the head so hard I lost vision in my left eye. From the sudden rush of warm liquid on my face, I knew I was bleeding. I also knew I had to get the fuck out of there. As soon as I could remember how to move.

Yuri didn't give me a chance to stand. While I was still dazed, he said something in Russian, punctuating it with a laugh. Two guys grabbed my arms and dragged me along the sidewalk, down into the alley.

As soon as I could get my feet underneath me, I dug my heels in and tried to pull free from one or both. The guy on my left was the stronger of the two, so I worked on freeing my right until Ivan turned and kicked me in the center of my abdomen.

While I struggled to regain the ability to breathe, the guys started dragging me again until Yuri told them to stop. They hurled me at the side of a building like a human slingshot. I slammed into the weathered brick and slid down the wall.

Get the fuck up, Roan. Get the fuck up *right* now.

No matter how many times I yelled at myself, my body wouldn't do what I wanted it to. My legs collapsed every time I tried to stand up and my left eye was still blurry. Nausea churned my stomach and my head was pounding. The realization I was going to die right then and there hit me hard, and there wasn't a goddamn thing I could do about it.

Like a pack of hyenas, the four of them spread out and came at me in unison. When the strikes started coming, I tried to fend them off. Even if I managed to push one away or get in a hit of my own, the other three were right there to beat me back.

By the time I crumpled to the ground, literally laying amongst the trash that spilled out of the nearby dumpster, I couldn't move. Every muscle was sore and my body felt like one giant bruise. All I tasted was my own blood. And fear, sharp and bitter. Both my energy and my adrenaline were gone. I alternated between waiting for death and praying Sasha would magically show up.

Yuri flipped me over onto my stomach and bent my arm up behind my back, straddling me. He said something in Russian and the three of them laughed, talking amongst themselves.

My fear renewed tenfold. Yuri's threat to fuck my face was a *not*-so-distant memory. As soon as I started struggling again, Yuri shoved my elbow up at an angle elbows weren't meant to go. Something popped in my shoulder. Hot, sickly pain flooded my entire arm and leeched into the rest of my body.

I screamed, clawing at the asphalt, trying to drag myself away to relieve the excruciating pain in my shoulder.

I was so focused on that, I didn't realize someone ripped my jeans down until it was too late. I tried to buck Yuri off of me, but he pushed even harder on my arm, wringing another agonized yell out of me.

He grabbed a handful of hair and jerked my head back, his stinking breath wafting over me. "Don't fight, suka. You know you'll like it." He laughed, a cold, vile laugh, before slamming my face into the pavement. My vision faded out again, this time in both eyes.

Without warning, something pushed inside me, cold, hard, and rough. Whatever it was felt like it was tearing right through me, an indescribable pain that surpassed the fire in my shoulder.

I refused to let myself make another sound. To make sure I didn't, I bit my lip so hard I drew blood.

From the moment it started, I stopped praying for Sasha.

I stopped hoping for a miracle.

Instead, I prayed for death.

# 44

## SASHA

Taking the stairs two at a time, I raced down the hallway as fast as I could. I jammed my key in the lock and turned it, feeling no resistance. Why the fuck was it unlocked?

Bile rose in the back of my throat as I pushed the door open and glanced around.

"Roan?" I eased inside, not even bothering to close the door behind me. The apartment looked ok, like everything was exactly where I'd left it. Except Roan.

Both the bedroom and bathroom doors were open; he wasn't in the living room or the kitchen. It was always possible he had his music turned up too loud, even if I couldn't exactly hear it.

Making my way toward the bedroom, I hoped he'd come out. I hoped he'd be laying on the bed. I hoped he was there, doing something, anything, but just *there*.

A quick glance around the bedroom completely dashed that hope.

The floorboard creaked behind me, along with a whisper of soft footsteps.

I unholstered my gun and turned, the trigger already halfway depressed.

It was Bohdana. Fuck! I didn't have time for her shit.

She looked at the gun and muttered something under her breath, as hard and unimpressed as ever. She was lucky I was too far away to hear her clearly or I might have let my finger contract all the way.

As much as I wanted to shoot the old bitch, I was more curious why she had the balls to be standing *inside* my apartment, uninvited and unwanted.

"What do you want?" I snapped, lowering my gun and closing the distance on her.

"Did you hear?" She blinked up at me with weepy eyes, magnified behind her gigantic glasses.

"Hear what?"

"About the boy?"

"What boy?" The muscles in my throat felt like they closed altogether, strangling me from the inside.

"Your boy. The nice boy."

I wanted to throttle her. Didn't she realize I didn't have time for this bullshit? I needed to find Roan and she was dicking around like I had all day. "Stop with the fucking riddles and tell me what happened!"

She swallowed, twisting a handkerchief in her hands before dabbing her nose with it. Had she been crying? When she didn't curse at me or call me a Moskal, I knew something awful must have happened, but for her to be *crying*? I was approximately two seconds away from shaking the information out of her.

"They found him in the alley," she said at last. Pulling a piece of paper out of her pink-flowered house coat, she held it out to me with a shaking hand. "I made them write it down."

It simply said Northwestern Hospital. It wasn't the closest hospital — it was the closest Level I trauma center.

Pushing her out of the way, I flew back down the stairs and sprinted to my car.

The next time I saw Misha, I was going to rip his fucking throat out. I didn't want Sergei's fucking files in the first place. I would have given it back to him once I knew what Viktor's agenda was. He didn't have to hurt Roan to prove his point. I *knew* what he could do — like me, his reputation preceded him. Preemptively hurting Roan was unnecessarily cruel, even by my standards.

I'd already murdered Misha a dozen different ways in my mind before I made it to the intake desk in the ER.

"Can I help you?" a nurse asked, glancing up from her computer.

"I was told Roan Sinclair was brought here?"

She typed something on the computer and clicked around before looking up again. "He's in surgery. You might want to take a seat. Someone will come get you when he's out."

"Can you tell me what happened?"

She shook her head and pointed across the way to a uniformed cop talking with a paramedic. "Try over there."

A cop? Great. Just what I needed on top of this shitty day. Nevertheless, I made my way to the duo and cleared my throat.

The cop straightened immediately, giving me a once over while his hand casually drifted to his gun. "You need something?"

I ignored him and looked at the paramedic. "Did you bring Roan Sinclair here?"

The medic exchanged glances with the cop before answering. "Yeah, I was there. He a friend of yours?"

I nodded. "Can you tell me what happened?"

The medic grimaced, lowering his voice. "It's not good. Docs rushed him straight to surgery. We got the bleeding stopped but he lost a lot by the time we got there. He'd been worked over pretty good."

Sickness swirled in the pit of my stomach. "Who?"

The cop piped up beside me. "That's what *I'm* trying to figure out, but no one saw nothing, or so they say. You sound like you're from that neighborhood. Were you with him?"

Guilt hit me like a fucking sledgehammer. I should have been. I should have never left him alone. If I'd been there, Misha's men would have never gotten to him. "No…"

"His ID says he lives in Highland Park. Do you know what he was doing there? Meeting up with someone, or something? Work? Anything?"

I couldn't even form words. All I could do was shake my head.

"Well, if you think of anything useful, can you give me a call?" The cop pulled out his business card and handed it to me.

I took it without looking at it, my attention shifting back to the medic. "Did — did he say anything?"

The paramedic shook his head. "Sorry, man. He was out the entire time."

Nodding, I drifted away from them, reeling from the little information they had. I wasn't the least bit surprised no one talked to the cops; they knew they'd be next. As soon as I was out of here, I'd knock on every fucking door in a two-block radius and *make* them talk to me. Someone saw something and whoever did this was going to fucking pay. I didn't care *who* they worked for, Misha, Sergei, or the fucking president.

Misery and anger and thoughts of revenge kept me

company until an annoyingly familiar voice broke the quiet unease of the ER waiting room.

"Sinclair!" a girl shouted. "S-I-N-C-L-A-I-R! You people called *me*, remember? So where is he?!"

I looked over to see Francesca staring the nurse down, slapping her hands on the counter. The guy from Roan's house was there too. Standing side-by-side, I could now see the resemblance between the two. Her brother saw me and nudged her, nodding in my direction.

Francesca's head whipped toward me, her brown eyes widening and narrowing all in a split second. Forgetting the nurse, she stormed over to me, looking capable of murder despite her small size.

I rose to my feet to meet her. As soon as she was close enough, she wound back and punched me in the stomach, right where that asshole drop kicked me yesterday. Luckily, she gave me enough time to flex my abs, so all she got was a fleeting grimace.

"What did you do to him, asshole?!" She hit me again, her eyes brimming with tears. "I know it was you, you fucking psycho! Hurting him once wasn't enough? You had to put him in the fucking hospital?"

Her brother rushed up behind her and grabbed her from behind, dragging her away. "Frankie, don't!"

She wasn't listening. "You better fucking leave, right now, before I call the cops and tell them everything!"

I cocked my head, brows furrowed. What the fuck was she talking about? She thought *I* did this? Was she insane?

Frederick tightened his grip around her, shooting a cautious glance in my direction. "It's not worth it. Ok? Fuck this guy. We're here for Roan."

"I don't care who you are," Francesca snapped at me, ignoring her brother's attempt to calm her down. "If he dies, I'll fucking kill you. Do you hear me, Sasha? Yeah! I know your name and I know what you did to him, you sick fuck! I know you fucking kidnapped him, manipulated him! And now this? *This* is *your* fault! Even if he survives, you've fucking ruined his life!"

"You're right," I said quietly. It was all I said before I turned and walked in the opposite direction, forcing myself to take slow, even breaths before I exploded.

Everything she said was true. Even if I didn't physically hurt him this time, it was because of me that Roan was here. I *did* ruin his life, because I was selfish and weak. He was the one good thing in my life, for however brief a time, and I destroyed it.

## 45

# ROAN

Disappointment was the first thing I felt when I opened my eyes.

Overwhelming disappointment.

I didn't want to be alive.

I didn't want to be in the hospital.

I wanted to be fucking dead. Dead people didn't have to deal with questions — fucking humiliation after humiliation.

The doctors asked questions.

The nurses asked questions.

The police asked questions.

Everyone asked questions and everyone got the same answer — silence.

I talked too much.

I asked too many questions. Sasha was always barking at me to stop talking. For once in my life, I fucking listened. I didn't listen to him before — I didn't stay put when he told me to stay. Now? It was too late. I learned my lesson. But at least I could save myself further shame and humiliation by keeping my fucking mouth shut.

"Are you feeling up to visitors?" a nurse asked, soft and mom-like.

Everyone had been sympathetic, but she'd been the most *empathetic*. She's the one who chased the cop away when he wouldn't shut up, bugging me over what I remembered and if I'd press charges and couldn't I just help him out a little and give him *something* to work with? No. No I couldn't.

She's the one who made sure I was cocooned in a pile of blankets and pillows to try and relieve some of the pressure on my battered body. She's the one who dimmed the lights and pulled the shades and yelled at the doctor to lower his voice.

And now, she was crouched beside the bed so she was eye-level with me instead of standing over me like *they* did.

I closed my eyes instead of answering. As nice as she was, I'd already made up my mind. I wasn't saying a fucking word to anyone.

The whisper of her scrubs traveled across the room and the door clicked open and shut.

I exhaled, opening my eyes again to stare at the sliver of the city I could see underneath the shade.

It was nighttime already. Already? I'd been out for hours. Brought in unconscious by the ambulance, kept unconscious by the doctors. Time passed. The world moved on. But I was suspended between that alley and the death that had been denied to me. Once again, I was fucking helpless. Weak. Powerless. Pathetic.

I couldn't fight back.

I couldn't die.

What the fuck was the point of any of it?

Someone gasped to my left. I knew without turning it was Frankie.

I closed my eyes again, hoping she'd go away.

"Roan?" It was Freddy, because Frankie had already started crying. "Are you awake?"

I didn't answer.

I didn't move. I couldn't move even if I'd wanted to. The drugs they had me on made me a slug, a lump of flesh just *existing*, just like before. What was the point of being able to run a four and a half minute mile if my legs wouldn't carry me to safety when I needed them to?

"Look what they did to him," Frankie whispered between sobs. "What kind of people do this?"

"He's alive. That's the most important thing." No, it wasn't, but I wasn't going to argue. "Come on," Freddy continued. "Let's go get something to eat. Get some flowers and stuff. By the time we come back, hopefully he'll be awake."

"Ok." Frankie's footsteps approached the side of the bed. I held my breath when she leaned over the railing and kissed the top of my head. It took everything in me not to flinch.

Thankfully, her sniffling and Freddy's squeaking shoes disappeared.

Opening my eyes again, I watched the lights pop on in the skyscrapers across the way. The sky behind the buildings was a haze of orange and purple. A perfect summer night.

A shadow shifted in the corner, blotting out my tiny view of the city, until it loomed over me.

"Solnyshko."

It was Sasha. Fuck. Even if I could only see his hand from the position I was laying in, I'd know his voice anywhere, that deep rumble and the mysterious word that seemed to be some sort of pet name. He never did tell me what it meant and now I didn't fucking care.

It was too late to pretend to be asleep, I knew he

already saw me. But I didn't have to look at him and I didn't have to talk. Those two things were still in my control. The *only* things I could control.

He lowered the side rail and knelt on one knee next to the bed. When he reached for my hand, I pulled it back and hid it beneath the blanket.

"Roan..." His voice cracked.

I almost caved, but I didn't. For once, I was strong.

I kept my gaze straight ahead, minimizing the sadness I saw in my periphery. Yet another reason I should be dead. The fact a man as strong and proud as Sasha was on his knees, on the verge of tears, over me? It made me sick to see what I'd reduced him to. I didn't deserve his sympathy. I deserved his anger. I didn't listen. I never listened. How many times had he told me?

"Talk to me," Sasha said softly.

Swallowing thickly, I cemented my tongue to the roof of my mouth.

"Do you know who did this?"

I wished I didn't. God, I wished I didn't. The fact I knew most of them, that I saw their faces, added to the misery. I wished they were unknown to me. Nameless, faceless strangers I could forget. But no. I recognized three of the four and knew two by name — Yuri, the fucking lunatic who attacked me, set me free, and came back to utterly destroy me. And Ivan, the nice guy turned evil because Sasha cut off his fucking fingers — *because* of me. No matter how I looked at it, I was the cause of *all* of this.

"Was it Misha?" The guy from the club? No. He'd been the only genuinely *nice* Russian I met in the past few weeks.

"Dimitri?" No. I didn't know who the fuck that was. At least, I didn't think I did.

"Roan, look at me." The snarl was back, barely

masking the quiver in his voice. His fingers dug into the sheet so hard I was sure he was going to rip it to shreds. "I said look at me!"

I refused. It was bad enough hearing his voice break, I couldn't bear to witness the look on his face too.

"Was it Yuri?" He sounded as desperate for answers as I was for him to go the fuck away.

A tear slipped out of the corner of my eye. I squeezed them shut, hoping he wouldn't see it with the low light and that I could stop the burning in my eyes.

"Roan, was it Yuri?"

After a few more agonizing moments of silence, he lowered his forehead to the bed, his shoulders shaking with each ragged breath.

Russian whispers floated around, like he was praying, but their meaning was absolutely useless to me. I no longer had a desire to learn Russian. I didn't want to know what they were saying while they took turns assaulting me with garbage from the alley. As if the act itself hadn't been humiliating enough…

The concussion, the broken ribs, the dislocated shoulder, the broken blood vessels in my eye — that pain was tolerable. Being held down, being invaded, degraded, mocked? That pain was…

Fuck!

Adding to my complete embarrassment, more tears streamed out beneath my closed lids. I couldn't even control *that.* I couldn't control *anything* when it came to my body, what it did or *didn't* do and what happened to it. So much for being a man, for being the "strong" one of the species. The protector. What a crock of shit. I was a disgrace to my gender.

"I'm going to kill them," Sasha announced, lifting his

head. "I promise you, Roan. I'm going to kill every single one of them."

I knew he would.

Too bad he wouldn't start with me.

## 46

## SASHA

Seeing Roan like that made me sick to my stomach. I'd left men like that — *worse* than that — so swollen and bloody, their own mothers wouldn't recognize them after they healed.

But they weren't Roan.

My Roan.

*Mine.*

The one *I* was supposed to protect.

I failed at my job — I failed him. I should have taken him with me. I felt it in my gut and I ignored it and now look.

The details of what happened were still out of reach, despite my best efforts. If this was Russia, I'd steal his chart and look. But it wasn't. It was America and all of the information was locked away on their computers and tablets. I had a feeling throwing a wad of cash at the staff wouldn't solve the problem either.

The doctor wasn't entirely without heart, though. With enough persistence he gave me a little more than the medic had. Beyond the fact Roan had been severely beaten, he said they'd given him blood transfusions and performed some sort of emergency colorectal repair. I had to Google the word and nearly crushed my phone when the search results loaded.

There was only *one* way he'd be injured there. And for it to be bad enough he required emergency surgery? I didn't see red. I surpassed red. I saw fucking black.

Yuri was the only name that caused a reaction in Roan. It wasn't an outright confirmation, but it was the only thing I had to go on. Combined with Lada's scared phone call, it was enough. Now I just had to find the fucker.

Once the Starlings returned to sit with Roan, I disappeared back to the underworld. As much as she may have hated me, I knew Francesca wouldn't let anyone get near her friend. He was as safe as he was going to be, which meant I had some time to hunt Yuri down.

Much to my annoyance, Yuri wasn't in any of his usual haunts. So, it was time to work my way down the chain of command, which meant my next stop was Gregor.

I pounded on front door repeatedly until Karine opened up, her eyes wide. "Sasha, wh—"

Shoving past her, I dropped my duffel bag by the door and tore through the house, shouting for her husband.

"What the fuck — Sasha? What are you doing here?" Gregor asked, storming out of the back bedroom.

"Where's Yuri?"

"Why?"

"Because I want to fucking know, that's why."

"I don't know." I might have believed him if his gaze didn't flick to his wife.

Unholstering the gun from the small of my back, I walked to Karine and threw my arm around her neck before she could scamper off.

"Sasha, no!" Gregor took a step forward. I jammed the

gun into his wife's temple and he stopped walking, holding his hands up in surrender.

"Where is he?" I repeated.

"Let her go, ok? She didn't do anything," Gregor said, licking his lips.

I'd sooner shoot myself than let my leverage go, and he knew that. Did he really think he could *reason* with me? "Were you there?"

Gregor's eyes widened. "What?"

"Were you with him today?" If I had to repeat every question, this was going to take for-fucking-ever and I didn't have that kind of time.

"Just let her go and we can talk." He gestured to the kitchen table, looking hopeful.

I motioned to the chair with the gun, keeping my arm wrapped securely around Karine's throat. She was so small, I could drag her with one arm easily, her toes skimming the carpet as I moved.

"Where are you taking her?" Gregor asked, half-rising from the chair he just sat in.

"Sit the fuck down," I snapped, smashing the barrel of the gun right under Karine's jaw. She gasped, digging her nails into my forearm.

He did as he was told while I backed up to the door. "Get the bag," I said to the trembling woman in front of me, releasing her throat.

She nodded, whimpering, and grabbed the bag. When she offered it to me, I tossed my head to her husband. "Over there. Tape him to the chair."

"Sasha, com—" Gregor stopped protesting when I snatched a handful of Karine's hair and ripped her head back. She shrieked and crashed against me.

"Tape him," I repeated next to her ear. "And make it fucking tight."

"How could you do this?" Gregor asked as Karine wrapped the duct tape around his wrists and ankles.

"To you, or in general?" I snatched Karine's arm and shoved her into the chair across from Gregor. "Generally speaking, you know me, Gregor. You know this is what I do. As for how I can do it to *you*?" I smiled, stroking Karine's cheek with my knuckles. She sniffled, shaking like a leaf. I made sure Gregor was watching when I slapped her as hard as I could, so hard the sting reverberated through my hand.

He swore at me and jerked in his chair.

She screamed and clamped a hand on her face, the tears flowing in earnest now.

"Oh, Karine, baby. I'm sorry. Come here." I touched her chin, tilting her face toward me. My handprint was as clear as day, red and angry, her tears glistening on the mark. "I don't have to hit you anymore. I promise. Just tell me what I want to know."

She looked at her husband, helpless and confused. The poor woman didn't know anything, but that didn't matter. "Gregor?"

I followed her gaze, waiting.

Gregor shook his head, hissing through his teeth. "You're a dead man."

"I've been dead for twenty three years," I replied flatly. My hand lashed out again, slapping Karine's flaming cheek. Before she could regain her breath, I seized a handful of her hair again and wrenched her head backward. "Was he there, Karine? Your husband? Did he help Yuri?"

She sobbed and tried to shake her head, but my death grip wouldn't let her. "I don't know. I don't know what you're talking about!"

The door swung open behind me. I whipped around,

taking less than a second to decide to pull the trigger at the male walking through the front door. The bullet caught him in the stomach and he pitched forward on his knees.

Gregor shouted and Karine wailed.

It was Kolya — another name on my list. Luckily for me, he was also Karine's brother and probably the reason Gregor was stalling, in the vain hope they'd, what? Overpower me? Idiots.

"Maybe Kolya will have more to say." I walked over to where he writhed on the floor, swearing at me, and ground my heel into the bloody hole in his stomach. "Where's Yuri?"

Kolya screamed and grabbed my foot, trying to dislodge it. I pressed harder until he stopped fighting and grunted out a few syllables that when strung together sounded like "With Viktor."

"He's with Viktor?" I confirmed.

Gasping, Kolya nodded. "At the lake house." Well, shit… That complicated things.

"Were you there today?" I asked, driving my heel down again.

Kolya cried out, but not before he looked at Gregor. I had my answer. I fired a round into Kolya's knee.

"Who else was with you?" I was pretty sure I knew that answer too, but I wanted to confirm Lada's information.

Kolya was too busy screaming and swearing at me to answer.

"Useless." I shot him in the head and turned back to Gregor. "Who else?"

"Fuck you, Sasha!" Gregor shouted. "You and that fucking rooster deserve to burn in Hell. Yuri told us you were fucking sick and he was right!"

Nodding, I moved back to Karine. She'd slumped over the table, sobbing into her arms. I grabbed the back of her neck and forced her upright again. She didn't even flinch when I lifted the gun and leveled it at her head, she just wept silently.

Gregor swore at me, still struggling to break free of the duct tape.

I fired a round right next to his wife's ear. Before the barrel could cool, I rammed it into her cheek and held it there while her skin burned. Her screaming renewed and she thrashed in her chair, unable to escape the vice grip I had on her.

Turning to Gregor with another grim smile, I slammed Karine forward, back onto the table, and nestled the barrel on the back of her head. "Who else?"

He seethed, but kept glancing between Karine and I, weighing his choices. Karine and I were both counting on him choosing wisely.

"Ivan," he said at last. "And Yuri."

"The four of you?"

Gregor nodded. "Now let her go."

"Of course." I pulled the trigger. Blood and gore shot out from beneath Karine's face and her body fell completely slack.

Gregor's shouting was completely unintelligible — howling and insults and promises of vengeance.

"How does it feel?" I asked, cocking my head as I stepped closer.

"Yuri is going to cut your fucking balls off, you fucking queer!"

With a smirk, I raised my gun and shot him in the head. Slinging my bag over my shoulder, I turned and walked out of the house.

Two dead, two left.

# 47

# ROAN

Day after day, I laid in the same position, staring at the same city skyline, until it was time to go home.

Frankie and Freddy alternated shifts at the hospital, sitting in my room, talking a million miles a minute about anything and everything. I didn't hear a word of it.

Instead of taking me to my parents' house, they planned on taking me to theirs. My parents didn't even know what happened. I didn't want them to. It was bad enough the Starlings knew, but since Frankie was listed as my emergency contact I had zero control over the hospital calling her while I was fucking unconscious.

I still hadn't said a word to anyone, despite the efforts of various people. Frankie, obviously. The doctors, nurses, and cops again. They even brought in a trauma counselor to try and talk to me; *try* being the keyword.

The only person who wasn't hounding me was Sasha. After promising to kill everyone, he left and never came back. For all I knew *he* was dead — or gone.

It was fine. It was what he wanted all along. He did his job for his shitty boss and now it was time for him to move on. Wasn't that his plan? Go to Russia, get married, and breed little criminal killers just like him so the cycle of violence could continue?

*Forget I exist.*

"So we've got the guest room all set up," Frankie yammered while Freddy wheeled me toward the front door like the invalid I was. "Freddy packed a bag of your stuff, told your mom where you were going to be, and then of course, *our* mom found out and told Consuela to make all of your favorites while you're there. But not over the top. Your doctor said you're on a restricted diet."

Freddy elbowed her at about the same time I closed my eyes and hid my face behind my hand. How fucking mortifying. I was furious when I found out they knew about my surgery. Even without revealing details, it was goddamn humiliating.

"Oh, shit," Freddy murmured. "He's still here."

"Stubborn motherfucker," Frankie hissed beside him.

We stopped moving suddenly. I dropped my hand and looked up, surprised to see Sasha standing in the way. So he *hadn't* left…

"I told you to stay the fuck away from him!" Frankie yelled.

Sasha did what he did best — ignored her. He closed the distance between us in long strides and took a knee next to me. At least he wasn't in a suit this time — back to his regular jeans and fitted black t-shirt. He didn't reach for me or say a word. He just knelt there, leaning on the knee that was still upright, looking at me, like a knight awaiting a command from his king.

I wouldn't meet his gaze, no matter how intensely he stared. I located a giant fleck in the tile in front of me and latched onto it. My whole existence was in that fleck, and as long as I didn't look away from it, I'd be ok. I could pretend the rest of the world didn't exist.

"We should really get him home," Freddy said quietly.

Sasha didn't budge.

"Don't make me call security," Frankie snapped.

"Solnyshko," Sasha whispered, dipping his head even lower to try and catch my gaze. "Please."

My breath caught in the back of my throat. In the time we'd spent together, Sasha never said please. *Never.* Not to me, not to anyone. He might as well have been begging me.

I forced my gaze away from the tile. It landed on his hand, tattooed and scarred, clenched into a fist so tight the veins and tendons popped beneath his skin.

His chest rose and fell quicker, drawing my attention upward. The muscles in his throat tensed, like they used to when we first met, a sign I now recognized as restraint.

Finally, I gave him what he wanted — I looked at him.

He didn't say anything. He didn't have to. The look in his eyes said it all. Fury, agony, despair.

Not pity.

Not disgust.

The world tilted. My vision blurred until Sasha was nothing more than a wash of color. Tremors wracked my body. I couldn't breathe. I couldn't move.

It wasn't until Sasha's arms wrapped around me that I knew I'd fallen. I buried my face into his shoulder, trying to muffle my sobbing against him. He stood up, holding me upright with one arm around my torso. His other hand alternated between holding the back of my head and running his fingers through my hair.

Frankie said something, but I couldn't hear her over my own pathetic breakdown.

Sasha's reply rumbled through his chest, and knowing

him it probably wasn't good. It was the last thing Frankie said.

I don't know how long we stood there. I didn't care.

"I have to go," Sasha said after a while, his voice right next to my ear. I shook my head, clinging to his damp t-shirt. I didn't want him to go. I finally felt safe and safety was the only thing I wanted at the moment. Running his hand through my hair again, he leaned back to look at me. "Go with your friends. I'll come when it's finished."

I blinked my vision back into focus and met his icy gaze with a furrowed brow. When it's *finished*? It wasn't already finished? What the fuck had he been doing?

"The rest of them die tonight," he said softly.

Any other time I would have balked at his bluntness. I would have been horrified knowing he was en route to murder someone. But now? I didn't give a fuck. He could kill the entire city and I wouldn't care. Caring got me nowhere in life, so maybe it was time to try things Sasha's way.

Caressing the side of my face, his gaze dropped to my mouth. I could tell he wanted to kiss me, but he was holding back. His reluctance sparked unexpected anger inside of me. Before this, if he wanted to kiss me, he'd fucking kiss me, regardless of what *I* wanted. And now he looked at me like I was a Faberge egg, one he was afraid was going to shatter at the slightest touch.

Taking hold of his face, I yanked him down to me, pressing my lips to his. After what happened, I needed to know how he really felt. I needed to know everything he would never say out loud. I needed to know if he still wanted me, even though I was damaged beyond repair.

His body went rigid for a moment before he relaxed again, returning the kiss with an uncharacteristic gentleness. It was soft, and scared, not repulsed. Even when he pulled away, it was with hesitancy. Resting his forehead against mine, he exhaled and closed his eyes, swallowing hard. "Roan—"

"Go," I said, cutting him off with a sudden surge of confidence. It was better to *tell* him to leave than to *be* told, like I had any say at all in the situation.

His head snapped up, pale eyes wide. It was the first thing I'd said in the better part of four days and honestly the last thing I expected.

"Do what you do, Sasha." I gave him a single nod and untangled myself from his arms, taking a slow, unsteady step backward.

Frankie's hand slid up my arm, her fingers curling around my bicep, providing a new source to lean on.

Accepting the order, Sasha inclined his head and turned away. Right before he got to the door, I called his name. He stopped, looking over his shoulder, the corners of his eyes tightening — just a flicker of an emotion I couldn't quite name.

"Make it hurt," I said, my hands balled into fists. I didn't realize I was trembling until Frankie's fingers squeezed me gently, a steadying pressure against the tidal wave of emotions crashing inside of me.

The corner of his mouth lifted into a dark smile. There was a visible glimmer in his eyes unlike anything I'd ever seen. The Wolf was off the leash and those motherfuckers had no idea what hell was coming for them.

## 48

## SASHA

TUGGING OPEN THE FRONT DOOR OF THE BIRDCAGE, I scanned the dim interior quickly. Given the fact it was lunchtime, it was mostly empty. Lada was behind the bar, sipping a cup of tea and flipping through a magazine.

"Get everyone out," I said, cutting through the tables for the back hallway.

She nodded, hurrying off to gather the girls and shoo away the handful of patrons.

As I rounded the corner for the office, Vlad stepped out, his brows furrowed. I hefted my pistol in my hand and smashed it against the side of his face before he had a chance to say anything. He flopped to the floor, blood oozing from the side of his head.

"Are they here?" I asked, crouching over him.

"What the fuck?!" he groaned, holding his head.

"Ivan and Yuri. Are they here?"

Vlad shook his head. "Only Ivan. Downstairs."

"Call Yuri," I said, patting the center of his chest and standing. "Tell him Ivan's dead."

His eyes widened. "What? Aleksandr!"

I ignored his stupid question and stepped over him, continuing on to the basement.

Luckily for Vlad, Ivan *was* there, checking over a new shipment of drugs. Seemed the errand boy was climbing the ranks. Too bad he picked the wrong man to follow.

As soon as he saw me, his eyes hardened. He reached for his waistband, but I beat him to the draw, shooting out his right knee. He dropped with a howl, holding his shattered kneecap. "Fuck you, Sasha, you fucking faggot!"

Holstering my gun, I leaned down and grabbed him by the throat, hauling him up so we were eye level. "How long were you in the alley?"

He sneered and spit in my face. I closed my eyes and wiped the saliva off with my free hand before drilling him in the mouth with a closed fist. "How long?" I asked again, squeezing his throat harder.

"Hours," he hissed, with a twisted smile reminiscent of Yuri's.

It was a lie. Roan wasn't alone that long. But if Ivan wanted me to think Roan suffered for hours, I'd be happy to oblige him.

"Then that's how long you and I will be together," I replied with an equally dark smile.

As soon as he realized I was dragging him to the utility room, he tried to fight back. It was pointless. Between his useless right leg and my bigger size, I had little trouble subduing him.

I bound his wrists behind his back before tossing the main line over a steel support beam and yanked on the rope until his shoulders strained visibly. He screamed and cursed me as he hung there, immobilized more by his pain than the rope. Once he was in an excruciating position, I tied off the rope on another post and circled around to the front.

Grabbing his chin and squeezing, I brought my face closer to his. "I'm going to take you apart, piece by fucking piece, you spineless little shit."

"Yuri will kill you," Ivan spat. "I told him what you are. What you and that fucking fag did in the basement. Yeah, I saw. You disgusting fuck."

So *that's* what this was about. Not the fucking flash drive. This was all because of me and my inability to control myself. As much as the guilt ate away at me, I didn't let myself dwell on it. I had work to do.

I shoved Ivan's face away and walked over to the table full of supplies we kept for occasions such as this. Picking up a pair of wire cutters, I squeezed them open and shut a couple of times, returning to Ivan. "Let's start with the toes and work our way up," I said with a smile.

---

Instead of leaving, like I told her to, Lada texted when Yuri arrived. I was annoyed, but the heads up gave me enough time to position myself on the side of the door before he burst through it, his gun drawn.

I grabbed his gun hand at the same time I kicked out the back of his knee. He went down hard. To make sure he stayed down, I kicked the side of his head.

"Glad you could join us," I said, disassembling his gun quickly and tossing the pieces aside.

"You motherfucker," he croaked, trying to push himself up off the ground.

I grabbed Yuri by his hair and dragged him to the beam next to the remnants of Ivan's body. Stringing him up the same way Ivan had been, I let him take a good look at his little snitch while I retrieved a knife.

Ivan learned I kept my word. I took him apart, piece

by piece. Toes, feet, sections of his legs, his dick, his balls, the rest of his fingers. The pieces were piled up in a heap, coagulated blood forming a dark red puddle around them. Between the trimming, I took the time to electrocute him, leaving burn marks over his torso, so I knew he felt the pain in every molecule of his body. Electricity was excruciating — I knew from personal experience — but it didn't kill him. That was probably the blood loss. Or shock. It didn't matter. He was dead now, hanging like a piece of meat that would soon make the creatures in Lake Michigan very happy.

"You're a fucking animal," Yuri hissed, looking at Ivan's bloody carcass with disgust.

I didn't answer him. Slicing his clothes off with the knife, I didn't care whether or not his skin was cut in the process. All the better if it was.

"Viktor is going to cut your fucking head off," Yuri said, trying to dodge the knife.

"Does Viktor know what you did?"

Yuri laughed.

"Laugh while you can. You'll tell me everything," I said, backing away from him slowly. "Just like Ivan."

Yuri spit at me, but it fell short. "Go fuck yourself, you fucking pedophile."

Unfolding a stainless steel hose, I made sure I stood out of the way so Yuri could see what I was doing, *exactly* what was in store for him. Thanks to some creative ingenuity, it was already hooked up. All I had to do was flip the lever.

Steam rushed out the end of the hose with a quiet hiss. I tugged on a pair of thick gloves and grabbed the end, dragging it over to Yuri's swinging body. Brandishing the hose in front of him, I let a cloud of steam fill the space between us, delighted at how wide his eyes got.

"My blood is clean. You're the one who will have to

answer to God for your filth," Yuri said, glancing at the steam, already beginning to sweat with how close it was. "You and your pretty boy. Good luck fucking that little bitch ever again. Or does he fuck you?"

If he thought taunting me would make me kill him faster, he was sorely mistaken. Roan wanted it to hurt — I was going to make it fucking hurt. Lowering the hose, I pointed the steam at his pathetic cock.

Yuri screamed and writhed like a worm on a hook until I turned the hose away from him.

"Does Viktor know?" I repeated calmly.

Moaning, his head flopped forward. His dick was red and blistered. It wouldn't be able to withstand much more. If I turned the lever up high enough, I'd be able to cut right through the fucking thing, but we weren't to that stage quite yet.

Yanking Yuri's head back and holding up the hose, I got in his face. "Your shriveled dick is the least of your concerns. I will fucking melt every centimeter of you if you don't start talking. Does Viktor know?"

"Yes," Yuri choked out.

"Did he know *before*?"

Yuri's eyes drifted shut. I let go of his hair and took a step back, returning the deadly white cloud to his genitals. His eyes popped open again, twisting in front of me as shrieks tore out of him.

Lowering the steam, I grabbed Yuri's face and held it steady, nose-to-nose with him again. "Did he know?"

"Yes." Motherfucker… Viktor, you lying, back-stabbing piece of shit…

"Whose idea was it?"

Yuri whimpered, his head slumping against my hand.

"Who?" I squeezed his face harder.

"Viktor's."

Nodding, I stepped back, absorbing the information. How long had Viktor known I was lying about Roan? It didn't matter. He knew, and he let his vulgar nephew round up a crew to destroy the one thing that mattered to me — the one thing that was outside of his control. The meeting was the perfect opportunity to go after Roan and I fucking gave it to him.

"Remember what I told you on the phone the other day?" I asked, returning to the steam valve and pushing the lever into the OFF position. Dropping the hose and peeling off my gloves, I unsheathed the filet knife again and strolled back to Yuri. "That I was going to rip your fucking face off?"

Yuri's lower lip trembled, but for once he didn't have a comeback.

I didn't give him time to fathom the pain he was about to endure before I sliced into his face. His screaming was practically deafening, but I didn't care. I kept cutting around the perimeter of his face, jabbing underneath the skin to sever the membranes and tissues. When I had enough loose skin to actually grab, I did, ripping the skin away from the flesh beneath with one hand while the blade slid along the inside, cutting as it went.

Yuri's whole body was shaking by the time I was done, blood pouring from his massacred face.

Holding up the mask of skin for him to see, I arched a brow at him. "You should have fucking known better than to cross me, Yuri."

Flinging the skin onto the pile of Ivan's body parts, I strode back to the steam valve. Pulling the gloves over my bloody hands, I pushed the lever open the entire way and grabbed the hose.

Circling around behind him, I clamped a hand on his

shoulder, speaking into his ear. "And you should have known better than to fuck with what's mine."

"Sasha…" The plea for mercy was evident in his voice, but all it did was fuel my fury.

Kicking his legs apart, I wasted no time ramming the hose up his ass, steam and all. His screams were inhuman and it was fucking music to my ears.

I left him like that, letting the steam liquifying his internal organs, and headed back upstairs.

Lada was sitting on the bar top, smoking a cigarette. She raised a brow, flicking ash off the end. "Is he dead?"

Faintly, I could still hear his unearthly screaming, muffled beneath the floorboards and the music playing. "Soon."

"Good." She held the cigarette out to me.

I gladly took it from her, my hand stained with her boyfriend's blood. "Thank you."

"Thank *you*," she said with a smile. "I knew you'd keep your word."

"Always." Taking a long drag from the cigarette, I closed my eyes and held it in. Exhaling slowly, I handed it back to her and headed for the door.

It was time for Viktor to learn the same lesson as his nephew.

## 49

# ROAN

"I'M SO BORED," FRANKIE WHINED, HER HEAD HANGING upside down on the bed. "Are you two going to be done soon?"

"Flank them!" Freddy shouted, thumbs moving quickly over the controller as our squadron spread out on the TV.

"In a min—come on!" I threw one hand up as my soldier's head exploded. "You were supposed to be watching for snipers!"

"Sorry, dude," Freddy chuckled, steering his character in a completely different direction from where mine bit the dust. "So have you heard from him yet?"

Frankie smacked her brother upside the head. He flipped her off over his shoulder and kept playing.

"No," I muttered, tapping out the button sequence required to move my character up a wall and crouch along a building. I'd been with the Starlings for three days already without any form of contact from Sasha. As much as I tried not to think about it, it was *all* I thought about.

"Are you worried?" Freddy asked as his character launched a grenade at a sniper nest.

Frankie flopped over on her stomach, glaring a hole in her brother's head. "Oh my God! Why are you bringing up that asshole?"

"Shut it, Frankie." Freddy paused the game and turned to me, his brown eyes soft and judgment-free, unlike his sister's.

"I mean…" What was I supposed to say? Yes, I was fucking terrified. Sasha was out there, doing God knew what. Would he get arrested? Would he make it out alive? If he did, would he come back? Maybe once he was done, he'd disappear. Maybe he'd have to, to avoid the cops. "I don't know. He's, um, good at his job. I guess."

"Being a criminal?" Frankie asked, wedging her head between Freddy and I to be part of the conversation.

"Cut him some slack. He didn't really have a choice," I replied quietly.

"What does that mean?"

"He doesn't talk about it, but I think he was trafficked as a kid. That's why he's so… hard. It's not about being a criminal, it's about surviving. It was him or them, you know? I don't know… Does that even make sense?"

Freddy nodded. "Totally. He's been conditioned by it. But you can't unlearn that, dude. Not without a fuck ton of therapy and actually wanting to change."

"It's not *who* he is, it's just what he does to stay alive," I grumbled, staring at the controller. "Once you get to know him, he's—"

"What? A completely different person? A big old teddy bear?" Frankie snorted.

"No, he's still an asshole," I snapped, but a smile pulled at the corner of my mouth. "But he's *my* asshole. He's actually funny. He cares, in his intense, overprotective way. And he understands people a lot more than I originally gave him credit for, even if he thinks feelings are all bullshit."

"I don't like it," Frankie said bluntly. "He kidnapped you, Roan. He beat you. He held you for fucking ransom. Those aren't the actions of a guy who 'cares.'"

"Did we say anything when you dated that dickhead on the football team?" Freddy interjected, glaring over his shoulder at his twin. "No. Did we say anything when you dated the fucking 'photographer'? No. So shut the fuck up. Roan is a big boy. He can make his own decisions without you chiming in like a nagging wife. Sorry he's gay, but he can't be your emotional boyfriend for the rest of his damn life."

I blinked.

Frankie blinked.

Freddy nodded curtly and resumed playing his game, as if nothing happened. I wasn't even sure *what* happened. Freddy had always been the reasonable one, but the reasonable one just gave his blessing to my relationship with Sasha, who, as Frankie correctly pointed out, was not exactly "boyfriend" material.

A few minutes later, Mrs. Starling appeared at the door, knocking against the frame. "Roan? There's someone here for you."

"Who?" All three of us asked in unison.

She chuckled and shook her head, gesturing awkwardly. "I don't know. Some big guy who asked for you by name."

I scrambled to my feet, dropping the controller on the bean bag. My heart thumped wildly as I followed Mrs. Starling down the hall to the foyer. As soon as I rounded the corner and spied the broad shoulders, swathed in a tailored navy suit, I felt sick.

It wasn't Sasha.

It was Misha.

"Thank you," Misha said, turning with a smile for Mrs. Starling. His bright blue eyes shifted to me, the smile remaining in place even though it didn't reach his eyes. "Roan."

"What are you doing here? How did you even know—"

He held up a hand. "Get your shoes. We're going to take a ride."

I folded my arms over my chest. Were all Russians this fucking bossy? "No way in hell. Not until you tell me why you're here."

He took a step closer, steepling his fingers in front of him. "It wasn't a request."

I held my ground, even if he could crush me as easily as Sasha. "I don't give a shit. Why are you here, Misha? Where's Sasha?"

"We need to talk."

"Great. Talk right here."

"I'd prefer to do it somewhere a little more…" He sucked a breath in through his teeth, glancing around at the glittering mansion. "Private."

"Where is Sasha?" I demanded, enunciating each word.

Misha's eyes tightened. "That's what I'm here to talk about."

A wave of nausea rolled through my stomach. "What about him? What happened?"

He strolled forward, one hand in his pocket while the other brushed his nose casually. He stopped in front of me, right in my personal space, his gaze locked on mine. "If you want what's best for Sasha, get in the fucking car. Now."

I swallowed down my fear and nodded. Without saying

a word to anyone, I grabbed my shoes and followed him outside to a waiting SUV. The driver opened the door for me and I climbed in carefully, mindful of my various injuries. Even though I could move around a lot easier now, I was nowhere near fully healed.

Misha sat next to me in the back. As soon as everyone was situated, he gave the word to leave.

"Where are we going?" I asked when it was obvious we were headed for the city.

"You'll find out soon enough."

"Is Sasha there?"

Misha slid a look at me that brought an immediate halt to my questions. Another thing he and Sasha apparently had in common.

I stayed silent for the rest of the ride, watching the buildings fly by, trying to keep track of where we were. When the SUV rolled to a stop and parked, I swallowed the lump in my throat.

We were at Delirium — the club I'd tracked Sasha down at and the place he told me never to return to.

The car door opened and I stumbled out. There was a line of people around the block, waiting to get in, but Misha walked past them all. The bouncer didn't even hesitate to push the door open for us.

Loud techno beats and flashing green and white lights bombarded us as soon as we were inside. Misha cut through the crowd with ease, like people knew to part for him and look away, in fear or deference.

My head was thumping by the time we made it into the kitchen. Then, my heart took over, beating wildly in my chest. I'd seen enough mob movies to know this was never a good sign.

"I think there's been a mistake," I said, looking for the fastest exit possible.

"No, no mistake," Misha said in front of me, not even slowing his pace. He pushed open another door, leading me into a room with thick insulation covering the walls. Soundproofing.

I turned around immediately, but the driver was behind me. He shoved me backward and Misha grabbed me from behind, one hand on the back of my neck and the other on my bicep.

"You've already been hurt once," he said quietly, his lips brushing my ear. "Don't make me hurt you even more."

"What do you want from me?"

"It's not what *I* want. It's what Sergei wants."

"Sergei Sidorov?"

Misha forcibly moved me a couple of steps and pushed me down into a chair, patting my shoulder. He walked away again, leaning against the padded wall, exchanging a look with the driver, who stood guard at the door.

Glancing around the small space, I tried not to panic. Sure, there was a very odd drain in the floor. And yeah, there was just this chair and one other, situated right across from me, interrogation style. But Misha had always been nice. He helped me find Sasha. He was polite while we waited, offering me tea and cake, and chatting amicably.

But he knew what happened. I mean, the bruises were still there on my face, and the burst blood vessels in my left eye were nowhere near gone. But the way he said it, that I had been "hurt," led me to believe he *knew*. And if he *knew*, did that mean he had a hand in it? Was it going to happen again? He all but said he would if I didn't start going along with the program.

I watched Misha carefully while we waited. He didn't seem the least bit interested in me. He spent the majority of the time texting, except for whenever he and the driver mumbled at each other in Russian.

When the door swung open again, I got to my feet, taking an instinctive step back.

The man who walked through had to have been Sergei Sidorov. Everything about him screamed power, from the slicked back salt-and-pepper hair to the high-end suit he wore. His eyes settled on me for a moment before he turned his attention to Misha, saying something in Russian that sounded like a question.

Misha consulted his phone and replied.

Sergei nodded and walked forward, his eyes flicking back to me. "Roan Sinclair. You have something that belongs to me."

Swallowing thickly, I glanced at Misha again. Standing behind his boss, he was stone faced, no longer an ally — if he ever was.

"I can explain," I said quickly.

"Please do." Sergei gestured to the chair I'd vacated. On cue, the driver darted forward, holding the second chair steady while Sergei eased his large frame onto it.

I stayed where I was, standing, poised to run if my traitorous body would actually listen this time. "Where's Sasha? I'm not saying anything until someone tells me what's going on with him."

Sergei cocked his head and looked up at Misha, asking another question with a gesture toward me.

Misha chuckled and nodded, murmuring his reply.

"He's coming," Sergei replied, squinting at me. "Now, sit down. Start at the beginning and tell me *everything*."

# 50

# SASHA

VIKTOR SHOULD HAVE REALLY UPGRADED HIS SECURITY when he decided to go after Roan. The alarm system was all too easy to bypass and the pair of guard dogs in the yard each ended up with a broken neck. The smartest move he'd made was bouncing between his various properties over the past couple of days. It was like a shell game, by the time I got to one, he was gone, off to the next, until I finally tracked him to his house in the suburbs.

I didn't even try to be subtle or stealthy as I approached the house.

Booting open the lovely French doors off of the kitchen, I stormed inside, scanning each room quickly for any of his bodyguards.

The ground floor was clear. It was also eerily quiet. This time of night, there should have still been people awake, people moving around. Despite the fact the lights were on, there was no activity in the house.

Apprehension settled in my stomach as I crept up the stairs.

The door to the master suite was cracked. Ignoring the gut instinct to leave, I headed toward it. I came here to kill that soulless fuck and that's what I was going to do.

Nudging the door open, I stepped inside, my gun lifted and ready to fire.

The light flipped on and the door slammed shut behind me. In my temporary blindness, something hard and heavy crashed against my back. I pitched forward and landed face-first on the plush carpet. The gun fell out of reach. With the weight still on my back, I couldn't retrieve it.

Blinking away the black and white fuzzies, Viktor came into view, standing next to Dimitri. My blood ran cold, freezing me in place. Whoever was sitting on my back secured a pair of handcuffs to my wrists, while someone else attached leg irons to my ankles. Once I effectively couldn't move, they stripped me of all of my weapons.

Viktor sneered in triumph. "Fucking goluboi."

"Come closer and say that," I growled up at him.

"Enough," Dimitri snapped, checking something on his phone before tucking it away again. "Let's go."

The two men behind me tucked their hands under my arms and hauled me upward, directing me back out the door. One of them held a taser up and squeezed the trigger. It cycled with a loud 'tick tick tick,' white and blue zaps of electricity sparking at the end. "Don't even fucking think about trying anything," he said, jamming the taser into the small of my back as they helped me down the stairs.

They stuffed me into a waiting van and off we went, the two of them in the back with me while a third drove.

Eyes closed and head tipped back against the side of the van, I went over what little I knew.

Dimitri was here, which was never good. He was

Sergei's judge, jury, and executioner. He heard complaints and settled internal disputes, usually with a bullet.

Viktor knew I was coming.

Dimitri knew I was coming.

They were *together*, waiting for me.

That meant there wouldn't be any sort of "trial" — Dimitri had already decided. As soon as we arrived at whatever destination they had in mind, I was going to fucking die. As long as I took Viktor with me, I didn't care. That motherfucker had been breathing for too long as it was.

Exhaling a slow breath, I kept my eyes closed, trying to map out where I was based on the turns the van had already made. There were only so many places they'd take me. Based on where Viktor's house was, I narrowed it down to a couple of the obvious choices. They were all fairly close, which meant I didn't have a lot of time to act.

Bringing my hands closer together, I took a deep breath and pushed against my left thumb as hard as I could. Having been broken time and again over the course of my life, it didn't take much to pop it out place. The sudden rush of pain wasn't pleasant, but it was preferable to death.

Grimacing, I opened my eyes and carefully pulled my left hand through the cuff, keeping ahold of it in my right. Glancing between the two men seated across from me, I assessed each quickly, trying to decide who was the bigger threat.

The one on the right was larger, but the one on the left had the taser.

Gripping the handcuffs, I lunged at the one on the left. I drove the single metal strand up under his jaw, the steel teeth tearing into his skin and spurting blood before he could even yell.

The guy on the right threw himself at me, but it was

too late for his partner. I was able to get my feet up in time and plant them in the center of his chest, kicking him backward into the double doors.

Grabbing the taser from the dead man, I turned for his partner, catching a boot to the side of the face. I shook off the pain and jammed the end of the taser against his thigh, pulling the trigger. He yelled and grabbed his leg, bending enough so I could grab his face. With one quick motion, I snapped his neck and threw his body out of the way.

The van jerked to the side and screeched to a halt.

Swearing under my breath, I clawed through the dead men's pockets until I found the handcuff key. The backdoors flew open right as I unlocked the last leg iron.

I launched myself at the driver as soon as he came into view. We fell to the ground in a heap, wrestling for his gun. It went off between us, the sound deafening and dangerously close to my face.

A second bullet fired, but it wasn't from the driver's gun. We both paused and looked to the side.

Dimitri's vehicle had pulled over too. He stood next to us on the shoulder, the gun pointed at me. "Quit fucking around and get in the car, Sasha," he said between his teeth.

Resigned to my fate, I climbed off of the driver and walked in the direction Dimitri pointed. I slid into the back of his SUV, still holding onto the bloody handcuff like a shiv, just in case. Not that it would do me any fucking good against a gun.

A third bullet tore through the night. I looked up in time to see Dimitri shake his head and walk back to the car. The driver was still laying on the side of the road, blood trickling out of his forehead.

Dimitri climbed in next to me, the gun resting casually in his lap. "Now let's go."

---

WALKING THROUGH THE BACKDOOR OF DELIRIUM WAS LIKE walking through the gates of Hell. The kitchen was sweltering and the bass from the club next door sank into my bones, like the percussion before an execution. And I knew, without a doubt, I was marching toward my own death. But first, I'd be weighed and measured by none other than Sergei Sidorov himself.

Dimitri led the way into a room off of the kitchen. I went next, with Viktor and the driver following us.

Sergei was seated in the middle of the room along with Roan.

Roan!

I surged forward, but two pairs of hands grabbed me from behind and held me in place. Trying to throw them off with a snarl, I glanced over each shoulder, recognizing Misha and his driver.

"*What the fuck is he doing here?*" I asked Misha in Russian.

Misha held my gaze for a pointed second, before he looked at Sergei. His boss had risen to his feet and was talking with Dimitri in low voices.

Roan was standing too, his arms crossed over his chest, his brows slanted over worried eyes. He *looked* ok, but who the hell knew what happened before I got here and who knew what was going to happen next.

"Sasha," Sergei said, drawing my attention to him. "I've been hearing *a lot* of things about you. A lot of… troubling things." Strangely, he spoke in English. I cocked my head at the language choice, stealing another quick glance at Roan.

I didn't say anything as Sergei moved closer. Misha gave my shoulder a squeeze before letting go and shoving me forward a step.

"Viktor tells me you are queer." Sergei looked me up and down, his lips twisting beneath the neatly trimmed gray beard. "He tells me you and your" — he gestured dismissively to Roan — "whatever, have conspired to steal from me. He thinks you are trying to oust him and set yourself up as a captain."

"Exactly!" Viktor exclaimed, taking a step forward. "And he—"

Sergei held up a finger, silencing the rest of Viktor's bullshit. "So, tell me, Sasha. Is the Wolf of Verkhoyansk, the terrifying butcher of men, a filthy, fucking faggot?"

I had a decision to make. If Sergei knew the truth, he'd kill me. But if I lied and he knew I was lying, he would kill me in a much more painful fashion. Since I was bound to die either way, I hoped my truthfulness would spare Roan. My gaze shifted past Sergei and settled on Roan as I answered. "It's true."

Roan covered his mouth with his hand, looking like he was two seconds away from throwing up. Even from a distance, I could see the wetness in his eyes, highlighting the purple color I loved so much.

Sergei nodded, running his tongue over his teeth, also looking like he was going to vomit. "And the two of you fucking faggots stole my property from the bank?"

"Yes," I answered tightly.

Sergei nodded again. "Where is it?"

I swallowed the lump in my throat. "My boot."

Misha immediately dropped to a crouch. I picked up my left foot and he unlaced it quickly, pulling it off. The flash drive fell to the floor. Misha shoved my boot back on and snatched the drive off the ground, handing it to Sergei.

Sergei looked it over and tucked it in his pocket, apparently satisfied it was the original. "What were you going to do with it?"

I shot a glare at Viktor and his stupid grinning face. "I was going to leverage it, to see if this piece of shit actually set me up."

Sergei followed my gaze. "Set *you* up? For what?"

"This," I hissed, gesturing at the confined space. "Someone has to take the blame for what a fuck up his nephew has been. It was Yuri's idea to rob the bank, Yuri who called the police and ratted out your warehouse. But it was Viktor who was trying to set himself up as the new boss, not me. It's the only thing that makes sense."

Sergei's brows lifted. "Is that so?" He turned to Viktor, the same curious expression on his face.

"He's a fucking liar!" Viktor said, his lip curling. "You can't believe a word he says."

"What has he lied about?" Sergei asked, spreading his hands. "He confessed to being queer, to stealing the flash drive. He's right about Yuri being a rat. Eduard found the proof in the phone records, records your man Gregor tried to hide from Misha."

Viktor blanched, covering it with a laugh. When no one laughed with him, he swallowed. "Sergei. You can't be serious. You think *I* am behind any of this? It's these two rapists you should worry about, spreading lies and disease and trying to make you look like a fool."

Sergei looked past him to Dimitri and tossed his head toward the door. The two men walked out together, closing the door behind them.

Without any hands restraining me, I darted over to Roan and threw my arms around him, careful not to crush his ribs. "Are you ok?"

He nodded, trying to push me away. "They're looking at you."

"I don't fucking care." I caught his face between my hands and kissed him, right there in front of Misha and the others. There might have been gasps and curses and murmuring coming from behind me, but all I cared about was Roan's soft moan against my lips. Dying with the memory of his lips on mine was all the comfort I needed. I'd kiss him in front of Sergei and happily take the punishment for both of us if it meant sparing Roan's life.

I hated to pull away, but I did, keeping hold of his face gently. "I kept my promise."

"They're all dead?"

I nodded.

His gaze dropped, a frown pulling at his lips.

My heart sank. He didn't look happy. Why did I keep failing him? Couldn't protect him, couldn't give him what he wanted. What fucking good was I? "What's wrong, Solnyshko?"

"I thought I would feel… something." He grimaced, his fingers twisting in my t-shirt. "Better? Relieved? I don't know…"

Not knowing what to say, I kissed his forehead and wrapped him in another hug. I tried not to think about how much time had passed, how much deliberation was taking place on the other side of the door. I just held onto Roan and breathed in the summery scent that was so *him*.

When the door opened again, I pushed Roan behind me and turned to face Sergei and Dimitri, making myself as big and tall as I could, like I was facing off against a bear in the woods.

"I've reached a decision," Sergei said, stepping closer to me. "Sasha, come here." When I didn't move, Sergei frowned. "I said come here. Come kneel before me and ask forgiveness."

"I kneel for no one," I replied tersely. The eight-point stars tattooed on my kneecaps practically burned at the command, rejecting it.

"You won't kneel to save your life?" Sergei asked, his gray brows lifted.

"Please just kneel," Roan hissed behind me, his fingers tightening on my shirt.

Turning to Roan, my molars clenched. He didn't understand. How could he? He didn't know what kneeling meant, what the stars represented, what I would be telling the men in the room by kneeling before Sergei. I was already subhuman because I was queer. Kneeling would only make it a thousand times worse. I'd truly be an animal in their eyes, debased and humiliated.

I had another decision to make, and quickly. I found the answer in Roan's wide blue eyes. Keeping my gaze locked on his, I dropped to one knee and then the other, facing him and him alone. The ultimate position of submission, the sacrifice of my pride, and the loudest declaration of my feelings for the boy in front of me. If I was going to die, at least it would be on my terms.

"I kneel for no one," I repeated, gazing up at Roan, "except the one I love."

Roan gasped, his breathing fast and shallow. Eyes wide, his gaze darted to something behind me, swallowing hard.

A gun cocked.

I was on my feet in a flash, shielding Roan as the first shot rang out. Clutching him to me, I held him tightly as two more rounds erupted behind us. He jerked against me with each one, but I didn't feel the shock of metal ripping through me. I had too much adrenaline coursing through me to feel anything.

The room was silent.

Roan was trembling when I pushed him out to arm's length, looking him over. He didn't have any blood on him. His gaze, however, was glued to something over my shoulder.

I spun slowly, careful to keep him behind me, and locked eyes with Sergei. He had a gun pointed at Viktor's body, sprawled on the concrete, the blood trickling down the slanted floor to the drain in the center.

"Lying sack of shit. Thought you could get rid of *me*? In *my* town?" Sergei snarled, spitting on Viktor's dead body. "Get rid of this," he said to Misha.

Misha nodded and started texting.

Dimitri looked at me from across the room, his mouth pressed into a hard line. His gaze traveled over me in apparent disgust before he turned and disappeared with his driver.

"Now that *that* is done. Let me tell you how it's going to be," Sergei said, stepping toward me, gesturing with the gun.

I pressed back into Roan, backing him up into the padded wall so I could cover more of him. Meeting Sergei's gaze head on, I lifted my chin, very much aware of the gun in his hand.

"None of this gay shit in public," Sergei said waving the gun between Roan and I. "Yes? If I see it, I'll cut your dick off. If I hear about it, I'll cut your dick off. What you do in private is *your* business. But queers are bad for *my* business. Understand?" No, I absolutely did not, but I nodded anyway, too stunned to say anything. "From now on, you work for Misha," Sergei continued, throwing a glance at the man behind him.

As soon as Sergei turned around again, Misha gave me a small smile and went back to texting.

"Yes? Am I clear?" Sergei extended his hand to me. I

didn't move. When he realized the gun was still in it, he chuckled and switched it to his other hand as if he'd simply forgotten to take his glove off and wasn't waving a weapon around.

"Yes. Thank you, sir," I replied, shaking his hand as firmly as I could. I was still in utter disbelief but I wasn't about to look a gift horse in the mouth.

"Misha will take you home. And you..." Sergei peered around me to Roan. I tried to block him, but Roan, pain in the ass as always, slid to the side, making himself more visible. "Don't forget."

"Thursday at one. Yes, sir. Thank you," Roan replied.

Sergei nodded, pivoting on his foot and striding away.

I jerked back, eyeing Roan's soft smile with suspicion. I didn't have to ask him what the fuck just happened, I was sure the look on my face said it all.

He shrugged a shoulder, the picture of innocence in spite of the little smirk lifting the corner of his mouth. "Apparently his nephew runs a theater and he's looking for a new composer. Thanks to all your stalking, Sergei saw my senior showcase. I guess he was impressed."

Was this really fucking happening right now? Not only were we both *alive*, miraculously, but Roan used our near-death experience to fucking *network*?!

Misha tucked his phone away and opened the door. "Ok. Let's go." He didn't wait for us to respond before walking out, leading the way through the kitchen to the Escalade waiting in the alley. I let Roan climb in first before I slid in next to him. My thigh pressed against his, the only form of contact I dared try. Misha sat across from us, a smirk on his face, but otherwise silent.

"I don't understand," I finally confessed as we set off for home. "Sergei… he is ok with…?" I pointed at myself.

"No," Misha replied loftily. "But he cares more about

his money than who you fuck. You're too valuable to lose, Sasha. Not many men can do what we do, as well as we do it. As long as you don't bite the hand that feeds you, you'll be fine."

"What about the others? This won't be a popular decision. I'm surprised Dimitri went along with it."

Misha chuckled. "After the mess we found at the Birdcage, I don't think you have to worry about anyone saying anything. If someone is stupid enough to complain or try anything" — he gestured to Roan — "feel free to remind them who you are."

The Escalade rolled to a stop in front of a luxe apartment building that was definitely not mine.

"Here you go," Misha said, leaning forward and handing me a set of keys. "My men do not live above fucking restaurants. Anton brought your things and you should find everything else you need. If not, you have a line of credit at the stores inside." I stared at the keys in my hand like they were an alien object. My mind was a fucking whirlwind, but Misha didn't seem to notice. "This is my building, these are my people. You're safe here, Sasha. So are you," Misha said, directing his attention to Roan.

"Thank you," Roan said, shaking his hand. "For everything."

Misha nodded, glancing back to me. "When I call, you answer. I'll give you some time, but we have work to do cleaning up Viktor's treachery."

Accepting the order with a nod, I opened the door and climbed out. As soon as Roan was safely on the sidewalk, I turned and leaned against the car frame. Misha slid forward, claiming the seat I was just in, so we were closer together.

"I'm tired of playing games. What *aren't* you telling me?" I asked quietly.

Misha bit his lower lip, squinting at me, like he was trying to decide if he was going to answer truthfully or not. A smile spread over his face slowly and he glanced away. "I already told you — I'm a wolf too. It's easier to survive when you have a pack." His bright gaze returned to mine, looking pleased with himself.

My jaw about hit the sidewalk. "You're telling me you…?"

He winked and reached for the door handle. I stepped back, letting him close his own door, too stunned to finish my question or even say a proper goodbye.

As soon as the Escalade pulled away, I spun and closed the distance on Roan. Seizing his face, I kissed him with abandon in the middle of the sidewalk while people milled around us. His fingers dug into my sides, twisting in the fabric and pulling me closer until we had to break apart for air.

"You said you loved me," Roan said in a breathless rush, searching my face.

"I do," I panted, answering the silent question in his eyes. And I *did*. Against all odds, I loved this kid. I loved his smart mouth, his reckless bravery, and the way he made me fucking ache to touch him, to just be near him. It was crazy, but for once I saw something in my future beyond pain and death — life. Because of him. For me, Roan *was* the sun, the center of my universe, the thing that gave me life. Without it, without him, I'd surely wither away and die. "I told you, you're *mine*, Solnyshko. I'm never letting you go."

"Are you kidnapping me again?" he asked with a wry grin.

"If I have to." I smiled and pressed my lips to his,

pouring every bit of love and affection I had for him into that kiss, so he'd know the truth and never question it. I pledged myself to him in that room — from that moment on, only death would take me from him.

As long as I drew breath, he was mine, and I was his.

THE END

## THE VENGEANCE OF ROAN SINCLAIR

### Chapter 1
### Sasha

Walking down the row of men, I surveyed each with a narrowed gaze. They were all cut from the same cloth — cold, ruthless, and, above all, lethal. Each came with a violent reputation and a skillset not suitable for the civilian world. They were just the sort of men I'd asked for and their respective bosses delivered.

"You." I stopped in front of a blond, head cocked. He looked like he could be Roan's body-double. Tall and lean with a youthful face. That was both useful and problematic. If anyone was looking for Roan, this one could lead them straight to him. Still, if someone had to die, I'd rather it be a stand-in than the real thing. "Over there."

The blond stepped past me and marched to the center of the room, waiting for me to select his opponent.

I glanced at the remaining men in line. "All of you. Go."

Pivoting on my heel, I folded my arms over my chest

and watched the five men swarm forward against the blond. His blue eyes snapped to mine briefly, accepting the challenge with a small smirk, before flicking back to his rivals.

The first man rushed forward. The blond blocked the punch and kicked the side of the man's knee out, dropping him. He wasted no time going for the second one, punching him so hard in the chest the man stumbled back, also out of the fight.

Three and four charged him at the same time. He focused his attention on the bigger of the two, twisted his hand in his shirt and yanked him in close to deliver a series of bone-crunching punches, regardless of the hits he took in return. Once the third man dropped in a bloody heap, he squared off against the remaining two.

I arched an eyebrow and slipped a hand inside my waistband, retrieving a knife. Catching the eye of one of the attackers, I slid the knife across the floor and resumed my stance, arms crossed.

The man snatched the weapon off the ground and lunged at the blond. He ducked and wove, deflecting the blade, looking for an opening to retaliate. With the other, unarmed, opponent circling toward his backside, the blond defender was running out of options.

"How's it going?" a quiet voice said next to me. I didn't need to turn to know it was Misha.

"We'll see."

"Better than Oleg?"

"We'll see."

Misha chuckled and glanced at his watch. "When this is done, we have a meeting."

I stole a glance at him out of the corner of my eye and nodded.

The blond was in a headlock now, trying to dislodge

the man behind him while not getting stabbed by the one in front. With a series of elbow strikes and kicks backward, the blond freed himself and threw his efforts into the one with the knife. They grappled with one another, blood slinging between them as the knife sliced back and forth, not caring who it cut with its curved blade.

Finally, the blond won out, twisting the man's arm backward and forcing him to stab himself in the shoulder with the knife the man wouldn't let go of.

Misha clapped politely.

I, on the other hand, strode forward in silence.

Sweating, bleeding, and breathing hard, the blond's chin tipped up defiantly.

A step away, I unholstered a gun and pointed it at his face.

In the blink of an eye, the blond's hands were on mine. One grabbed the gun while the other slammed into the inside of my wrist, bending it inward. The gun slipped from my hand. He flipped it to his dominant hand and took aim at my chest.

I assessed the blond again, giving him an approving nod. "You're hired."

He inclined his head and spun the gun on his finger, handing it back to me, grip first.

"What's your name?" I asked, holstering the weapon.

"Ilya Chernyshevsky."

Tossing a glance over my shoulder at Misha, I bit my tongue before I said something inappropriate. I should have known. From their appearance to their fighting style, Ilya was like a younger version of his uncle. It was so obvious now, I felt like a fool for not seeing the connection sooner.

Misha smirked and strolled toward the door, texting on his phone.

I withdrew my own phone, opening it to a picture of Roan. It showed him smiling, even though he was looking away from the camera. I don't even remember what he was so happy about, but it was one of my favorite pictures of him, probably because it captured him so well — warm, radiant, perfect. I could count on one hand the number of times I'd seen that smile lately. As a result, I wanted to live inside that picture, with *that* Roan, not the one I'd been sharing an apartment with for the past few months.

Holding up the picture for Ilya, I arched an eyebrow at him. "This is who you'll be guarding."

Ilya nodded, his face blank.

"If he dies, *you* die," I said matter-of-factly. "If he's *hurt*, you die. If he comes home with so much as a scratch on him, you die. Understood?"

"Understood."

"I don't give a fuck who your family is," I added when his gaze darted to Misha. "You work for me, not Misha. These are the terms. Take them or leave them."

"I understand, sir."

"Good. Meet me at the Adler Theater tomorrow at ten."

Ilya nodded once again and shook my hand with a firm grip. I felt the tiniest bit better knowing Roan would be in safe hands, no matter how pissed he'd be.

With the weight finally lifted from my shoulders, I turned and followed Misha out of the basement gym. We climbed the stairs to the ground floor and exited into an alley, climbing into the back of his waiting Escalade.

"Why didn't you tell me he was related to you?" I asked once we were settled and the car was underway.

Misha laughed. "I didn't know you'd pick him. You had some of the best in the business in there."

He might have found the situation amusing, but I sure

as hell didn't. Roan's safety, his life, was the furthest thing from a joking matter. "You know I won't hesitate to kill him if he fucks up."

"He won't." Misha gave me a pointed look. No doubt he'd trained Ilya personally and if the boy was half as good as his uncle, Roan would be nearly as safe as he was with me.

"Good." I gave my phone, and Roan's picture, one last glance before tucking it in the inner pocket of my suit jacket. "Where are we going?"

"To get information," Misha replied with a bright smile. "How is Roan?"

"Normal." The weight of Misha's stare was crushing. I finally looked up, right into his sky-blue eyes. As usual they were waiting, patient and knowing. "What do you expect me to say?"

"The truth."

I scoffed and looked away again, watching the buildings rush by as we drove deeper into the heart of Chicago. "The truth... I don't know what that is because he won't say. I see him. I feel him. But *he's* not there and I don't know how to bring him back."

"You know these things take time," Misha said gently. "You've seen what happens to men after they've been violated. It is a hard thing to come back from. Some people never do."

My knuckles cracked the harder my fist tightened. I knew it had happened, obviously, but every time I thought about it my blood boiled all over again. How could I honestly expect Roan to move past it when I was enraged nearly everyday at the mere thought?

Misha wasn't deterred by my silence. "Even after the body heals, the mind still carries the injury. All you can do is be there for him, no matter what he does to try and push you away. He may lash out at you, but in some way it's because he knows you can take it. And you *have* to take it, Sasha. If you want him to move forward, he has to know you can handle anything — like he had to. Otherwise, there is no future for the two of you."

I forced myself to nod, acknowledging the painful truth of his words. God knew I was trying to be there for him. It just wasn't enough. Some days I saw the old Roan, but those days were fewer and far between. I couldn't help but think perhaps he'd be better off if I did leave. Misha could talk to Sergei, insist on my returning to Russia, or any of the other European cities Sergei had connections with. That way Roan wouldn't be reminded, day in and day out, of what happened — and why. He could move on completely, without my world overshadowing him, a constant threat hanging over both our heads.

"Neither down, nor feather," Misha said, patting my knee.

"To the devil," I replied flatly.

I appreciated the well wishes, but I doubted luck was on my side in this instance. Getting Roan back to normal was going to take more than superstition, but damned if I knew what that was.

---

To read the rest of Roan and Sasha's story, make sure you grab your copy of THE VENGEANCE OF ROAN SINCLAIR.

Please don't forget to rate/review if you enjoyed the book! Every rating helps indie authors, more than you know.

## ABOUT THE AUTHOR

Award-winning dark romance author Ashlyn Drewek has always been a hopeless romantic. She's also fascinated by the dark, macabre things in life (you can blame a love of Halloween and Edgar Allan Poe for that one).

Most of her time is spent making up stories in her head or researching some obscure topic just because she's that much of a nerd. The degree on the wall says she's a historian, but the paycheck says she's a first responder.

Ashlyn lives in Northern Illinois with her patient husband, fearless daughter, and a house full of animals.

For information on news and upcoming releases, check out her website at www.ashlyndrewek.com to sign up for her newsletter, follow her on BookBub, or at any of the social media options below.

## ALSO BY ASHLYN DREWEK

The Leander Welles Series:

AWARDS
2021 Award Winner!

*The Mystery of Leander Welles — a dark, romantic suspense about a criminal psychiatrist who falls in love with her patient.*

*The Rationale of Leander Welles* — a dark, romantic suspense about an accused murderer who falls in love with his psychiatrist… or does he?

*The Damnation of Leander Welles* — a dark, romantic suspense about a cutthroat lawyer and an enigmatic millionaire and what happens when two dark souls join forces. A prequel to Book I and II.

*The Wrath of Leander Welles* - a dark, romantic suspense about love, revenge, and how far a psychopath is willing to go for both.

*The Fall of Leander Welles* — TBD

The Solnyshko Duet:

*The Kidnapping of Roan Sinclair* — a dark, MM romance about an American college guy who is kidnapped by a Russian criminal.

*The Vengeance of Roan Sinclair* — TBD

Paranormal:

*Out of the Dark* — *a slow-burn romance between a vampire detective and his human partner.*

*Malum Discordiae* — TBD

Printed in Great Britain
by Amazon

53037249R00199